Clive James was educated at Sydney University and Cambridge, where he was President of Footlights. In addition to his bestseller *Unreliable Memoirs* and its equally successful sequel *Falling Towards England*, he has published a novel, *Brilliant Creatures*; four mock-epic poems; three books of literary criticism; three books of television criticism; a book of travel pieces, *Flying Visits*; and his poems 1958–85, *Other Passports*. Between 1975 and 1982 he was television critic for the *Observer* and he has appeared regularly as a television performer.

Also by Clive James in Picador

CLIVE JAMES

The Remake

published by Pan Books
in association with Jonathan Cape

TO TOM MASCHLER

First published 1987 by Jonathan Cape Ltd
This Picador edition published 1988 by Pan Books Ltd,
Cavaye Place, London SW10 9PG
in association with Jonathan Cape Ltd
9 8 7 6 5 4 3 2 1
© Clive James 1987
ISBN 0 330 30374 0

Photoset by Rowland Phototypesetting Ltd
Bury St Edmunds, Suffolk
Printed and bound in Great Britain by
Richard Clay Ltd, Bungay, Suffolk

Contents

The true value of a human being is determined primarily by the measure and the sense in which he has attained liberation from the self.

Albert Einstein, *Mein Weltbild*

PART ONE

My Name in Lights

Galileo uses language not as a neutral instrument, but with a literary conscience, with a continual participation which is expressive, imaginative, and in the strict sense lyrical ... Even Galileo the scientist, in his ideal of observing the world, is nourished by literary culture.

Italo Calvino, from *Due intervisti su scienza e letteratura*, collected in *Una pietra sopra: discorsi di letteratura e società*

LAUREN WAS WITHIN HER RIGHTS, BUT LETTING ME DO it to her on the night she threw me out was one below the belt. Have I put that too abruptly? I vowed when I sat down to write this that I would pull no stunts. No games of spot the author, no alternative endings, no putting the middle first. Not even any attention-getting sexy first sentence. But getting thrown out on the street with my squib damp is where the story really and truly starts. Like most people with serious work to do I pick my literature off railway station kiosks and those supermarket racks at the airports where the paperbacks come out early. I think my taste is good. Ask me a question about Saul Bellow. He's got Sartre's eyes, hasn't he? Not just the bulge, the squint too. Ask me a question about Thomas Mann. About Heinrich Mann. Klaus. Manfred. You can pick up a lot, just shopping under the bright lights. But hardly any novel for which I lay down good money has a straight narrative any more. Watch out for anything translated out of Italian. The prize-winning novels of Luigi Database have plots like a Klein bottle and are called *If and When a Winter's Night Some Gravel Truck*. I bought one once at the bigger of the two bookstores in Changi airport and gave it up while I was still waiting in the lounge at Gate E 37. Didn't even get as far as the plane with it.

Novels by English dons who teach English literature have five plots plaited together, each plot about an English don lecturing about novels with five plots plaited together to an audience of clandestine philosophy students in Prague. The don gets laid by the Minister of Culture's bomb-breasted, nuke-nippled mistress and goes home to Norwich so full of guilt that the only way to expiate his crime is to write a novel with five plots plaited together. Technique. God save me from technique. Even the Australians are getting into the act now. Australian novels used to be fat and simple. Reading one was like watching *Breaker Morant* or *Gallipoli*, a good straight story about bronzed Aussies fighting the treacherous Brits. *The Thorn Birds* got me all the way from London to Sydney and back twice. Now the Australian novels are fat and complicated. I am too.

11

I'm an Australian, by the way. Already the narrative progresses. An Australian. Not a literary man. No, I'm not Napoleon. Am I a scientist? Yes, I'm a radio astronomer who performs on television. I'm the first television radio astronomer. That's my line. The first radio television astronomer has yet to appear. My name is Joel Court, and my wife Lauren threw me out because she caught me red-handed having a love affair with a star. Not so much *with* a star. I didn't make it with the actual *star*. But it was the failure to get there with the star that made me desperate for the girl. I know I'm not being clear. I'll unscramble all this later. Back to my wife Lauren. She let me make love to her that one last time because she wanted to use me as I had used her. Her words. There was a lot to them, but I couldn't see that at the time.

The star was, we all assumed, centrally situated in a mass of gas, rather in the way of that pulsar you've heard about, drumming away in the middle of the Crab Nebula like Buddy Rich. I won't say Ringo Starr because puns are a low form of wit and anyway Ringo holds the sticks at the end, pop-style, and goes *thwack thwack*, whereas Buddy Rich holds them in the middle like the good jazz man he is, so he can fire those precise rim-shots which are much more like what the little snare-drum-sized neutron star in the Crab must sound like when it flexes: *tick tick tick*. Or *would* sound like if it had an atmosphere, and you were there to hear it. Nobody, however, ever thought that the star in the middle of *my* nebula was clicking away exactly like that. Instead, it stuttered with a patterned randomness somewhere between chaos and predictability. Not much of a nebula even had it been close, the hostess gas-mass was a hell of a long way away.

From our viewpoint it went nova before recorded history. When the Crab appeared, the flare of the supernova was visible by day and much commented on by Chinese scribes, who called it the Guest. They drew it in the margins of their scrolls, perhaps playing for safety in case they were being tested by the government. When mine showed up, it was either recorded on the wall of a cave or never spotted at all. It always has been a bit of a blur. The one thing I and Veronica Lilywhite were ever in total harmony about was in calling it the Smudge.

Astronomical stock control gives it a number which I won't try to impress you with. It sounds like a car number plate. Nebulae prominent enough to get on Messier's original list all sound like motorways. The Crab is more correctly known as M1, but does that make you any the wiser? So how much wiser would you be if I gave you the registration number of a car purchased in Belgium and said that's it, that's the star I did myself in over? And how much would a mass of technical talk make me sound more real?

A lot depends on what you think of well-researched novels I don't mean Flaubert. Nobody begrudges him his long cab rides through Paris to map out the precise topography of *L'Éducation sentimentale*. But *he* was creating the past of his country, not a persona for himself. On my way to South America once, where I was going in order to be filmed talking in the middle of a radio dish built into a volcano, I started John Updike's *Couples*. It was clear that all of Updike's literary friends had been changed into carpenters and dentists so that they could penetrate each other's wives without fear of libel. Was this strategem, which no doubt has its justification and might even be inevitable, made any the less glaring by the thoroughness with which the technical vocabularies of dentistry and carpentry had been mugged up? Did all the talk about window sashes and quartz-filled bicuspids go an inch towards persuading you that the author had ever picked up a bradawl or a hypodermic syringe? Only the pretender strives to make himself believable. For the genuine article, it is enough not to be unbelievable. Unless I put the Smudge somewhere in your back yard or say that I took a ride through its inner suburbs while sitting on a comet's tail, you'd be better off just accepting that it's been out there for a long time, sending us its annoying little signal, the discreet roar caused by its central power-house, that enigmatic noise-maker we called the Glimmer.

We called it the Glimmer because we couldn't get an inkling. The Smudge is no show-stopper optically and of course the Glimmer couldn't be detected at all until the first big radio telescopes started collecting everything. Even then it stayed unremarked, because it didn't pulse. It took a long while for someone to spot that what wasn't a pulse wasn't just noise either. The anomaly would have stayed entombed in years of print-out if a squad of nerds in America hadn't uncovered it during one of those apologies for a research project that the Bible-Belt universities put their losers on twenty at a time, like prayer meetings. What they dug up was no thrill. If the Smudge was unexciting, the Glimmer was an outright bore. A pattern would start, then stop. Unfortunately it would hardly ever stop at the same place. Not *never* stop at the same place – that would have been a pattern in itself. Just hardly ever. While everyone normal at Cambridge got frantic about the sexy neutron star inside the Crab, only the mad people sat still for being nattered at incoherently by the infinitely repetitive Glimmer with its meaningless variations on an undetectable theme. As a high-flyer, with my very own television programme, I was doing my junior colleague Veronica Lilywhite a big favour by devoting to this unglamorous phenomenon a considerable, if necessarily limited, proportion of my valuable time.

Veronica had come down out of the North to spend the rest of her life at Girton, first as an undergraduate, then as a graduate, then as a don, and, one day in the future, as a dead body. She was the kind of frump who made you wonder why they ever bothered to locate the place so far out of town, because no man except her dim bulb of a husband would have travelled more than a hundred yards to get near her. Dressed for evening, she wore printed silk caftans and wooden clogs. Her normal daywear was three pullovers, except in summer, when it was two pullovers. Although she made a lot of statements and was perfectly capable of making another one by means of her apparel, her sartorial display was not necessarily a political gesture. She was like that *before* feminism. It was a special sort of Cambridge female stereotype going back to when women had to pass an unattractiveness test before they were allowed in. And if they stayed on as dons, or were invited in at that level, it wasn't enough to be off-putting. They had to be crazy too. There were a few exceptions to disguise the plot. My first summer in Cambridge I saw Bobby-Anne Righter at a Girton garden party and slavered appropriately at her length of leg. At one stage there was a medieval Romance philologist at New Hall who looked like Sigourney Weaver, and an assistant

14

lecturer in Spanish at Newnham whom Goya might not have thrown out of bed. But these were Potemkin villages. More typical was the senior lecturer in jurisprudence who let her children run wild from an early age on the principle that to be hit by a car or abducted by one of the area's plentiful supply of sexual perverts could only increase their awareness. The police would bring her brood home to her in the evenings after they had been rescued from playing in Trumpington Street or found tearfully wandering on Jesus Green with their short trousers around their ankles. She would count them twice, not because she couldn't count but because she didn't know how many she had.

Veronica had almost as many. I think there were four of them. She looked after them well enough, in a pebble-dash nightmare of a house on Alpha Road. Her husband was no doubt of some assistance, in the rare moments he could snatch away from his political activities or the hard job of publishing his poems on a hand press. He had a small private income, a large, badly organised beard, and sandals on over his socks. The political activities consisted mainly of circulating petitions which demanded the removal of American atomic bombs from East Anglia and the immediate conversion of multi-storey car-parks into low-cost housing. His presence in the living room gave Veronica plenty of incentive to be sitting in the kitchen with her exercise books, filling them with calculations. Once when we were still friends she showed me the exercise books. They were of the school-smelling, pathetically neat sort still made in the Chinese People's Republic by some forgotten capitalist factory whose workers must all be a hundred years old and have bound feet. She had scores of these exercise books full of figures, and scores more ready for more figures to come. She was trying to sort the whole thing out by sucking a Biro. Occasionally she cycled into town to run a main-frame computer programme, but only when she needed some big-time number-crunching that she couldn't do on her home micro, which for some strange reason, probably ineptitude, she had never managed to get connected to the main-frame. Then it was back to the exercise books, the crossings out and the startings again. One book I picked up and flipped through had pages of games of noughts and crosses in it. She laughed like someone caught playing hopscotch in a cathedral. I didn't precisely think she was nuts, but I did feel justified in spreading the word that she was producing the mathematical equivalent of her husband's poetry, which lacked flair in a way that only the truly diligent can achieve.

Jim Lilywhite was a pain in the neck, but perhaps I spent too much time saying so. Composed as if nobody else had written poetry before, the junk he cranked out was innocent, but not beautifully innocent. There was a terrible arrogance to it: the conceit of claimed humility. I started thinking the same about Veronica's home-baked maths. Worse, I started saying it. But she had offended me too often by her lack of love for the subject. The cold truth, in my opinion, was that she didn't have the soul for astronomy. She knew next to nothing about its history and I doubt she knows much more now. You could tell by that house of hers, with not even a map of the heavens to eke out the plywood veneer furniture and the wallpaper that looked like paper you stick on the wall merely so that you can see paper instead of wall. Apart from the handprints of innumerable children there was nothing to look at except one of those crucifixes that Brancusi might have made if he had attended an evening course in woodwork and had had no talent. A Catholic astronomer. Had anyone else since Galileo been that?

My wife would be the first to admit, or even insist, that our own house, a blond brick and tinted glass high-tech extravaganza in a close off Madingley Road, was a bit over the top in that respect. A bronze bust of Newton, a stone head of Einstein, a silver-plated worm-drive from the first Hale Observatory optical telescope, a working model of the CSIRO 64-metre radio telescope at Parkes – I had everything in there except the mirror of the Mount Palomar 200-inch reflector, which would have made a perfect floor for the dining area if lit from underneath. I gave excellent dinner parties, right to the end. The whole Cambridge scientific brains trust would be packed tight around the polished mahogany with the highlights of silver cutlery bouncing off their spectacles and bald heads. Lauren's black sequinned Kansai Yamamoto evening top would light up with a million pin-points. *Ex oriente lux*. Clive Sinclair was practically the dumbest man present.

On Saturday nights our driveway was packed with Porsches and BMWs. German cars with air-dams and digital glove-boxes were crawling all over Cambridge by that time. The booming microchip economy of Silicon Fen had flooded the flat land with money. Cambridge science had always been exciting and now there was glamour as well. The business sections of the posh Sunday newspapers called it the Cambridge Phenomenon. I suppose the glamour was meretricious, but I liked it. Maybe I liked it *because* it was meretricious. Alan Turing had won the war in secret. One man at King's had ensured that the Germans would in future invade the world with nothing more lethal than sports cars. But he had remained unsung. Later on, you could make a big discovery and be famous too. Crick and Watson turned Cambridge into Lourdes: aspiring scientists made pilgrimages to the Eagle, where the two breakthrough brothers had sat quaffing pints while ogling nurses; and to Old Addenbrooke's, where they had picked the nurses up; and to the language schools in Station Road where they had picked up foreign girls sent by doting parents to study English. Giving the alien lovelies a crash course in pillow talk, our clever pair were inspired to crack the double helix. It was a buddy movie before its time. Butch and Sundance.

Later still, you could not only be famous, you could get rich. The windowless green-field factories came to the Science Park so that the whizz-kid entrepreneurs could get access to current research. It wasn't long before the researchers joined the industrialists on the board. For a heady moment it was as if the brain drain had gone into reverse. There had been a local outbreak of order in Britain's otherwise inexorable entropic slide towards heat death. The Science Park was the Klondike with central heating. Gold fever. I suppose it was the wrong way for an astronomer to think. It wasn't as if we had anything to sell. A physical chemist playing with the glassy metals would have NASA waiting outside in the corridor with cheque book poised. Being an astronomer was a vow of poverty. Even if you could prove that an astronomical H_2O maser was a sure sign of gas condensing into a protostar, there was no way of cashing in on the discovery unless Steven Spielberg wanted to take an option on the material. But I had a well-off, well-groomed American wife, and amid the general excitement of go-go Cambridge it was hard to turn down the television companies when they gave me the chance to build my income up a bit nearer to matching hers. To be fair to myself, I would probably have done that first little series of shows even if I had had to pay the producers instead of them paying me. Loving the subject, I loathed the way it had been treated on the box. Some of the daytime Open University programmes were all right: I had done one or two of them myself and soon mastered studio technique, which mainly consists of not trying to put out the viewer's eye with a stabbing forefinger. The science shows for mass evening viewing, however, were almost invariably dire, and for some reason the ones about astronomy were the worst.

If you were lucky, an American popular science writer stared significantly at Raquel Welch's chest while helping her to grapple with the concept of a binary star system. If you were unlucky, a British popular science writer with a speech impediment explained general relativity to Dudley Moore, who made small noises of understanding from inside the helmet of a silver space suit. Late at night there was a weekly programme that took a less patronising approach, but it was still based on the hallowed British principle that the presenter of a specialist series should reassure viewers by looking as if he might breathe up a horse's nose at any moment, or pull a white mouse out of his ear. There was room for someone who sounded reasonably normal. Two weeks into my first series the TV critics were calling me the David Attenborough of the Asteroids. I can't say I hated them for it. Three weeks into the series, I was having an affair with the programme's research assistant, a blonde called Gael who wore pink overalls, career-girl glasses and a worshipping smile. At twenty-five she was fifteen years younger than I was, so with a wife and two children on my conscience you can imagine how I felt. I felt terrific.

Late every night before each studio day I would call in at Gael's basement flat off Bayswater Road to be briefed and debriefed simultaneously. She had read physics at St Andrew's and there was a photograph of her in her red gown on the little table beside the lacquered bamboo bedhead. I got to know that photograph very well – rather better than I got to know Gael, as it turned out. But for a season things couldn't have been neater. Neither the show nor its most salient fringe benefit detracted from my work in Cambridge. If anything, my energy and concentration were increased. A measure of fame and a dollop of sexual luck can have that effect separately, let alone together. In the group effort to resolve the enigma of the Glimmer and thereby find a rationale for the variable radio sources associated with supernova remnants, the strategic thinking was largely mine. Cracking the problem was going to be my Contribution to the Subject. My name would be in lights – a big, if usually unspoken, consideration for all pure scientists. Getting there first really matters, if having your discovery named after you is the only lasting reward. Jimmy Connors might have been the one who said 'Second is nowhere' but he wasn't the only one who thought it. We were a team, but it was *my* team. Right, gang? Not just in Cambridge but in three other British universities keen young high-flyers were linked to me by telephone and terminal, feeding me ideas but following my lead. If it took us all to do it, it would still be my approach. Understood? OK, let's go to work.

Veronica dropped out, and I can't even pretend that I resented it. She, on the other hand, quite clearly resented me. Not that she knew anything about Gael. For Veronica, however, my appearing on the tube was quite extracurricular enough. I had always taken for granted, been rather pleased by, her disapproval of my house, wife, car and clothes. Anti-flash was a moral principle with her, not just an oversight. Nobody could overlook Jim Lilywhite's socks and sandals. They were a political manifesto, and tolerating them was tantamount to an endorsement. She found me light-minded anyway, so when my mass media activities started necessitating brief, planned absences from inspiring and supervising our group, she took the opportunity to sideline herself. I made a point of not missing her. My carefully chosen, highly motivated swot squad was linked into an international mass assault on those pulsars evincing a compact complexity of features. Among these features was a pulse so intermittent that it amounted to Restless Behaviour, a trade term for fluctuations which in the normal course of events might have been safely ignored, but in the case of these little beasts seemed characteristic. We classified them as would-be pulsars because that appeared to be what they would have been if something or other was not screwing up the signal. Apart from the Crab and Vela it had been dishearteningly tricky to get a remnant that matched up with a pulsar, but you could always turn disappointment on its head by saying that whatever interfered with a straight radio signal was the same thing that stopped you getting a snapshot – i.e., all the dust, junk and fuzz of a big star that had catastrophically shrunk to a little one. When these things suddenly contract into a trillionth of their original volume they give off an awful lot of fluff. I used to dream of the Glimmer as a football-sized neutron star cackling away brightly like an early-morning disc jockey while the Smudge hung around like a wet blanket. It *had* to be a remnant. For were not the number of detectable pulsars and the number of detectable remnants roughly the same? Get out of that. Any lateral displacement could be put down to the initial bang.

Nothing could better account for an irregular signal than an irregular medium. Of course, we couldn't have it both ways: if the pulsar was displaced laterally from its remnant then it couldn't be the remnant's debris that was getting in the road. But in the case of the Smudge we were looking into a part of the galaxy where there was every reason not to be able to see what was going on, and for almost every other would-be pulsar the same applied. We could only listen, and wait for the X-rays, which meant waiting for more satellites to go up. We needed more evidence about what was in the way. Veronica was the only one pig-headed enough to behave as if there was nothing in the way and the evidence was already in. She just went on dumbly doodling with the Glimmer's ropy signal as if the thing was saying what it meant instead of choking in a dust-bath. Old habits die hard, we all thought. Veronica had got her start as a junior dogsbody working on the complete radio history of Nova Lepantes, a monumental group effort which has been going on since 1970, yielding a log-book the size of a library. Now she had the chance to be just as boringly single-minded again, all off her own bat. She had her scores of little Chinese notebooks full of Arabic numerals and wanted to be alone with them. The Glimmer was her baby. The other would-bes and all her colleagues could go hang, me first. I felt the same about her. I promise you, it got to where I was saying her name as a swear word. On Christmas morning I was helping my son Benjamin assemble a plastic model of the Millennium Falcon and when I snapped a radar dish off its pivot I said, 'Veronica!' Benjamin dropped the glue.

But Veronica was right. The Glimmer *wasn't* sending a simple signal made complicated by interference. It was sending a complicated signal with no significant interference at all. The damned thing was a multiple. She worked out the full set of orbital elements. Not just a sub-set. The whole thing. That was what she had been doing in her childish notebooks without leaving her ratty kitchen, while I had been roaming the world from Effelsburg to Kitt Peak, from Serpukhov to Arecibo. In chukka boots and straining blue jeans, with my hands tucked into the side-pockets of my chamois bomber-jacket, I had been photographed with some of the world's most desirable precision instruments. The dishiest of the dish aerials suffered differential expansion from the heat of my body as they stood proudly behind me, their wave guides tilted snootily skyward. The fan beam of many a large array bathed me with secret love. I travelled the five kilometres of the Cambridge interferometer for a series of helicopter shots with a gyro-stabilised camera that showed me magically appearing and disappearing in front of each aerial, like a star. Not a radio star. A television star. You should have heard me. You should have seen me. You probably did, on the cover of the *Radio Times*. I was explaining, with a humble yet confident smile, that it would probably take an interferometer the width of the solar system to crack the problem of the complex sources. The wind was ruffling my layer-cut hair while I was explaining. And while I was explaining, Veronica was publishing.

Her results weren't particularly well expressed. There have been neater papers. Something of her wallpaper and her husband's socks, a certain atmosphere of food scraps trodden into the unsealed tiled floor of a small kitchen, got into her expository prose. The central effect, however. was, I have to admit,

21

impressive. She had made decisive use of the line radiation data. By adding the radio recombination line data to the continuous emission data she got the beginning of her picture. From there on it was perseverance, no doubt bolstered by prayer.

She was as absurdly, thickly confident as Magellan, who had a map reference of the passage to the Pacific that he didn't realise was only the River Plate. When he arrived at the River Plate with his crew already dying like flies he should have packed it in. But he wasn't clever enough. Veronica wasn't clever enough either. She didn't know when to quit. The radio signal was too irregular to have a structure. It wasn't a shell, it was a filled distribution. Unless – and this was her act of faith – it was a *set* of shells. The binary star W. Ursae Majoris has two stellar cores in one envelope, like a pair of fried eggs whose whites have joined up. Veronica's multiple, if her sums were right, must have more cores than a carbuncle, all zooming around each other in a basketwork of orbits. But what *were* their orbits? The separate cores, she crazily assumed, didn't add up to a pulsar. They were *all* pulsars. There was no interference apart from the standard tat offered by the interstellar medium. The little demons were interfering with each other! Fluctuations, she decided in her confident madness, were to be accounted for by coincidence – accumulated eclipses that strengthened or weakened the signal depending on how many of the sources were in line. But how many sources were there?

There wasn't an interferometer in the world – and by that time the whole world was an interferometer, with all the major telescopes linked up – that could separate a point-source pack of little pulsars and count them. Veronica did it by counting on her fingers. In the Mond Console Room behind Pembroke she ran main-frame computer programmes for brute-force calculation. If the main-frame crashed she would go back to her micro. Once the big sums had been done, she went back to her exercise books, filling them with drawings that looked like Leonardo's unsuccessful designs for a marketable executive toy. Eventually she abandoned even the exercise books. All the figuring that mattered she did by mumbling to herself. If not this, then that. The driver into the side of whose bus she rode her bike one afternoon at Bowes and Bowes corner complained that she had seemed to have something on her mind. In New Addenbrooke's hospital she looked dreamily preoccupied even as her husband fed her his special lentil soup from a wooden bowl. Recuperating at home, she stared entranced at the toes protruding from the cast on her right leg. She wiggled them in sequence.

Finally she got the answer, and nobody seriously argued with it. Like the double helix, the elegance of her solution silenced criticism. Objecting to the structure of DNA would have been like quarrelling with the zip fastener. Veronica's multiple had the same authority. It was a set of five pulsars all swooping around each other like the logo on a packet of Ariel Automatic washing powder. It might have been designed to go on the cover of *Time* magazine, where it soon appeared, with an impressive portrait of Veronica staring dreamily through it, looking like whatever happened later to the lead singer of one of those early 1970s English folk rock groups who ate muesli in soft focus. Veronica's multiple was red meat for the journalists. At first they called it the Pop-group Pulsar. For a while it was referred to as the Rolling Stones. But in the scientific world nobody tried to improve on the soaring euphony of its official title, the one that will go into all the books until our time ends: Lilywhite's Quincunx.

Veronica would have been famous, if she had collaborated with the publicity machine that assembled itself around her like earth-moving equipment around a bomb crater. But she did a Garbo, and thus became more than famous. She was a legend, a myth, a charismatic figure, a numen, an avatar. I had my own views, which I did not forbear to vocalise, about why she played hard to get. You couldn't imagine, I laughingly insinuated, that even Veronica would be cloth-eyed enough to let herself in for one of those colour supplement 'A Room of One's Own' features that showed the latest silicone-bodied, sabre-toothed female junk novelist coolly at ease among the severed, chromium-plated pudenda of her previous husbands. (That was a lot to insinuate, but I rehearsed.) I conjured visions of Veronica proudly showing off her linoleum-topped child-proof dining table and plywood-framed Van Gogh sunflower print while her husband toiled in the dim background at a new petition for turning Cambridge railway station into a day-care centre. Everybody laughed. But nobody stopped admiring Veronica. Neither did I, underneath. Between underneath and on the surface, however, were several grinding, crunching strata of disappointment, resentment and indignation. When you feel like that, it is better to have it out than to let it fester. Unfortunately it was some time before I met her again face to face, and by then she must have heard that I had been propagating snidery. I would rather have not seen her at all, but for the upcoming second series of the television programme it had been decided to do something about my group project on the remnants, and we couldn't do that without featuring Veronica at some length: without treating her as the star, in fact. My producer welshed on his promise to go and see her.

She received me in her parlour, where the sunlight, already filtered by the anti-Cruise Missile poster Sellotaped to the window, was eaten up by the gutta-percha-textured wall-to-wall carpet substitute richly strewn with small odd socks and bits of connector set variously combined. Jokingly I asked Veronica if the wooden toys of Willy Fangel had helped in her calculations. She smiled at that, but not so as to bare the gums, and those partly exposed teeth-tips, it turned out, marked the limit of what she would concede. She would contribute no opinions on the general topic, just a short exposition of her own discovery. I offered the view that the time for keeping herself to herself had passed. Perhaps rashly, I allowed my tone of voice to include the suggestion that going off on her own had been a touch antisocial in the first place.

'Do you honestly think,' she asked in the voice of one precluding an answer, 'that if I'd asked for any help you wouldn't have grabbed the discovery?'

'Oh come *on*, Veronica.'

'Oh come *off* it, Joel.' She swallowed some air at that point, as if in disapprobation of her uncharacteristic play on words. Veronica was no verbal gymnast; a quality, or lack of it, which gave her sincerity an extra punch. 'Look what happened to Rosie Franklin.' She meant the X-ray crystallographer whose name is so seldom mentioned along with those of Crick and Watson.

24

'What about Jocelyn Bell?' I countered, meaning the Cambridge astronomer who had found the pulsar in the Crab after painstakingly screening out all possible man-made sources for the signal – a triumph of tenacity over imagination, in my view, although tactfully I forbore to say so.

'Yes,' said Veronica, with a nod whose weariness I would have liked to think was theatrical, 'and she did it by plugging away on her own.' Point proven, said Veronica's flapping clog, whose dark-blue leather upper was held to the wooden sole by a line of rivets. I tried to imagine her underwear. Raw calico with staples? Jute?

So Veronica's personality didn't bulk as large in my second little series as her personal discovery did. I, on the other hand, was on screen all the time, looking less at home now that the show had moved decisively out of doors. In studio I had found no difficulty in speaking to camera. Out on location, walking and talking simultaneously, I looked a bit less of a natural talent than I had fondly imagined myself to be. The show still sounded pretty good if you compared it to the usual pop science drivel about Old Man Gravity and the putatively catastrophic effect of anti-matter on Peter Ustinov. But all that eye-witness footage of me and the telescopes made me look a bit prat-like when it was edited together. I found myself abruptly turning towards cameras that had unaccountably snuck up on me from the side. When I made wavering, long-lens appearances through the heat haze of the Californian deserts, those blue jeans of mine looked thoroughly stuffed, not just in the arca of the crotch but all the way down each leg. About twenty extra pounds of anxiety had wrapped themselves around my body. It was the first time in my life that the French phrase Easy In His Skin had not applied to me. Still dubbing the last shows when the first ones had already gone to air, I began to feel hot, hurried, old and angry.

My anger was not directed wholly at Veronica. I tried to take credit for directing some of it at myself. I was kicking myself for having been too clever. If I had been dumber, I would have tested out the possibility of the Glimmer's signal being the unadorned article. It was the same mistake I had made when doing my Wechsler-Bellevue IQ test at Sydney University twenty years before. My score should have gone off the clock. It stayed on the clock because I got stuck trying to complete a series that went something like AF CH FK etc. I did the clever thing, looking for a relationship between the letters in each pair. But I should have done the stupid thing. The only relationships that mattered, it turned out, were those between all the first letters, and, separately, those between all the second letters. The solution was so elementary I hadn't considered it. It was an insult to my intelligence. My rage was pure, intense, disabling and long-lived. I would bore people with it. It wasn't that I bored them without noticing. I saw them shuffling their feet and exchanging tolerant smiles, but I bored on regardless.

This time it was worse. Eaten up with disgust at my own naivety for having been too sophisticated, I got on Gael's nerves. Perhaps I should have taken a tip from my daughter Donna's behaviour when playing Trivial Pursuits. French is one of her best subjects at school, so she guessed straight away that a 'tastevin' must be a wine-taster. But she didn't see how that fitted into the Sport and Leisure category. Suspecting a trick, she changed her answer, hazarding that it might be a fencer. When it turned out to be a wine-taster after all, she sulked for the rest of the game, the rest of the day and half the following week. She got that from me. She drove us up the wall.

I should have realised I might be doing the same thing to Gael. But I was so careful to dress up my agony with jokes. Some of them were quite good. If Veronica got the Nobel Prize, I suggested, she would be able to afford a pair of shoes for her husband, who could give up poetry and hand out circulars full time. I tried that one out on Gael and she quite liked it, without ever having clapped eyes on him, so I knew it would go down a storm in Cambridge. But there were a lot of other jokes that she apparently liked less, especially when I woke her up to tell them. Also, the second series being something of a critical disaster, Gael had to bear the brunt of my frustration in that regard as well. Just when I was getting used to journalistic jibes about my tight blue jeans, there was all this flak about how stiff I looked on the move. That smart bastard in the *Observer* said that when I walked he thought the single-frame advance on his VCR had got stuck. Deep down I had to admit there was something to it, so on the surface I went berserk. I blamed the production team, of whom Gael was the nearest representative. Desiring her more than ever as everything else went wrong, I naturally assumed that *her* commitment to our affair was increasing too, and could thus put up with some abrasion. This turned out not to be so, but I was never with her long enough to spot that she had begun to cut back on the total amount of tenderness from which I had reserved a fixed percentage for abuse. To my mind, our sweet set-up continued functioning normally. Indeed it felt all the sweeter, narcotically sweet, as things went sour at home, where I had become hard to live with. I showed Gael how hard I had become to live with at home by becoming harder to live with with her. But she didn't have to take it. She claimed later that she had dropped many hints. I found this difficult to believe. I found it equally difficult to believe when she asked me not to call any more. A bad patch, in my then view, had been dramatised by her into a crisis. Understandable preoccupation on my part had been magnified into a deal-breaker. Worse than that: a heart-breaker. My need for everything about her became overwhelming as she moved out of my reach. The attractive force of the receding object increased rather than diminished. I had promised her nothing. Now I promised her everything.

Each week for the past six months I had come down to Liverpool Street by train, taken the Central Line to Queensway, walked to Gael's little flat and spent a perfect evening there while pretending occasionally on the telephone to be in my sad little hotel at Shepherd's Bush near Television Centre. Not long after midnight I would go to the hotel to field any emergency calls that might have come down the line after me. There was always the chance that Donna had set fire to her nightgown when burning the Trivial Pursuits set, or that Benjamin had got his head stuck in his Darth Vader helmet. Anxiety is never absent from these affairs. But while holed up with Gael, in the days when I was riding high, I had been as happy as I had ever been in my life, and now that I had suffered a setback she at least made being miserable tolerable. It was a weekly injection, and like an addict I reacted badly to the threat of its being withdrawn. Think what I would lose. Her tank of goldfish with the light behind it. Her poster of Sam Shepherd in *The Right Stuff*. (Nothing strained about *those* blue jeans.) Her flat wicker basket of mauve and pink pebbles on the glass table. Her bottles and boxes and sprays, which would be named in detail if this were any American novella influenced by *Franny and Zooey*. Her knickers, chosen with me in mind, which had been specifically put on for my visit. Her.

It was revealed that she had other plans: had always had them. There was a job open in California. Not in pure research: it was too late for that, and on her own account she would never have been up to it. But there was an outfit in Pasadena which made in-house training videos for the information technology industries. Software about software. An American headhunter had decided she was just the ticket: knowledgeable, pretty, classy, English. His invitation accorded with her secret desire to get in front of a camera. Actually this desire was no secret. She had often told me about it. I hadn't taken it seriously because it didn't accord with either my wish or the realities of British television, for which the women on screen were required, with few exceptions, to be as underqualified as possible, so as not to threaten the men who put them there. Nor did I take Gael's ambitions with full seriousness even now that the chance had arisen of their being fulfilled. I interpreted the whole revelation as a stratagem to win my commitment. The prospect of losing the last prop to my confidence was too much. Gael gasping and blushing flashing-eyed beneath me was the symbol of my power. Very well, then. The next time I arrived on her doorstep I had a suitcase in each hand. Packed in some haste, they would have revealed strange discrepancies on analysis. There were fourteen pairs of boxer shorts but no socks, for example. These statistics could not be verified at the time because I was never given the chance to unpack. The suitcases got into the building but not through the door of her flat. They stood outside, on the tough green carpet of the common parts.

We ourselves stood inside, face to face but a yard apart, while the two goldfish, Crick and Watson, maintained a similar lack of connection in a different medium. I was weighed down by my Burberry coat, which had the detachable lining zipped into it and so would have made me hot even in winter. It was summer. I was wearing the coat because I had not wanted to leave it behind. Gael didn't ask me to take it off. On the high point of the curve of my left ear where it joined my head, sweat sprang out of the skin and bifurcated into rivulets, one going down my neck and the other down the line of my jawbone. Or perhaps it was my right ear. How could I remember so precisely? Why should you trust me? She was asking herself the same question. No she wasn't. She had already found the answer.

'You never really gave me a thought,' she said. Crick put his nose up to the surface.

'I did. I thought of nothing else.' Watson headed for the bottom, tanks flooded, engines off. Stand by to receive depth charges.

'Not about me. Not really. I was just another prize you were picking up. Another University Medal. Once you'd got me you did the absolute minimum.'

'But that was the deal.'

'Wet.'

'Wet what?'

'Shirt collar. Your collar's getting wet. Look, you have to go.'

She was right. Any observer would have seen that I had to go. The chairs and the sofa were empty but there was nowhere to sit down. So I muscled the bags out into the street and after twenty minutes of counting occupied taxis I hailed an empty one that got me back to Liverpool Street just in time for the Cambridge train to show me its blunt rear end as it pulled out. The black man in the blue-dyed Afrika Korps cap smiled his admiration for the speed at which I had run in the Burberry coat with a big strapped burgundy leather suitcase in each hand. I took the coat off, folded it, mopped my face with the exposed lining, and lugged the bags upstairs to that overhanging tea-house effect, which in its heyday might have had Celia Johnson and Trevor Howard sitting in it gazing at each other with helpless decency, but which in recent times – all the time I'd been in England – had been given a new image every couple of years in a series of doomed attempts to lure the more up-market passengers who couldn't face breaking bread with the *mobile vulgus* down in the cafeteria. It had been a bistro and a brasserie, a Europa bar and a coffee-house. On this occasion it had a health food emphasis. You could get slices of pumpkin cake on heavy grey-blue stoneware plates, and coffee poured from a Silex into a mug like a tankard. The striven-for atmosphere of weight-watching energy was, as it was bound to be, utterly undone by the insolent somnolence of the girls behind the counter, but it wasn't a bad place to sit and wait until your train was cancelled. Certainly it was better than either of the bars, where along with the hordes of crew-cut squaddies travelling in mufti I would have become incapable of catching the next train when it was finally, after arriving half an hour late, ready to go out again an hour late, so as to arrive at my destination two hours late exactly.

On the way up to Cambridge the locomotive broke down only once. The second long delay was because of a broken signal. So by the time I had shuffled forward to the head of the taxi rank outside the station I had had plenty of time to think. I thought: why didn't we have two cars? We could easily have afforded them. Then I could have left one car for Lauren, taken the other to London, and I would have been mobile, instead of standing there alone with two suitcases and not a cab in sight. I got home just before dinner. Nobody except Lauren realised that I had even been away. While they all watched *Minder* I phoned Gael from my study and kept getting her answering machine. Leave a message after the beep. I left a long apology, in about thirty instalments. It was after eleven before the children went to bed, and then Lauren turned away from me for half an hour before she let me have it.

She let me have it, and then, before I had even finished the usual pathetic sagging, shrinking and crinkling, she revealed that Gael had rung her up. Lauren put it in American. 'You know that researcher of yours that you told me was so hideous you can't look at her? The one with two heads and the bad breath? Guess what. She gave me a call.' Gael had spilled the whole thing while I was building up my right forearm lifting that stone mug of coffee at Liverpool Street. The full Take Back Your Husband aria. So it was time I had a taste, said Lauren, of how it felt to be cynically used. Too smart for my own good as usual, I said it felt fine. She accused me of having exploited her. Not Gael, her. I had the answer to that. If I was an exploiter, I asked charmingly, why didn't I have a car of my own?

Next morning, after Lauren had driven the children off to school, I was in a cab to the station with the same two suitcases, but this time I left the Burberry behind, because I couldn't quite believe that I was being thrown out for good. The official story for home consumption was that Daddy would be going away to think for a while. Daddy believed it, so why shouldn't they? I bought a first-class ticket and tried to get into the same compartment with the Duchess of Kent, but a big man in a blue suit stood up and blocked the doorway. He was very nice about it and I understood completely.

Money would be short, so I went to stay with Chance Jenolan. I could have afforded a cheap hotel, but my credit cards drew only on my personal account, not the joint account. Though the personal account was replenished from the joint account when necessary, the replenishment could easily be stopped by Lauren, and I wasn't quite sure how she could be stopped from stopping it. She had always looked after the money side. I suppose I was a bit helpless from that viewpoint. Anyway, when I rang Chance during the thankless night between Being Used for the first-and-last time and being thrown out on my ear, he said come on down. 'You'll have a clear month before Angélique gets here,' he had said sleepily. 'The Mole will be in and out, but otherwise it'll be just you and me. Bluey and Curley's Reunion.'

Angélique Visage was Chance's live-out wife. She came over from Paris to hide conspicuously in between films. The Mole was a new one on me. It might have been a pet rodent, but judging from the capital letter I had heard when Chance pronounced the name, and knowing his world-class track record, the odds were that it was some sort of woman.

Less of a woman, it turned out, than a girl. Chance had his principal London residence in the Barbican. Though I had been to his flat twice before, I still got lost following the yellow line from Moorgate to the Arts Centre. When the yellow line forked, I followed it each way, and both ways turned out to be wrong. Finally I found the right stairwell, completed a long upward

31

journey by lift, and arrived seeking entrance to his front door just as he was letting her out of it.

'This is Antonia Blunt,' said Chance blearily. 'She's a student.'

Chance being clad in a badly creased silk dressing-gown, bare feet and a two-day beard, I could see why he was careful to specify his friend's occupation. Otherwise I would have thought she had been sent by an escort agency in order to fulfil his fantasies of innocent young womanhood. She had Disney eyes, Swedish teeth, glistening straight-combed, square-cut chestnut hair hanging half-way down her back, dark-blue satin court shoes, sheer stockings, a well-tailored dark-blue suit, a row of pearls over her roll-neck white silk blouse, and an executive briefcase. She could have been a trainee stockbroker, if you did not discount the possibility that she was about to have a new ballet created for her by Kenneth MacMillan. Shoulders back and toes turned out, the straightness of her stance lent an extra measure of easy cachet to Chance's casually non-possessive slouch. He signalled to her with a drowsy raising and lowering of his right hand, whose fingers were seen to twiddle minimally in what had to be, but was not one iota more than, a wave of farewell. She smiled at me with piercing sweetness and stepped away along the carpeted corridor as if she were going out on stage at Covent Garden to trade securities, or arriving on the floor of the Stock Exchange to dance a *pas de deux* with Baryshnikov among the hexagonal kiosks.

'That,' said Chance as he ushered me languidly inside, 'is Antonia Blunt. Usually known as the Mole to avoid embarrassment. Had any breakfast?'

At that stage I could only guess at the degree of influence the Mole had had on Chance's life, but judging from the living area, which I had last seen a year before after one of his first nights, he had undergone a neatening process which could plausibly be put down to her example, if not to her active interference. There were still books in several languages lined up double on the shelves and stacked all round the edges of the floor, including the lower wooden frame of the sliding glass wall looking out above the ornamental lake. But the dining table was actually free to be dined off. Even in this, the grandest type of Barbican flat, the kitchen could be inspected from the dining area, since nothing separated them except a sort of counter. The counter was occupied up to shoulder height by stacked books and videos, but the kitchen gleamed. On and under a set of deep low shelves in front of the counter, banks of silver video and stereo equipment glittered dust-free. The staircase led upwards to three more floors – Chance's flat was really a town-house in the sky – and it seemed a fair inference that they too were in an unprecedently pristine condition for which only a continuously busy feminine hand could be responsible. 'The Mole's made a lot of difference around here,' said Chance, confirming my impression. 'Cleaner can't find anything to do any more. Mole does it all.'

'You're a lucky man.'

'She's as bent as a cleft stick but it doesn't hurt to have her on my team. Good for the image. More coffee in the machine.'

'You mean *she* isn't *normal*?' I asked plaintively as I poured.

'Isn't bent *instead* of normal,' said Chance as if he were losing interest. 'Bent *as well*. Clean, though. Puts gloves on before she goes on the tube.'

'She does television?'

'Underground. Won't get on it unless she's wearing gloves.'

'I can quite see how the Northern Line might be beneath her.'

'You can have the spare bedroom on the first floor next to my study. A lot of her stuff there but she won't get in your road. When she stays overnight she usually kips up on the second floor near me. I'll just answer that.'

The telephone had squealed. Chance was still speaking into it half an hour later after I had taken my bags upstairs, unpacked my stuff and been extensively to the nearest bathroom. My digestion was out of kilter so I had to spend some time sitting there looking at a monumental accumulation of bottles and aerosols arranged on shelves like a window display in Burlington Arcade. It was an extravaganza that made Gael's lay-out of accoutrements look like a first-aid kit. Could they all belong to one woman, even if that woman was Angélique? Some of them must be the Mole's. Chance's life, like the Mole's allegedly bipolar sexuality, never had something *instead* when it

33

could have it *as well*. He had always been like that, ever since I had first known him.

'. . . if you want a no-strings yes from Bob,' Chance was saying, 'you'll have to wait for winter. Have to strap on a pair of skis and ambush him on his own mountain.'

Listening in as I surveyed Chance's collection of compact discs – he seemed to have them all – I guessed fairly quickly that he couldn't be talking about Bob Hope, who would have to be ambushed on his own golf course. So which Bob would have to be ambushed on his own mountain? Bob Dylan? Bob Crosby? Bob's your uncle? The breathtaking thing about Chance's name-dropping was that he never dropped names. He wasn't doing it deliberately. He just talked that way.

'. . . can work it out in New York on Thursday. Got lunch with Tony and Teresa. She's ours for three weeks between the next two seasons. But the only way we can make a window is to forget about Santa Fe . . . '

Tony Martin? Teresa Brewer? Then I caught on: Tony Harrison and Teresa Stratas. This time he wasn't directing a movie, he was producing an opera. I caught on but I didn't catch up.

'. . . if Joan and John won't write it . . . Glenn will do it if Tom says yes . . . I think they'll ask Mike . . . '

Joan of Arc and John Donne? No, Joan Didion and John Gregory Dunne. But which Glenn? Glenn Miller? John Glenn? And which Tom? Tom Thumb? Mike Mazurki? Already I was being lulled by the thin, wild blue atmosphere of Chance's high-flying hustle. His manoeuvring was so stratospheric that it made the earthbound pressure on anyone who listened feel like a welcome burden. Chugging along near ground level suddenly seemed the thing to do. With Chance being so entirely successful, somebody had to be only relatively successful. Why not me? Flagging cabs and seeing them go by with people in the back, running for trains and missing them, I had been feeling like a wimp. The British novel I can stand least is the one about the wimp. Whether phoney Waugh or post-punk, the wimp hero is characterised by his incapacity to make anything happen. Usually, in the course of the text, the author turns up under his own name to observe the wimp's disintegration and give him sage advice. God save me from any novel in which the author gets a mention. Not even Firbank could get away with that. God save me from the wimp. I'm not like that. I'm not a patient. I'm an agent. I'm an Australian, one of the Wizards of Oz. We can sing the mad scene from *Lucia*, win Wimbledon ten times in a row, revolutionise Fleet Street, restructure female consciousness, nick the America's Cup, marry Rachel Ward. Chance himself, the embodiment of our hybrid vigour, was living proof that we, the Robust Australopithecines, can bend iron bars with our teeth and fly faster than speeding bullshit. Poet, novelist, performer, and lately director for both stage and screen, he lucratively practised all these art forms and one more besides – the art of pursuing the whole lot simultaneously. The year I arrived at Sydney University in the early 1960s, Chance was just leaving. His fame enveloped the place like the solar wind. Five years difference in age seemed like an aeon at that time. I had been in awe of him. Since then the gap had closed, but not to anything less than open wonder. The time I had thought of him as a genius was long gone. But I admired him all the more as an operator. Admired and needed. My confidence was shaken and I was hoping to catch some of his.

'Shostakovich cello concertos are on the machine,' murmured Chance after putting down the phone. 'Mole's discovery. Listen to the second movement of the first one while I get dressed. Know how to work it?'

After he disappeared upstairs I figured out the mode switches on the Mission Control console and had time to listen to the whole disc while reading most of the way through Chance's soon-to-be-forthcoming collected poems, half a dozen copies of which were stacked on one of the big black leather sofas. The book was called *The Rubaiyat of Omar Sharif*. I already knew much of its contents fairly well, or at any rate as well as I ever want to know modern poetry, which on the whole makes me feel comparatively tolerant of the modern novel. But Chance's poems had never sinned through lack of accessibility. If anything, they jumped into your lap, typifying the gossipy familiarity of the current trend which unashamedly submits itself to showbiz glitz. But Chance made a kind of discipline out of the indulgence. He had, after all, been at it a long time. In fact he had presaged the whole thing. When we were students he had filled the Sydney University newspaper *honi soit* with villanelles in praise of Tuesday Weld and elegies on the death of John Farrow. (Look him up and you'll find that Mia Farrow's father was an Australian. Yes, my country is linked by marriage to Frank Sinatra.) They were in the book. There had been no need to throw anything away. It had all worn well. Costume jewellery never dates. In the photograph on the front of the jacket, Chance looked younger than he had done in the photograph on the back of his most recent novel.

'That lovely?' he pretended to inquire as he returned from upstairs. 'Mole found it. Plays the cello herself. Skis. Dances. Cooks.'

I took another look at his jaw-line. It was still fleshy, but definitely less so. The photograph wasn't lying.

'What does she cook?' I asked him. 'Lean cuisine cardboard?'

'Nar, I'm eating like a horse,' said Chance, rubbing his newly reaped jaw as if my glance had made it itch. 'Just a *sensible* horse.'

'It's magic, like a face-lift.'

'You'll never catch me having one of those. Don't want to end up with my cock hanging out of my forehead. So tell me what happened.'

After handing me a glass of flat champagne he lounged back on one of the sofas like a breakfast television guest whose turn had come to listen. This impression was reinforced by his suede, corduroy and cashmere casual attire. Unseasonable but suave. For most of his life, Chance had had no spare time to be anything but a slob. When I came up to Cambridge as a graduate student, he had already gone down – after a starred first in the second part of the English tripos and the unprecedented triple presidency of the Marlowe Society, the ADC and the Footlights – to increase his glory in London. Though he had loathed everything about flower power, the unwashed blue jeans and matted long hair of the period had appealed to him logistically. He had always resented time spent on having his hair cut. In recent years this problem had been made less urgent by encroaching baldness. Now that I came to look at the top of his head, he seemed to be keeping it at least as neat as Elton John or Phil Collins, but presumably he could be doing that himself, with nail scissors. The improvement in his clothes, however, could only be ascribed to an act of will. Watching him on television over the years, I had seen him gradually abandon his earlier persona as the man determined to preserve his scruffy integrity. If all his stellar appearances could have been edited together and transmitted at high speed, you would have seen an open shirt collar suddenly cinched by an acrylic tie, then the tie becoming silk, then the shirt itself acquiring a set of those Turnbull and Asser cuff-links that look like scout woggles for leprechauns or – revolting thought, instantly suppressed – the interlocking orbits of Lilywhite's Quincunx. Sideboards would have grown shorter, eyebrows neater. And the jowls heavier, but now even that sole remaining retrogressive tendency had gone into reverse and started moving forward, one last arrow of time belatedly joining the rest of the shower that was heading towards the past-like future in which Chance Jenolan, instead of falling apart, fell together.

I had only one hour to tell my story and hear his opinion of it. After that, he warned me, he would be going with Bruce and Peter and Fred to meet Charles for lunch. After a moment's semi-automatic puzzlement I guessed that Bruce and Peter and Fred were his fellow-Australian film directors. But who was Charles? Charles Chaplin? Charles Lindbergh? Charles the Bold? Oh. Of course. Conscious that I was eating into the timetable of a man who filled his diary the way Leonardo da Vinci filled a notebook, I gave the compressed version of my woeful saga. Only occasionally grunting and glazing over, he stared through the slowly sipped-away contents of his champagne glass as their glow waned in the waxing morning light, there being increasingly less of them to catch fire. It was an heroic effort on his part. Though not without generosity when reminded, very rarely did he concern himself with the affairs of others unless he was looking for material. I completed my exposition wondering if I should ever have begun it.

'Don't worry,' he said as if reading my mind. 'You won't recognise anything I steal. Sweet story, incidentally. Standard plot but nice nuances. Terrific part there for Brooke Adams or Karen Allen. But it'd never make a movie. Too much like real life.'

'I know that, for Christ's sake. It *is* real life. Mine.' With relief I noted that his socks were odd. Excellent quality, but definitely from two different pairs.

'Mine too. That was how I screwed up with Paula.' He meant his first wife, the one before Angélique. 'I went apeshit about Gunilla. Remember Gunilla?'

'Yes.' I remembered her vividly. A fashion model too lovely to look at with the naked eye.

'I can't. Girl whose chief attribute was not being Paula. That and youth. Absolute airhead. If I'd fucked around more beforehand she wouldn't have come as such a revelation.'

'Yes.' It was hard to see how he might have found it physically possible to fuck around more beforehand than he had, but I was lying low.

'That's why it's always the good blokes who get divorced. Bad blokes aren't thrown for a loop by their first teenybopper blow job. I don't really live here much.'

He was looking at his acreage of windows as if explaining to me why he'd never got around to having curtains fitted. The greenhouse effect was intense. I could see him weighing the choice, testing it between his thumb and forefinger, of removing his cashmere sweater or making the advertised move towards lunch. He got up, shrugged off the sweater and replaced it with a tweed jacket that had been lying over the back of a chair, on which there was a stack of fat envelopes and spiral-bound scripts.

'All unsolicited, these. Allegedly terrific ideas for novels or screenplays the author wants me to help rewrite. Or write. This guy here . . . ' Chance pulled a springback folder from half-way down the pile, ' . . . wants me to publish his novel under my name so it'll get reviewed. He says, "I did not get reviews, needless to say, for my previous novel because of course I was not a member of the literary establishment as you are. Not that I want to be a member of the London gang. We can't all be Australians." You can tell *he's* got integrity.'

'What's it about?' I asked, trying not to be sorry that the dialogue had moved off the topic of my preoccupations and on to his.

'Usual stuff about the loss of identity. Interweaving plots.

Have to go.' He threw the offending manuscript back on top of the pile, from which it slickly slid off and fell to the floor, where it lay waiting for someone, presumably the Mole, to pick it up and put it back with its doomed fellows. 'Spare keys in top kitchen drawer. Treat the place as home until Angélique gets here. She mightn't even stay. Likes the Dorchester.'

'When will you be back?' I tried not to blubber like a man overboard viewing a retreating lifeline.

'Tonight. Stuff in fridge. Make yourself some lunch. Mole'll get dinner. Relax. Use the phone. Forget the guilt. Robert Stack and Carole Lombard.'

'To Be or Not to Be.'

'A while since I've played that game with anyone as quick on the draw as you. Good to have you around. Don't feel superfluous. I'm gone.'

The game was called Stars. I couldn't believe that he hadn't played it to a high standard with his theatrical friends, but perhaps he had become a bit of a flatterer, or was just stroking my ego to look after me. Long ago, when he had first picked me up, I had helped him formulate the game's rules. 'A game,' he had said, 'consists of the rules by which it is played. Wittgenstein.' Stars is easy to play badly but quite tricky to play well. You should spot the film after hearing the names of a minimum number of its cast members. The more names you need to hear, the less you score for a right answer, but if you jump the gun and name the wrong film your opponent gets full marks. Burt Lancaster and Tony Curtis. Did you guess *The Sweet Smell of Success*? You guessed too soon. You should have waited until I said Gina Lollobrigida. It's *Trapeze*. There are all kinds of tricks you can work if you've seen everything and have a good memory for the early screen appearances of future stars. A good memory, which Chance and I had in common, brought us together for long orgies of conversation dotted through the years. The long conversations mainly consisted of bartered names, jousting facts and figures. Probably it was a way of not meeting: *Doppelgängerschrei* allayed by small talk. I think he thought of me as the boffin who operated in the one field closed to him, and I know I thought of him as the lucky man who participated in the artsy creativity of which I was doomed to be a spectator.

Being thus debarred had been no hardship when I was still sure that a greater form of knowledge would one day include my name in its annals. But now I was less sure and I envied my *alter ego* his sureness, not to say his ego. I envied him his living conditions too. Not that the décor could be called luxurious. Everything looked incomplete. Miles of walls were white with nothing on them. The place was even bigger than I remembered. There were whole rooms unutilised, with little in them except rows of plastic shopping bags full of stuff that had obviously remained un-unpacked since the day he moved in. The main bedroom had a bed big enough to play polo on but you wouldn't have picked it as a possible setting for Angélique Visage, even if she had been starring in a Jean-Luc Godard movie about a terrorist cadre based at La Défense. Not even the room which the Mole was allowed to call her own looked as if it had been given much loving thought. Clearly she lived somewhere else, and came here only to read and rest. There were a few books which had to be hers, because only a student would read them. *Restructuring Joyce: the Artist in the Portrait.* Pencilled comments filled the margin. 'But is not Stephen's apprehension of the void the precise equivalent of Beckett's concept of zero? See *Endgame*.' I went through her clothes in the cupboard. There were only two pairs of shoes. There was a drawer full of knickers and bras which I tried to examine as if they were merely underclothes instead of provocations to desire. I felt defeated enough to succeed, although her daintiness was already a pleasure to be anticipated as well as remembered. Where did Chance get off, affecting to be casual about a girl like her? Who did he think he was, Hugh Hefner? In a flat handkerchief box there was a sheaf of love letters, which I put off reading after checking the signatures and sampling the first paragraph of the top one. They were from Chance, of course.

Dear Spy,

Missing you like blood. Bangkok is aptly named. Last night I woke up rigidly thinking of you, tried to guess where the bathroom was before turning on the light, and . . .

But it wasn't my moment to enjoy someone else's happiness, and anyway I swore this wouldn't be an epistolary book. (Novels with a lot of letters in them are a real cop-out, don't you agree?) Up yet another flight of stairs, the top floor of the flat was all one big square area, two of the walls glass and one of those rigged to slide, so that you could walk on to a concrete balcony and look out over the City of London. You could see what the modern architects were doing to it that the *Luftwaffe* hadn't. Actually I like the NatWest tower. Somewhere in his make-up, every scientist has a soft spot for Fritz Lang. The new Lloyds, however, couldn't help making the odd remaining Lutyens cupola look cherishable by comparison. There was one sticking up out of the periphery of Finsbury Circus – the one with an Expo-style latticework globe of the world on top – that reminded me, by its dome and drum, of the optical telescopes along Madingley Road. Suddenly I hated Veronica. It was a disturbing experience to look at a building and loathe a woman. I turned back into the room and remembered it as I had seen it last. There had not been much in it except about thirty people, the thoughtful overspill from the floor below, where there were about fifty more. It had been the late evening aftermath of one of the preview nights of Chance's biggest National Theatre success, his production of his own adaptation of *The Ring and the Book*, one of those gigantic subsidised semi-musical saturnalias from which the hard-worked originators receive no reward except a gigantic percentage of the gate when it runs commercially. Chance privately called it the Clowning Version, but if he was ashamed of trivialising himself he didn't let it show. And indeed the four-hour spectacular had been – deadly praise – a Delightful Evening in the Theatre.

The party was better. For one thing, the cast was not present. Everyone else was. They were all there. You couldn't move for Michaels and Toms, Peters and Davids, Kates and Helens. Standing there a year later, it still angered me how much fun Lauren had contrived not to have. She had got herself stuck with an old drinking pal of Chance's who had evidently been kept on out of pity, to circulate in a cold ellipse at due distance from the hot light – a flaky writer of some kind called Clive James. Apparently he lived somewhere near by in a basement flat. In the corner of the room where he and Lauren had stood boring each other, there now gleamed one of those exercise tables on which you could lie down while lifting weights with every part of your body. You could do a snatch-and-press with your arse, a clean-and-jerk with your cock, lift bar-bells with your balls. There were two exercise bikes and a treadmill with chromium handrails. There was a rowing machine. Chance had everything it took to keep his waistline from reflating. There were machines for other uses too. There was a two-screen video editing unit and a Panasonic minicam on a tripod. There was a Nashua copying machine the size of a refrigerator. There were machines adding up to a complete audio pre-production studio. Some of them were just names to me. What did a Roland SBX-80 Sync Box do? There was an Atari 24-track Sequenced Emulator which had a VDU sitting on top of it. The VDU was saying something. It was saying Track Midi Fast-Access Flags NO-NAME Unselected. There was a Yamaha smart piano which was obviously just aching to give you a Buddy Holly hit in the style of *Tristan und Isolde*. With all this stuff, Chance could choose the face and voice he wanted. But the main emphasis was on his choice of body. This was where he had acquired his new air of languor. He had always had self-control, but it had looked like energy on a hair trigger. Now he made Gary Cooper look like Jerry Lewis. He was so relaxed he was asleep. This was how he did it. Through sweat and strain. What was he after? Lost youth? He had never wasted a day. I retraced my steps downwards.

The study which had no room for the Nashua copier had acquired an Amstrad 512 since I saw it last. Compared with the stuff upstairs it was only a toy. I remembered Chance's tight-lipped tirades against word processors and doubted that he had mastered this gizmo much beyond the extent of using it as typewriter. I checked one of the floppy discs: empty. Beside the VDU on the big desk was a golfball electric typewriter that looked lived in. On the floor were a couple of old ordinary typewriters he had cast aside, probably because their ribbons had gone pale. A golfball typewriter was getting perilously close to being up to date, but it was still satisfactorily user-unfriendly. Chance liked, he had said, to feel some resistance from the medium. Suddenly I loathed that golfball. I stood there fixated by it, floating silently above it, landing on it. *Roger, Tranquillity: we copy you on the ground.* Words sweet in my memory had turned sour. My obsession had betrayed me. It could never happen to Chance. He made his own rules, his own worlds.

Look at his desk. Neat, free of dust, but crowded to capacity. The chaos he made order from. It was big enough for ping-pong but there was nowhere for the ball to bounce. Sitting in his swivel chair, careful not to swivel in it lest I feel like a usurper, I surveyed the heaps of manila folders, proofs, carbon copies, tear-sheets. Along the far edge of the desk there was a two-level platform full of reference books. There was a floor-to-ceiling case of more reference books behind me and still more in the other set of shelves that climbed half-way up the opposite wall. *Gradus ad Parnassum. Der Sprach Brockhaus. Dictionnaire Étymologique. Dictionary of American Underworld Lingo. Enciclopedia Concisa Illustrada. Biographical Encyclopaedia of Science and Technology.* Almost everything I knew was either encoded into the last-mentioned book or else would appear in a further edition, to be raided by Chance, who didn't know it and didn't have to, as long as he had access to the words. All he needed was a technical-sounding term and he was off. Long ago he had sought me out because I shared his facile knack. Our first uneasy friendship must have been made possible for him because to some extent I shared his green fingers for a phrase. But he had gone on with it, made it his profession. Superficial, but it would never fail him. Would never fail him *because* it was superficial. The world wanted his glittering surfaces, so as to be entertained, so as to flatter itself that it had been understood. The world also wanted my depths. Needed them more than his shallows. But it had turned out that I could not produce the depths, and now, to my own reluctant eyes, the sparkle of the shallows had intensified to a dazzle.

Above the bookcase on the opposite wall was a cork pinboard full of personal photographs and minor trophies. But Chance had never been much of a one for parading his credentials in front of visitors. There were no posters on display for his books, his programmes, his films or his productions. There were plenty of framed old Hollywood glamour photographs, but even more of these were leaning against the walls on which they would clearly wait for ever to be hung. Without exception they were from before his time. The Garbo portrait was especially appropriate. He had always been good at, and had grown increasingly better at, doing a Garbo. The hollow phrase 'rarely gives interviews' had a solid ring where he was concerned. Some said it was because he had too much to hide, others that his unforthcomingness was based on a precise calculation of how much the traffic could stand. But if, as seemed likely, the keepsakes carelessly stuck to the pinboard had been put there solely for his delectation, their resonance for anyone else who penetrated this crammed sanctum could only be enhanced. His press passes for foreign assignments were up there like place-cards. There he was on the Dick Cavett show with Mary McCarthy, all three of them laughing. An amateur photograph, obviously taken at Glyndebourne and presumably by him, showed Frederica von Stade giggling with shocked delight. Elsewhere he had his arm around Peggy Ashcroft. Torn out of a magazine, a colour picture of Fellini with his face made up half-white was dedicated with a felt tip *al mio discepolo*. Another colour photograph showed Chance and a strikingly handsome silver-haired man both in swimming attire, holding a surfboard each and posing histrionically with an arm slung around each other's shoulders. Angélique stood beside the silver-haired man, staring at the camera with her hand shielding her eyes, as if it were the sun. In another picture she sat at an *al fresco* table with Jean-Paul Belmondo, his features altered, no doubt by her, to make him look like Toulouse-Lautrec. There were posed photographs of Chance's children, and of the Mole looking not much older. There were buttons and badges saying KRAZY KAT, CAESAR'S PALACE DATSUN, and I'M PULLING FOR BAZZA! It was a gleaming jumble. The whole place was a visual shambles. How could any dwelling be so cleanly austere and yet so full of objects that didn't fit? A junk yard had more coherence.

On the level of language, however, there was unity. Even the images contributed to the tone. Everything had, or was, a name. Nothing was here that Chance couldn't rework into a poem, a novel, a script, a screenplay, a lyric, a libretto. Nothing he couldn't mangle, mince, pulp, process, rehash, reconstitute, regurgitate. His books were grouped functionally, not out of love. I loved literature and had the library to prove it. In Cambridge, my shelves of novels were a talking point for my dinner guests. You know those little Novel Library editions with wallpapered boards and the NL monogram? I had collected the whole lot, including that perfect set, almost impossible to find, of Jane Austen, six volumes with the same black spine. It was one of my three best sets of Jane Austen and not even Lauren was allowed to touch it. I kept my literature immaculate out of adoration. That was the main reason why I wouldn't grant admission to any recent work of fiction whose author believed in his duty to deconstruct character, atomise style, etc. *Bel Ami*, whose author had put a lot of effort and every resource of style into constructing its main character, had a right not to be contaminated. Cousin Pons, Cousin Bette, Anna Karenina, Effi Briest, Tom Jones, Wilhelm Meister and others too numerous to mention had their names up there because they were people. They might be fictional people, but they deserved a better death than to be annihilated by the invisible gas of sciolist theory. I kept them dusted as if there were plutonium drifting on the wind.

My science books and papers were inherently harder to keep spotless, because sometimes I had to work at home, but by and large I brought the same reverence to my vocation as to my avocation. Where it stood majestically on its very own oak shelf, my complete set of the Cambridge edition of Newton's papers – bound for me in full leather by Lauren as a Christmas present – had a tiny light fitted behind it so that it was edged with radiance when we sat down to a candlelit casserole. I allowed joking suggestions that there was a certain resemblance to a Forest Lawn shrine or a fluorescent niche in the Temple at Salt Lake City. But I was mad about my subject and proud that its masterworks gleamed there in the dark, in rich half-calf, stamped with silver and gold titles, with old brass instruments for bookends. Chance just dumped his subject on the floor until he needed a piece of it. If the stack toppled, the Mole or the cleaner put it back together. Chance's organising principle operated only to expedient ends. A cairn of books and pamphlets on the floor beside the swivel chair suggested that he was doing something about Brecht. *Dreigroschenroman*. *Brechts Dreigroschenbuch*. *Dialektik auf dem Theater*. A glossy picture book called *Leben Brechts* published in East Berlin. *Brecht über Lyrik*. Lotte Lenya's memoirs. Chance must have been writing an article about his *bête noire*, or contemplating an adaptation, or casting the filmed biography. I visualised Klaus Maria Brandauer in the role, with Meryl Streep as Helene Weigel. I was beginning to think like Chance. No, I wasn't. Never could, thank Christ. Christ I was tired. Forgetting about lunch, I lay down for a while on the narrow bed that was supposed to be mine.

PART TWO

Lost in the Barbican

From this viewpoint the labyrinth is not something which has grown from nature, it is a work of art. This means that it is a human copy of something. Daedalus built it. What kind of plan did he follow? He thought: there is a Minotaur, and I must invent something which he can move freely in, but not get out of.

Friedrich Dürrenmatt, *Die Welt als Labyrinth*

'WOULD YOU LIKE SOME TEA?' FOR A STRANGE MOMENT I thought the Mole was an air hostess. Enough light spilled between the drawn curtains for me to look up and see her polished hair as she sat on the edge of my bed. She had taken off her jacket. I could see enough of her long-sleeved, roll-neck silk blouse to deduce that her breasts were as large as they could be without being out of proportion. Longing has a mind of its own that works at high speed even when the rest of the brain is dazed. I lifted one hand – I was lying on top of the made bed, with nothing over me – and brushed the back of it across where her nipple must have been in its lucky cloth cage. The sensation of touching hard rubber would have been unexciting if I had been touching hard rubber, but since I knew I wasn't, it wasn't. Concentrated softness is not hardness.

'*Tea*, I said,' she said with put-on haughtiness. 'Just for that you'll have to come downstairs for it.'

Less bleary-eyed after splashing my face in the bathroom, I was able fully to appreciate the way she graced the kitchen. I couldn't believe the time that showed up digitally on the VCR machine. I had to check it against my watch. Most of the afternoon was gone. While I had been asleep, the Mole, it transpired, had been to lectures and tutorials.

'Amanda,' said the Mole in much the same tone as I might have mentioned Veronica.

'What about Amanda?' Obviously I was meant to ask. It was the least I could do for someone making tea with such care. Making it a treat, and looking a treat while doing it.

'Amanda is such a wally. She's in my tutorial group and she is *such a wally*.'

'In what way does Amanda's wallyhood manifest itself?'

'Sugar?'

'No thanks.'

'I wouldn't have given you any anyway. Too much of you there in the middle. She's just such a dumb-dumb. The stupid things she says. It takes up half the time. We've only got an hour, and half of it goes on discussing her stupid remarks.'

'Like what?'

'The stupid things she *says*. You'd swear she'd only read the Cole's Notes. She says things like, "It has been said, has it not, that there is a frequent use of coincidence in Hardy's novels." It's the "has it not" that gets me.'

'I can see how it might.'

'She thinks I fancy her, too. Fat chance.'

'Is she pretty?' I asked with feigned casualness, as fascinated as I had ever been by anything in my life. This was prime information. Stars more red than they should be are going away from you. Stars more blue are coming towards you. I had learned that when I was a child. But until now, in middle age, I had never experienced a girl like this as a totality, the way she looked and the sounds she made. Coming towards me. Not going away.

'Not my type,' said the Mole firmly, adding a parodic snooty nose to show that she knew she was being superior. Her nose, I estimated, running mental calipers over it, was at least a size too small, but well chiselled without looking like a bob-job. Its smallness was probably a help in making her so photogenic. Cecil Beaton had said that even Grace Kelly would not have been so photogenic if her nose had been larger.

'Too dumb?'

'No, it's not that. I could fall for a clueless girl if she was pretty enough. Just like you in that regard. It's just . . . '

'Too boring?'

'Too pretentious. She isn't *content* to be clueless. Chance says that saying nothing is better than saying something that means nothing.'

'Does she share your . . . has she made a pass?'

'God no. She's as straight as a road. But a girl who knows a girl I knew told her about me. And what a wally *she* is.'

'The girl you knew?'

'The girl who knows her. Damn. I forgot to get the white wine vinegar.'

Deputised, or having volunteered, to cook dinner for Chance and me, the Mole had brought home a range of simple but high-quality foodstuffs to supplement what was already in the refrigerator. But the list of what she still needed ran to nine items when she had finished writing it down on the back of a handbill announcing a charity raffle in the vestry, if not the chantry or the pantry, of St Giles's Cripplegate. She assured me that all these things could be acquired at Safeway. Under the list she drew a map of how to get there. It looked like an integrated circuit, but by following the turns meticulously I became merely confused instead of desperate, and eventually arrived at the Arts Centre, from which the supermarket was almost in line of sight. By now it was nearing five o'clock and the huge shop was crowded. You could see the impact which modern merchandising had made on the old street of small shops and its intimate way of life. No impact. Old women who would once have gathered to yap endlessly in front of the greengrocer's now gathered to yap endlessly at the corner of the vegetable counter. The only difference was that they had trolleys and you couldn't get past them. Another sociological axiom knocked on the head.

Alienation, though, became a reality after I had collected my specified items and made a bid to get out. I was ready to pay cash. Those in front of me in the queue for the Express check-out (9 ITEMS OR LESS said the sign illiterately) had all opted out of the cash nexus. Everybody had a cheque book and wrote in it at length. One woman must have written a short story on her cheque stub. These long delays for prose composition were punctuated by longer delays when the price had to be found for items which had been placed in the trolley without the presence of a price sticker having first been verified. When the check-out clerk found one of these items on the conveyor belt she had to examine it for a long time from all angles. Clearly she was only a trainee. Why had a trainee check-out girl been assigned to the Express check-out? Would British Rail assign a trainee driver to an express train? Yes. After mentally photographing the item in four dimensions, the clerk asked the clerk on each side of her what they thought it might cost. They were trainees too. Then she pressed the button on her Tannoy and sent out a call for help. In the course of time a young man approached and she showed the item to him. He, also, examined it from all angles, as if making an independent assessment of what it actually was. He went away. While he was away, the customer's pen

51

was poised over the cheque book, waiting for *le mot juste*. Either the young man came back after a long time or he did not come back at all. The only way you could tell he was not coming back at all would have been to wait until he didn't. The disembodied voice might have been his, however, which eventually mentioned a price in the check-out clerk's ear. Slowly she turned and transmitted it vocally to the customer. At last the cheque was filled out and handed over to the check-out clerk, although for some reason the transfer seldom took place before the cheque stub had been filled out to match. The cheque having changed ownership, the clerk now began to study it as if it were a love letter already familiar and now to be cherished for its every delectable quirk. Having tested its merest syllable against her fond memory, she slowly added some observations of her own with a ballpoint pen. My impatience was as pure as fear. It had been a long time since I had been in a supermarket. When I finally drew abreast of the check-out clerk I was surprised – or would have been surprised, if I had not been consumed by anger – to see that the cash register subtracted the total price demanded from the amount of money I offered and told her how much change to give me. The last check-out cash register I had seen had not been quite so smart. The human being was now entirely superfluous. So what was she still doing here? Then I found out. 'Ear!' she announced loudly. 'You've a sinus?' I looked blank, like a man who has just wasted half an hour of his life and then been asked a question about his facial anatomy. 'You've a sinus what's on a telly?' As I told her that I was indeed the scientist on the telly, I strove to convince myself that here was a sample of the mass attention I had sought, and that I should not despise it. But self-pity had joined frustration, leaving no room for self-reproach. Not since my wedding day had I been obliged to queue for provisions. For years they had all been delivered to the house in a cardboard box. Lauren had organised it. To a large extent she had paid for it. But to an even larger extent she had organised it. I got a sudden urge to call Cambridge.

I was impressed at the time – I'm not just saying it now – that I could harbour a new desire so distant from the need

52

to burn down Safeway. All you want from a store except a conflagration. But it wasn't their fault. Hence my rage. It was my usual rage at not having spotted the obvious. The non-express check-out queues were the ones to join. Those people with trolleys loaded like Jumbo jets full of pilgrims were the experienced shoppers, less likely to choose items without price stickers, more likely to have their cheques and stubs filled out before the clerk had finished the tally. Getting behind two or even three of the big spenders would ensure quicker progress than queuing up behind five or six of the small fry. I had missed the too-obvious point. Failed the IQ test. Overinterpreted the stellar signal. Ah, Veronica!

Back in the flat, I handed over the provender to the Mole and entertained her with a calm account of my adventures. She was padding barefoot around the kitchen in a silk dressing-gown. When she laughed I tried not to notice that she was wearing little underneath. I left her to her work and went to Chance's office, where a telephone call to Cambridge revealed that Lauren refused to talk to me. My daughter was not at home but my son explained that she was not talking to me either. He then advised me to stay off the line for at least a week. 'It's raining shit up here.' I told him not to swear and he told me that I was no longer in a position to give orders, merely to suggest a course of action. I could tell he got that from his mother.

I could also tell that he was relieved when I said I had to cut the call short, on the grounds that it wasn't my telephone. Back in the kitchen that wasn't mine either I was enrolled by the Mole, who wasn't mine either, to open a bottle of excellent wine – a Château Fonplégade Saint Émilion Grand Cru 1967, which was not mine either. Chance had boxes of the stuff stashed in the cupboard. The bottles had never been unpacked and laid down somewhere cool. The most that had been done for them was to lay the boxes sideways. But the Mole assured me that everything got swilled down before it could spoil. 'Anyway, he gets most of it as presents. For speeches and things like that. They give it to him instead of money and then we all drink it.'

'Who's we all?'

'Oh, everybody. Everybody comes here. Keep cutting the garlic while I do the vinaigrette.'

'Do we need this much?'

'It's good for you. It brings out all the poison.'

'Too late for that.'

'Stop being so dramatic.'

'Stop being so bossy.'

'It's my function. Chance loves how I boss him around. I wish he'd let me live here all the time. I could really get this place organised.'

'Are you trying to talk him into it?'

'More or less.'

'Well, here's hoping.'

'*He's* hoping? No, I am.'

'No, *here's* hoping.'

'Here's hopping?'

'No. It's an expression. *Here's hoping*. It means that something is to be hoped for. Don't you know that expression?'

'No. Should I?'

'Stick with me, kid. You'll learn a lot of ancient slang.' Such as: stick with me, kid. We might not feel old when the policemen start looking young. We might not even feel old when we meet girls born after the Second World War, and then after the Korean War, and then – like this one – during the Vietnam war. But when they can't understand a word of what we say, *then* we feel old. Pervaded by an embarrassed feeling that my vocabulary had gone out of date like flared trousers or the crinoline, I put off until another day my projected inquiry into just what exactly the Mole did for Chance apart from getting him organised. It went without saying that she slept with him, but on what basis? Was she a bed-warmer for Angélique? Did she want to be his next wife? Perhaps Chance was the one to ask. Perhaps neither. Hanging on by the skin of my teeth, I was in no position to demand an account of the sleeping arrangements. I already felt guilty about not having made a bigger contribution towards paying for the supplies which the Mole was expertly transforming into the kind of meal she had been taught to create at her Swiss finishing school. Could Lauren cut off my credit and cash cards? And if she could, would she? If she did, I would find out soon enough. If she didn't, I could never find out she wouldn't, unless she talked to me. I would just have to go on using them until they became useless. And even if they didn't, they would always feel as if they might.

This interior monologue had nothing in common, except for its self-generating circularity, with the Mole's exterior monologue, which mainly concerned the other girls in College Hall, where she lived, as opposed to here, which she only visited, except out of term time, when she lived here instead of there, but not really. The other girls were introduced to me one by one and their characters differentially sketched. The star catalogue very quickly became too fascinating to ignore. Sexuality, proved or suspected, was given prominence. There were wallies you couldn't imagine doing it. There were super wallies you could imagine doing it with anyone, even a Dutch businessman just back from Nairobi. There were some classy girls who were unfortunately straight as roads. One very pretty girl was ready for anything but unfortunately she had hands like plates. The Mole demanded refinement. She liked beautiful hands. She had them, too, but while she was saying this I was doting on her long, straight dancer's feet. She made my heart feel like a microlight aircraft, like a solar-powered car with bicycle wheels, like a silver-foil-clad satellite spinning up from the Space Shuttle. She took me out of myself. It was one of her many gifts.

'I'm going to have a bath,' she said, with the intense but detached interest in herself that I could already see was usual, 'and get changed. Put on some music.'

'What would you like?'

'Take your pick.'

There being too much to choose from, I put on the Shostakovich cello concertos again, selecting the second, slow movement of the First Concerto and turning up the volume so that she would be able to hear it upstairs. As the cello unspooled its first long thread of melancholy, the word 'Yum!' came floating down, haloed with tiled resonance, like a sweet echo. Usually I don't enjoy being introduced to things. And really I knew quite a lot about music, for a passive listener. I could read it, for example, which Chance couldn't. In childhood I had put in my years as a flute prodigy. But my tastes ran only as far as early late romanticism, and those poor persecuted Russians had always struck me as *too* late. It would be unsettling to find myself newly receptive, starting again. Trying not to be swept up, I poured myself a *Punt e Mes*, freighted it with ice and sought quiet distraction. Though it was still not dark outside, it was already seven o'clock. I turned on the television for the Channel 4 news, keeping the sound down so that the Mole would hear only music. A standard rape and murder came at the top of the show. A relatively minor bombing was beaten into second spot. Apparently an Arab terrorist had blown himself up in Athens airport, killing or maiming the entire family of the leading Egyptian expert in bone cancer. The unintentional massacre was being claimed as a victory anyway, by a break-away group sworn to punish Yasser Arafat's flirtation with Zionism. The Princess of Wales was on early, bending close to old women in wheelchairs. The eternal sadness of the Russian cello made temporary sense of it all by evoking worse fears and even more arbitrary deprivations. With the lights off in the room, the large television screen and tiny diodes of the audio stack illuminated little beyond themselves. Swamped with shadows, I looked out and down through the glass wall into the oncoming evening. Across the walkway above the ornamental lake, people were arriving for the night's performances at the Arts Centre. Incongruously eager in that setting, they moved like extras in *Metropolis* or *Things to Come* released for a meal break. But the brick esplanade in front of the Guildhall School of Music had emptied of its daily students and there was no one in the little park except a solitary jogging figure in trainer shoes, sloppy joe and white shorts, his excess bulk detectable even at that range. Rather theatrically I kept watching him instead of turning around to greet Chance's arrival.

'Pathetic sight, isn't he?' asked Chance at my shoulder. 'One of ours. Bit before your time. Knew him at school. Name's Clive James.'

'Is that him? Lauren got lumbered with him at that party you had here. Sad sort of guy.'

'The last freelance literary journalist. Does sports reports to keep going. Writes critical essays. Odd bit of television guesting on book programmes. Strictly hand to mouth. Writes poetry that sounds the way reproduction furniture looks. I have him up here for a meal when he's starving. Not that he shows any signs.'

'Sometimes malnutrition makes them swell up.'

'Mole'll make sure it doesn't happen to us.'

The lonely runner had convinced me, as if by telepathy, that I must do something about my own weight. Chance was a model of what could be done if the Mole was available to help do it. She hadn't precisely dressed up, but she had dressed well, mainly in black silk jersey. In the dark room she was the hardest thing to see and the easiest to look at. With the machines shut off and no light added except for some cupcake candles, our small round dinner table took on the overtones of a Supper at Emmaus by Rembrandt, unless I mean undertones. The food was sickeningly healthy. There was a salad to start, followed by a salad, with salad on the side. Proud to have had a hand in preparing this, I was glad enough to help eat it, but without the red wine I might have missed red meat. Not all the light in the Mole's childish face was indebted to the candles. She had a triumph to report. Apparently she had been the star of her tutorial on the novel. All I had learned about this was the bit about Amanda's wallyesque opinions on Hardy, so I was jealous. The Mole had held back the best of her news for Chance: clear proof of love. Here I give only an extract from her monologue. You must imagine the verve; the way she kept talking even while coming and going with plates and wooden bowls; the pleasure of self-discovery. Chance listened, not just with the nearest thing to patience I had ever seen him muster, but with an apparent determination to enjoy the fleeting moment even if it took an hour.

'And I was the only one who was really talking about *Les Gommes* because all the others were only saying what they'd seen in this book on the *nouveau roman*. Except the hopeless wally Amanda who hadn't even read *that*. And *I* said, Chance are you sending me up?'

'Contrary. Fascinated. Wondering if you're going to go

straight up in the air and hang there humming like a flying saucer.'

'Your eyebrow was raised.'

'Astonishment. Go on.'

'And *I* said, obviously the narrator is trying to make this distinction between art and reality, keeps showing, you see, what happens is, while the protagonist is chasing around looking for the perfect rubber, not *that* kind of rubber, Joel, you're as bad as him, the *shoe* kind, he sees in the window the model of an artist, um, painting this picture of a Greek temple, and looking at, or *sposedly* looking at . . . '

'Sposedly?' asked Chance. 'I'm sprised.'

'*Supposedly* looking at, shut up, a scene of, a photograph, ironically representing reality, of a twentieth-century crossroads. And *I* thought that just as an artist, and the model artist, is representing a representation of a reproduction, because it's a copy of a painting, the *actual narrator* talks about a *model* artist, which is a representation, as if it was *reality*, and gives a series of contradictory reactions. Do you see?'

'Yes. I see,' said Chance, and I believe he did. He knew all about this: he had already heard, long ago and from less engaging sources, the dull clear signal of which the Mole was giving him a version wildly scrambled, vividly chromatic. She was practically dancing by now, half-way to her feet, waving her beautiful arms, doing Balinese poses with her fingers to give these airy notions the life she thought they deserved. Perhaps they did, if they could do so much to excite her.

'The model artist seems to be static . . . '

She froze, being static.

' . . . but if you analyse it closely . . . '

She narrowed her eyes and held one finger in the air, analysing closely.

' . . . most nineteenth-century novelist novels, I mean realist novels, pretend to narrate reality, but this doesn't. It shows that reality can *never* be represented, and that's what metafiction does, what self-reflexivity does, it shows, that, um, and the *main point* about metafiction is that it's the actual writing, the *process*, rather than the *product* . . . '

She leapt a foot high and a foot sideways, landing in a crouch, with the emphatic forefinger held forward, almost touching Chance's nose as he pretended to deliberate.

'. . . that produces the realism! Good point? Am I clever? And everybody else had just read those chapters about the *nouveau roman*, but they hadn't read Robbe-Grillet, and they hand't got the point *at all.*'

Suddenly she laughed, not about anything she had already said but about what she was going to say next.

'Do you know what wally Amanda called Robbe-Grillet? Robert Grill-it! Seriously! I mean, that girl has *no clue.*'

'Not like the Mole,' drawled Chance proudly, as his *protégée* – was that what she was? – sat down with her chest heaving and her face on fire. Ethereal, flush'd and like a throbbing star, said Keats, who had felt the cosmos in his lungs, *flammantia moenia mundi.* The flaming walls of the world. My flaming oath. Knowing that I was a dog in the manger, I employed my trick memory for a devastating quotation.

'It was decided that Emma must be prevented from reading novels.'

'But Flaubert meant that she shouldn't have been reading *sentimental* novels,' said Chance with a sudden access of polemical force, a snapping into focus. 'Robert Grill-it and the rest of them aren't sentimental. They might be a mob of posturing jerks, but they're not giving the customer an easy ride. Look how they've helped to wake this Mole here up. Emma's novels put her to sleep. *They* were the *real* white arsenic.'

Chance's habitual cropped and compressed speech had suddenly expatiated into bravura. I could tell that one of his famous filibusters was coming on. Without wishing to prevent this, I did my best to forestall it, making my case for the way literary studies had become pseudo-science, a sophistical poison which had corrupted first the teachers, then the students, and finally the writers themselves. In all humility I strove to suppress, or at any rate soft-pedal, the consideration that my viewpoint was a vantage point. I was a real scientist contemplating the havoc wrought by voodoo; an astronomer dismissing astrology. Careful not to hurt the Mole's feelings, I nevertheless argued with some cogency, even if I say so myself. Was I not doubly qualified, the expert in real critical inquiry on the one hand, and the ideal common reader on the other? Also I had my act well polished from many a Cambridge dinner table, not excluding high table at my college. Trinity, especially between terms, was a watering hole for the kind of conference-trotting post-humanists who could decode a text in nothing flat but couldn't read a book to save their lives. I had always made a point of reminding them – or, in some cases, apprising them for the first time – that on my territory they were fish out of water, whereas I on theirs was a duck in it. The Mole had no choice but to hear me out. Chance chose to, for half a glass, and seemed actually to enjoy my peroration.

'And finally,' I said, 'in this short version of what should be a long and, it goes without saying . . . '

'Apparently not.' But his smile was tolerant.

' . . . more subtle argument, I have to point out something about the exact sciences which decisively separates them from anything pretending to be science. The exact sciences don't try to sound scientific. They sound the way they do from necessity. Occam's Razor applies. They *are* Occam's Razor.'

'I know what this *is*!' piped the Mole, about an octave higher than her usual excited voice, which was never very low. 'But I can't say it out loud.'

'It means there should be no needless multiplication of entities,' I said helpfully, doing a good job, I thought, of saying it in the way she would have said it if she could have said it. 'The determination of structuralism, post-structuralism or any kind of literary analysis I've heard of except plain ordinary criticism – their determination to sound scientific is the clearest indication of what's wrong with them. And the whole thing feeds back,' I concluded rather feebly, 'into literature itself and screws it up, so that when a man like me tries to take a holiday from the flux of facts and re-create himself in the hard, enduring subtleties of humanely observed and considered life, all he finds is more damned theories, only this time without any rhyme, reason or motivation beyond the aggrandisement of some pretentious author who doesn't realise that his theory of reality, or whatever it is that his theory is *of*, is, and must be, immeasurably less interesting than his instinctive understanding, whose nuances he won't, he can't possibly, register or even conceive

60

of in the first place if he spends his whole time representing the representation of a reproduction, saving your presence, Miss Mole.' She looked a bit less awe-stricken than I would have liked.

'No wonder they gave you so many medals,' said Chance in a show of honest admiration. 'You said "flux of facts" without a tremor. And you've made a strong argument generally. But it's bullshit, for the following general reasons.'

'Tell me the general reasons,' I said, miffed.

'I'm going to tape *Auf Wiedersehen, Pet*,' said the Mole, rising.

'It's not fair,' I said. 'While she's fooling with that machine, you're rehearsing your eloquence.'

'No need to,' said Chance with a temporary return to ellipsis. 'Got most of it learned off.'

'All set,' said the Mole. 'We can't miss this episode. Patrick hasn't told Gudrun that his wife's coming over for a visit.'

Lifting his full glass, Chance took the kind of deep swig that you have to bite off at the end. It was just a taste of his old habits, when I was the young star student and he was out there in the great world, holding court at Vadim's in King's Cross the year before he went to England. Hot nights, T-shirts, khaki drills, Hong Kong thongs. My first dissipations. Why were you a Catholic, Joanna?

'You're more right than you realise about literary theory,' Chance began. I recognised a favourite technique of his, but for the moment I sat silent. 'You could have gone further, and said that in literary matters any technical analysis which precedes judgment makes judgment impossible. Assessment of quality is either *a priori* or it doesn't happen. It's a whole-soul response. If you study *One Hundred Years of Solitude* for its representation of reflexivity or whatever, you'll end up like a certain Mole who thinks it's a work of art instead of a load of crap.'

'It is *not*,' squealed the Mole with delighted anger. I was very jealous. This was evidently a standard disagreement between them.

'You will come to believe,' Chance went on, 'that the author of *One Hundred Years of Ineptitude* is doing something marvellous when all those undifferentiated characters walk out of one end of the village and keep walking until they walk in at the other end of the village some time later, not having walked around the world but merely having been forgotten by their supernaturally gifted author between chapters. You will come to believe that the author is practising some kind of *conscious minimalism* when he calls two women by the same name – as it might be, Maria – and differentiates between them by making one of them pick up dirt and eat it. As Maria eats dirt despite the protests of Maria, a third woman, called Maria, arrives from the East having previously left for the West, whither she had gone to visit her cousin, Maria. You will persuade yourself, because the alternative is unthinkable, that the author, Ferdinand Imelda Marcos . . . '

'Gabriel García Márquez!' the Mole insisted, aware that she was whipping a humming top.

' . . . is practising a realism *beyond* realism . . . '

'Magic realism! That's why it's called that!'

' . . . a magic realism which does away with the tired notation of verisimilitude. You will not allow it to occur to you that he is, in fact, a fuckwit.'

One night a week, sometimes even two nights, I had been drawn to the foot of Joanna's staircase in Sancta Sophia, to meet her and take her up to the Cross and back again afterwards to somewhere dark near the college to pet heavily with my hand between her thighs and one finger gone missing, a fevered amputee. But not even that thrill would have been enough to keep me away regularly from my log tables, slide rule and gooseneck lamp. Only this live bait could lure me towards Bohemia – the prospect of Chance Jenolan unleashing a long solo, like Paul Gonsalves in 'Diminuendo and Crescendo in Blue', Duke Ellington at the Newport Jazz Festival, 1956.

'Witchdoctors like Derrida dismiss themselves by the way they speak,' Chance went on. 'It's the language of sophistry and nothing sensible can be said in it even by accident. But you can go further. An apparently more lucid pundit like Barthes is usually talking flapdoodle too. Quite apart from the fact that he isn't as good as he's supposed to be at noticing things. He noticed, for example, that the Hollywood movie of *Julius Caesar* was full of American actors who signified that they were Roman by combing their hair forward. But he noticed wrong. The Hollywood movie of *Julius Caesar* was full of English actors and anyway Romans *did* comb their hair forward, so what else could the actors have done, comb it backward? Barthes's acolytes didn't notice how rough and ready his noticing was, because they themselves noticed even less than he did. And that was really why they liked him. Because he let them off real criticism, in which it is possible to be inadequate, to go wrong. The real reason why any form of structural approach, up to and including deconstruction and whatever the Hell comes after that, is not and can't be science, is that you *can't go wrong.* Nothing anyone says, using those methods, can be disproved. As Joel will explain to you some other time, Mole, this is the very opposite of science.'

'Will you? Will you tell me about that?' Momentarily dragging her eyes away from Chance's mouth, she smiled straight at me, as if digging money out of Daddy. I would have told her anything. When Paul Gonsalves played his tenor sax solo at Newport, the Mole must have been about minus eleven years old. An arrow through the heart.

'But as Joel will also tell you,' Chance went on, 'falsifiability is only what separates science from non-science. It doesn't separate sense from nonsense. There is no inherent reason why somebody taking a structuralist approach shouldn't discover real things, and no reason for you to fear, Inspector Mole, that your investigations into this field have been without fruit. As I was careful to say before: though Derrida always talks baloney, Barthes only *usually* talks baloney. It's not entirely uninteresting to be told, as Barthes tells us, that a sonnet by Baudelaire has a preponderance of two initial consonants in its opening quatrain. On the other hand, how interesting is the symmetry which the author has created unconsciously, compared with the symmetry, or lack of it – the real structure, if you like – which he has created consciously? How interesting is our theory of the book compared to *his* theory of the book? And here we reach the point where Joel, having run out of gas, pulled off the highway and pretended to admire the view.'

He knew I was enjoying his performance, but couldn't know I was also enjoying the memory of him a quarter of a century before, in his first-floor front room in Glebe with the cast-iron balcony caked with green paint, before anybody except a few eccentrics thought of preserving the old architecture. The Duke Ellington Newport LP was an old American pressing with a thick cardboard cover, split along one edge. 'Listen to this bit,' Chance had said as Gonsalves drove on, surprised by his own inspiration. 'Hear that slap-slap sound? It's Joe Jones, hitting the edge of the stage with rolled-up newspaper.' Yeah. Go. The raw wine we drank was called Red Ned. When Chance's girl arrived I had to leave. Barbara. I walked all the way home to Bellevue Hill and they must have been exhausted before I got there.

'You can reject the theories of the critics but you can't reject the theories of the creators. They make real discoveries which, once known, can't be, if you'll forgive me, un-known. Once you've read what Henry James says about the author's point of view, you can't get back to a state in which you never heard him raise the question. And not reading his critical articles and reviews won't get you out of hearing him raise it. The whole question is all there in his novels. One of the things his novels are about is how the novels were written. You might say that such preoccupations are part of what makes him a monumental bore . . .'

'Is he?' inquired the Mole. 'Don't I have to read him, then? Oh good.'

'He is, but you do. Start with *Washington Square* the way I told you. Part of what makes him a monumental bore, but he took the novel forward. The arts don't progress, but they do develop. And ignorance about the question of the author's intentions won't be enough to get you, or him, back to a state of innocence where the author's intentions don't matter. It's true that the artist must retain his simplicity, but he can do so only by perpetually returning to it, back down the corridor of sophistication.'

'The second simplicity,' I contributed.

'Exactly. The musicologist Alfred Einstein, whom the Mole is under no obligation to distinguish from the physicist Albert Einstein, since she can play the cello and I can't, said that Mozart attained the second simplicity. Having learned everything, he was able to work again from pure instinct. Every artist must aim for that. But unless he's talented to the point of genius like Mussorgsky or Le Douanier Rousseau, he can't stay pure by dodging school. Every real novelist dreams of an unselfconscious novel. Imagine how much easier it would be for a character to give a long speech that the narrator remembers in detail, if it just didn't occur to you that the speaker's propensity towards monologue and the narrator's uncanny memory will both have to be justified. And yet isn't that why we find Aldous Huxley's novels not only unfairly neglected but unintentionally funny? Not just because his characters talk like encyclopaedias. Real people, including Huxley himself, have talked like encyclopaedias. But Aldous tried to pretend that Gustave had never existed. What dates *Point Counter Point* now had already dated it when it came out. It was a technical throwback. Because the real complexities of counter-pointed dialogue were all there in *Madame Bovary*, never to be simplified again except as sentimentality. And as much as you might want your straight uncomplicated narrative, Joel, Gustave is there to prove you can't have it. There are whole stretches of *Madame Bovary* to prove that you can't have it. Whole chapters with no identifiable authorial voice at all. All done with the shift of viewpoint, with transitions, with the play of tone. Impossible not to be delighted by all that. Impossible not to see what he did as an increase of opportunity to get at the truth. More ways to do what a novelist *should* do – write a book that can't be turned into a movie. More ways to be *good*. And, of course, more ways to be bad. Just like in painting, where if there had never been any evolution towards abstraction, the field would at least have been cut down to people who could draw. But any duffer could set himself up as an abstract expressionist, and now any writer with nothing to offer can call it self-reflexivity. The *nouveau roman* makes a virtue of leaving out things that the author doesn't really know how to put in. Which is why, although the Mole doesn't know it yet and we won't tell her, the *nouveau roman* is washed up. Even the Frogs are fed to the teeth with it. They'd rather read Simenon, and they're right. But Simenon is no primitive. He's technically sophisticated to the nth degree. A novel's technique has to be part of its subject, and no way out of it. There can be no such thing as a novel written merely to be enjoyed. The very idea is sophisticated. Naivety can't be willed.'

The Mole gazed at his moving mouth adoringly, as Barbara had once done. The lovely, frail, un-Australian-looking Barbara, who would have been in her middle forties now, but cancer had taken her last year – very quickly, I had heard, like a shark attack. 'You can have exactly one of these each,' said the Mole, holding an unwrapped sweetmeat towards the admired mouth, 'and don't ask me where I've hidden the box.' We were well into the coffee by then.

'Numb of whiff . . . ' Chance went on.

'Don't gobble.'

'None of which means that any artist in any field mustn't do his or her best to make the great return from self-awareness to selfless inspiration. The work of art that has nothing except its technique for subject matter is a dead duck, like almost all *avant-garde* music since *Verklärte Nacht*. If Benjamin Britten walked out of a concert by Harrison Birtwhistle, why should I stay? And don't tell me that Debussy wanted to do the same to Stravinsky.'

'I wasn't going to,' I said for punctuation.

'I, for one, would be sad,' said Chance, 'if this here Mole were to spend her life reading nothing but Robert Grill-it and working on her theories about the representation of a registration. I like to think that *War and Peace* will make her less eager to explain the book and more hospitable to the possibility that the book is explaining her. But meanwhile she is sharpening the powers of attention that she will one day bring to greater literature, and she has learned that even those simple narrative forms which she, like you, truly adores, are the products of conscious art.'

'Can we watch *Auf Weidersehen, Pet* now?'

'Knew you were going to say that.'

'Can I have my feet tickled?'

'A voluptuary.'

They spoke as if I didn't exist. With the screen and one last candle the only lights in the room, I sat in an armchair and Chance sat at one end of the long leather couch, the Mole lying along it with her feet in his lap. He tickled her feet constantly except when he reached for the remote control to zap the commercials.

'Mole knows everything about these characters. Also an expert on *Coronation Street*, *Dallas* and *Dynasty*. Ought to be doing a media studies course somewhere, except who needs it? Ask her something about the sex-life of Dex and Alexis. Alexis wrecks Dex with sex. Ask her . . . '

'It's starting again. Shut up and tickle.'

When it was over they got up to go to bed. The Mole bent to kiss my forehead and disappeared upstairs. Chance lingered for a moment. 'Stewart Granger and Robert Taylor,' he said.

'I can't.' I couldn't.

'And Ann Blyth.'

'*All the Brothers Were Valiant*.' Two men, one woman and a lot of sea water.

'Nice work. Talk properly tomorrow.'

'Good night, you lucky bastard.'

'You'd be surprised. Night.'

I stayed to finish my glass of port and have another. Chance's television set got the whole world. It was connected to a dish aerial up on the roof. I watched CNN for too long and went to bed with hot eyes. Tears made them feel better.

Late next morning I woke up with a sore head and some perspective. I had, after all, known the Mole only twenty-four hours. Not long, even by her standards. Chance was gone. 'Fend for youself,' said a note. The Mole was gone as well. She had gone to learn more of what she needed to know before Chance told her she didn't need to. Was that their arrangement? A pattern began in which I rose late each morning, asked myself these questions, and set about answering them by sipping guiltily at a paragraph or two of one of her love letters. Why didn't she keep them in her college room? She must have been afraid that a friend would read them.

Dear Mole of Discretion,

Don't think it's fun here in Cannes. The fun does not come in cans here in Cannes. It comes in very expensive bottles. First of all, I miss you. Angélique misses you too,

67

but not the way I do. She spends her day being interviewed by French television in their *al fresco* studio on the Croisette, opposite the Majestic. They ask her about her new film in which she is a professor of philosophy in love with Gérard Depardieu who plays a multi-storey car park, or possibly works in a multi-storey car park: I am not sure and find it hard to care. Nobody could be more magnanimous than she is about playing a role that Catherine Deneuve didn't need, Stéphane Audran wouldn't touch, Fanny Ardent was too tall for, Nathalie Baye not old enough and Isabelle Adjani too animated. Yesterday at Eden Roc I talked to the American producer Gus Disting about Robert Browning. He thought I meant the man who invented the gun. Meanwhile I crave you. I'll be the cello and you be Pablo . . . '

But I promised to quote no letters. Nor will I quote from the diary which I started about then. I could have bought a floppy disc and composed my diary on Chance's idle Amstrad, but I had a regressive urge to use pen and paper, to make a book. Venturing out as far as Chancery Lane, I bought one of the same Chinese notebooks that Veronica had done her figuring out in. Flying Eagle Brand. Made in China. Everything I learned about Chance and the Mole I put into it, making daily entries. It was a deliberate exercise in anti-solipsism. That feeling I had with them, and especially with her, of getting out of myself – I wanted that when they were not there, and the diary gave it to me. It got the spotlight off me. It put me in the cooling dark. I had enough time on my hands to lose track of it. The diary gave me direction. My *crise à quarante ans* became a story. There were characters, and a kind of narrative, except that nothing much happened to the narrator. The weather moved further into summer, with the odd fine day to bear the calendar out, before clouds came scudding back behind the tall towers. The Mole moved from term time into the long vacation, already studying hard for her final year. She went to her parents in the country for three or four days at a stretch – an aeon, an epoch.

Chance moved mysteriously. He had an office at the newspaper which had first refusal on his work, and another office at the television company which transmitted his programmes, but if you called him at either you were told he was probably at the other. If he went to Paris for lunch or Salzburg for the weekend, I would find out when he got back. He would say in the morning that he was going to the National Theatre for talks with Peter and come home in the evening saying that he had been to Glyndebourne for talks with Peter. The discrepancy gave me two chances to guess that he had not meant Peter Rabbit, but the vagueness went beyond cool. He was becoming secretive. The Barbican was his fortress. I wondered why he had let me into it. Dear Flying Eagle Brand Diary, why has he let me get so close? Am I the eunuch in his harem, or just the human back-up to his answering machine?

Shostakovich was our composer that summer. It often goes like that, a musical fad binding you together. At Caltech it had been the Lovin' Spoonful. The year I met Lauren we all sang 'Nashville Cats' out in the Mojave Desert under a sky streaked with meteors – portents, I now realised, of the Mole's birth. Lauren still called me a Nashville Cat in bed, or had done until recently. We both suffered so for John Sebastian when he forgot the words at Woodstock. Bartók was our serious man. The Third Piano Concerto. Written in America, Lauren reminded me. She loved her country all the more, the more I loved it less, in that year of Search and Destroy, of helicopters over the Mekong Delta. *Thwack thwack*. She gave herself to her bio-chemistry, to her music and to me. I could never get her genuinely interested in jazz but she loved pop. It pleased me to chase classical with pop, like Scotch with beer, and I was glad the Mole had the same instinct. Not that I could even recognise the names of her fave raves. I had always thought Sade was a poxed old French libertine whose idea of a good time was to pour hot wax on a serving girl's flayed rump. It took the Mole to tell me that Sade was a black girl singer who pronounced her name Shah-day. But trusting the Mole's musicality I listened and was well rewarded. 'Frankie's First Affair' was at its prettiest when the Mole was gently dancing to it, but sometimes I put it on when alone, although not as often as I searched for my favourite bits of the steadily unfolding Russian. The

Eighth String Quartet put me in a trance, which I suppose was hard to distinguish from my usual state of immobility, except that instead of just not moving a muscle I had glazed eyes as well. One bleak wet summer afternoon the Mole came in and found me like that, wrapped in Russian sorrow. His sorrow for millions of his murdered countrymen and mine for myself. *All my symphonies are tombstones.* Where had he been all my life? How had he managed to accomplish so much with everything going against him? Thought I, who had had everything going for me, and accomplished nothing.

'You shouldn't listen to that on your own,' said the Mole. 'It gets you down.'

'It's the pommy weather. You call this a summer? Look at that grey filth.'

'Let's take Chance's big umbrella and go for a walk. I know where it's tropical.'

She did, too. The Barbican arts complex looked like a hardened missile silo mixed up with a Cape Kennedy firing room. In addition, there was an off-world element, a sort of scaffolding-and-glass canopy sticking up at one side like a detached section of the Beaubourg parked in space. From outside, this high-tech gazebo was only just identifiable as some kind of botanical conservatory. Mainly you saw just the glass and the pipes: the green stuff might have been stored scenery from *A Midsummer Night's Dream*. From inside, I now learned, it was a real forest, growing on several levels, with pools and streams and spilling terraces. The doors were locked but a man behind them, who was arranging a hose that squirted from hundreds of pin-holes only a few inches apart, turned when he heard the Mole knocking on the glass and smiled as if his day was made. Straight-backed in her blue suit, she put her high heels into the third position, clasped her hands palm-down in front of her as if reciting, and bobbed down about an inch in silent supplication. The doors opened as if she had said 'Sesame'. Their guardian bantered heavily about how the responsibility would be all ours if we were attacked by the jaguars or the alligators. Then we walked on, the Mole having taken my arm, I pacing our step with the tapping ferrule of the folded umbrella, slowly along a brick pathway between ferns. The air was already hot. Beside the first pool we paused to watch the carp.

'Big and lazy,' I said for something to say.

'I'm glad you think so. When Chance first brought me here I said I thought they were big and *he* said they were only little ones. Because he'd seen the ones in Kyoto. He said these ones were just bait.'

'Usually he's pretty careful about not crushing you though, isn't he?' More so than he ever was with me, I could have said.

'He's getting better. I stick up for myself. It does him good.'

'You've improved him. You should charge a fee.'

'I do.' I didn't like the sound of that, but it turned out she meant something different. 'I pick his brains all the time. And he can be very patient with me, considering how impatient he is really. I ask him really dumb Amanda-type questions and he tries to answer them. He says it's good for him and I should keep it up. It keeps his mind off his troubles.'

'And what are those?' What are those compared with mine, I meant. From the first big pool there was a streamlet about six inches wide leading to a smaller pool. One carp had made the transition and obviously had no idea how to get back. A big fish in a little pond. Perhaps the man with the hose would come along and turn the poor fish around, like a locomotive on a turntable.

'It's so hard for him. He has to spend so much time deciding. Everyone wants something from him. Nothing is simple. I think that's all I'm for. I'm a rest for him.'

'Does he love you?' I asked, as if I had never read his letters.

'In a way. Yes. I suppose he does. I think he picked me up as a toy for Angélique, because you know she's a bit inclined that way too.' No. I didn't know. But of course. How could anyone so obviously unambiguous be anything but ambiguous? People who didn't spend their whole day working for a living picked these things up straight off. The rest of us came chugging along, miles behind the action, arriving so exhausted at the old news that we greeted it, slack-jawed, as a revelation. 'But I couldn't really bear it with her. She's so *rough*. Nothing like as refined as she looks. And then Chance discovered that he just liked having me around.'

71

'Do you love him?

'As much as I've ever loved a man

'In your long career

'Don't be so snide. I meant, as much as I *can* love a man

'Because you like women best.'

'Oh no. I like both kinds. But I do love *a* woman best. Have done since school.'

'What's her name?'

'Penelope

'How often do you see her?'

'Never. I don't see her any more. But I can't get over her.'

'Does Chance know about this?'

'Oh yes. Of course. He's a terrific help. If we go along those stepping stones we come to the rude cactuses.'

She went ahead, turning once to put her finger to her lips, as if we were sneaking up on something. The cactuses were indeed rude. Jade loofahs that had penetrated porcupines, avocado dildoes that had been up echidnas, they ruined the mood in which I could probe further about the grief of lost love, but I profited from the gaiety and held her hand on the way home. Our clasped palms retained a pocket of hot moist air, while the rest of our bodies readjusted to the chill evening. For a little while I felt less marginal, as if I were included. But hearing that she wasn't fully his didn't make her mine, so to care for her could only mean more desperation. Out in the open, we crossed the metal bridge over the ornamental lake and climbed the stairs to the main walkway, where two police constables, one of each sex, came strolling towards us, as if on a gangway into Noah's Ark. I dropped the Mole's hand and took the arm it was attached to. She giggled.

'Am I meant to be your daughter?'

'Belt up.'

'Do you think I could meet her?'

'I'm not sure that even I'm allowed to.'

'Are you afraid I might seduce her?'

'I'm just afraid generally.'

One morning I was up early to phone the children before school. There was no school. It was half-term. I had lost track. In fact I had never had more than a vague idea of when school started and stopped. Lauren had taken care of all that. But Donna must have been working on some assignment, because she asked me a question.

'Daddy, where's the Bristol Channel?'

'It's out West in Wales somewhere. Near Bristol. Where did you think it was?'

' I thought it was part of the *Channel*. You know, the English Channel.'

'Haven't you had any geography lessons about England?'

'We have geomorphology.'

'Yes, but don't you learn the *names*?'

'Oh sure. Isthmus. Promontory. Spit.'

'I mean the *names*. Like: Wales, Bristol Channel, Cambridge, Madingley Road.'

'We learn to recognise the shapes

'Can I speak to your mother?'

'She said she doesn't want to

'Tell her it's about school.'

Lauren's voice, for the first time in so long that it was like the first time ever, sounded primly in my ear. She had always been proper. Her deportment was a containment building. Never any beads and headbands for her. Even at the height of the student thing, her biggest concessions to social revolution had been straight-legged corduroy jeans, Weejuns penny loafers and an English pullover. When her friends had big posters of Marcuse on the wall, her idea of an icon was Linus Pauling. There were plenty of hippy girls from rich families. But Lauren's family was as strait-laced as only old Hollywood could be, holding on to its Eastern manners as if the West was still a frontier. They had a barn in Connecticut to which the house on Mulholland Drive was only an annexe.

'Yes?' She bit the word off at both ends.

'They aren't teaching her any geography. They're teaching her geomorphology instead.'

'You mean you aren't for it?'

'How could I be for it?'

'Well, it's science.'

'Jesus, what's the point of knowing how to recognise a fucking isthmus if she can't find her way there to see the fucking thing?

73

What's she going to ask them for at the fucking railway station? A day return to the fucking geomorphic formation?'

'Don't be foul. As it happens, I think you're right. I'm not getting what I thought I was paying for. A common condition all round.'

'How much money have I got?'

'Haven't you called the bank?'

'Too scared.' I mixed an element of contrition into this, but it came out sounding merely cute, so I back-tracked. 'Couldn't you make her go to ballet again? She's so round-shouldered. Was when I last saw her, anyway.'

'Look, I don't really want to discuss anything.'

'Couldn't . . . '

'No, we couldn't. I'll look after everything that matters and you just look after yourself, OK?' She hung up before I even got a chance to ask Benjamin about how he was making out with his Amstrad. I had wild dreams of linking his machine to Chance's by telephone so I could send long messages at night.

By day I explored the geomorphology of my environment, its concrete cliffs, its caves and canyons. The Barbican was a 1950s architect's idea of the shape of things to come. Like all visions of the future it had dated fiercely. If the rents had not been kept high it would have been a vandalised, windblown wreck like Le Corbusier's original folly in Marseilles. A thousand times bigger than that, the Barbican was riddled with design faults down to the smallest detail. You needed a diamond-tipped drill to hang a picture. The ornamental lake was just too shallow to keep fish healthy and just deep enough to drown a child. A leaking roof in a sub-podium flat meant that half a square mile of brick walkway had to be taken up and put back. It had all been done in good faith, which led to the most unsettling aspect of all. Designed before security became a consideration, the place had a hundred separate entrances and they could all be opened by anyone's door key. Chance's fortress had no defences except confusion. Despatch riders trying to deliver parcels would be admitted by the car-park porter and then wander the corridors for ever in search of their inner destination. You would see one of them in his copious black rubberised clothes and impenetrable helmet, and then half an hour later, in a different part of the building, or the same part of a different building, you would see the same one again, his radio squawking as he checked doorways through his visor. Once in, there was no resistance, nothing to stop you circulating. Thus I could wander for hours from level to level of Heathrow-scale car-parks, through power-rooms where huge machines saying *gumph gumph* masticated the effluent of many garbage disposal conduits, over catwalks and under waterfalls, along residential corridors that looked like Alcatraz with carpets. There were secret gardens at ground level, monochrome from lack of light. High up in window boxes swathes of flowers spilled, hanging gardens from a brutalist Babylon. I saw things through windows: a bald man in white pyjamas aiming karate kicks at a punching bag, a naked fat woman stroking her breasts with a cat.

In the nearest car park, on the second level, there were three Lincoln Continentals parked side by side, filmed with dust, their tyres soft. The car-park attendant said that they had belonged to the embassy of a small African country which had changed governments, and that some geezer would eventually come to take them away. 'Better be three geezers,' I said helpfully, 'or the same geezer will have to make three trips.' But I was already alone. One of the Lincolns had a bicycle twisted into the back seat.

Dear Star-nosed Rodent,

Rio is everything I hoped for and worse. This had better be the best carnival ever staged. My designer, who was supposed to be taking notes with his minicam, ate some of the hotel food, so now *I'm* carrying his minicam. The brown boobs on the girls at the Oba Oba Club bounce with a resilience you might quite like, but even the hoofers have a shelf life of about a week. Any other beautiful girl stays firm for three days maximum, then turns squishy. The fruit rots on the vine here. The wet heat sucks the life out of everybody except the muggers. I'm in the oldest hotel on Copacabana beach, of which you have no doubt heard. But you will not have heard that the sand shelves like a cliff at the surf's edge, that the waves fall vertically to

75

obliterate anyone crazy enough to go in swimming, and that no swimmer could get to the water anyway, because he would be mugged as he stepped on to the beach, even if wearing nothing but a G-string. His balls would be removed and sold at the nearest squash court. Even in the early evening, to walk on the footpath along the esplanade is to have one's wrist-watch instantly misappropriated, possibly with the wrist attached. Muggers operate in gangs of six. On the classier Ipanema beach, further down the coast, they don't mug you on the sand. They come right into the hotel lobby and do it there. As I stand near a policeman and gaze out over all this mayhem, my eyes fill with tears because of the hydrocarbons pumped into the air by thousands of tiny cars each driven by a would-be grand prix star wearing a gold medallion and a watch that looks like the one I lost the previous evening. I lift weeping eyes to the mountains and find them teeming with hovels which give off visible puffs of hepatitis germs like a sick man smoking. Up there, even the goats have Aids. As I lift my eyes even higher, I see, as if through a film of oil, a sky scarred by hang-gliders, drug-runners' helicopters, satiated vultures and Europe-bound airliners in which I am not a passenger. So I go back to my room, draw the curtains, turn up the air-conditioning from INADEQUATE to FEEBLE, lie down on the off-white sheet and take myself in hand, thinking of you, *sancta simplicitas*, your polymorphous perversity, your non-proselytising advocacy of life's joy. I know who you miss most and I don't mind. It even excites me. But I need your full attention. When you shrank from Angélique I felt the possible loss of you like a blow to the heart. Then I found out that you wanted me for my essential self. Lucky, lucky me. Don't worry: I know you like the hoopla, too, and I'll make sure you get some of that. You'll see the Copacabana muggers one day, in all their glory. But the important thing to me is that you enjoy my voice. You identify it and enjoy it. While I – this will be difficult for you to understand – am having trouble finding it. Can't hear it. All the time I get better at husbanding my energies, at doing more with less sweat, or anyway less with more

76

effect. And you, born organiser, help smooth the way. But you can't imagine what I would stand to lose, if I lost my response to the small things, the way Angélique took away my taste for water. Writing becomes harder for me all the time. This is my longest piece of prose for years. There is an article about that bastard Brecht on my desk that I must have started when he was still alive. More of that later, however, because . . .

He didn't stop there, but perhaps I should. Nothing can tell us what two people are like when they are alone together, not even their letters to each other in which they evoke that very thing. The same subject came up, with a twist I didn't anticipate, when Chance took me out to lunch. The Mole had been away for an endless long weekend, Chance had been home for two days in a row, and perhaps he couldn't face another of my healthy snacks. All the ingredients had been bought within the guidelines of what Chance called the Mole's gruel rules, but there could be no doubt that I lacked her flair in their final preparation. 'Garrick's got a table for two in the Coffee Room,' said Chance. 'Somebody must have died.'

'Are we getting a taxi?' I asked in the lift. I was increasingly reluctant to set foot outside the perimeter.

'Car,' said Chance, which was not strictly true. Admittedly it was only a Granada, and therefore nothing beside the three Lincoln Continentals, the Rolls-Royces, Jaguars, Mercedes and Porsches that stretched away into the concrete distance of the car-park level as if they had been stored against atomic attack. But the Granada had a telephone in the back and a driver called Eric in the front.

'Garrick, Eric,' said Chance, and Eric saluted with a silver hook instead of a hand. It was just like the movies.

'What I like about the movies,' said Chance as we purred down the concrete ramp into the traffic, 'is their *fundamental* illiteracy. Not just the routine illiteracy of the hacks, but the way even the geniuses are at war with words. Got a tape of an interview with Francis Ford Coppola I must show you. He says his pictures aren't made to please the *hoi polloi*. Eventually you realise he means the élite. He says 'part and partial' when he means part and parcel. I *love* that. Can't resist the evil attractions of all that. The way it's got nothing to *do* with real writing. The *Godfather* movies are wonderful, but not because anybody involved can write. They can construct a scene, but they can't compose a sentence.'

'Come on,' I protested, already aware that he was deliberately winding me up out of my depression. 'There are some very intelligent writers even in Hollywood. In fact *especially* in Hollywood.'

'How many times have you seen *Tootsie*?' he asked, his eyes resting on a neatly clad lady legal type – silk blouse, dark suit, lacquered shoes with bows, rather Moleish but a bit older – who was contemplating the problem of crossing London Wall without the benefit of traffic lights. She smiled at Chance as if he were an old friend. 'These women look more American all the time.'

'Twice in the cinema,' I said, honestly trying to be accurate, 'and four times on video.'

'About the same for me. It's a miracle, isn't it?'

'It's perfect.'

'Who wrote it?'

'Sydney Pollack directed it.'

'Yes, but who *wrote* it?'

'Wait a second.'

'If I wait an hour you won't be able to tell me. Nobody I've ever asked ever could. Nobody remembers the writer.'

'Weren't there two writers?'

'Three.'

'So what does that prove?'

'Proves that if Sydney Pollack and Dustin Hoffman have each other plus three writers, they don't make another disaster like *Straight Time* or *Bobby Deerfield*. Pollack is a marvellous director. *Three Days of the Condor* is put together like a compact disc player. Not just the way it's edited. He edits in the camera. Deserves his fame. But he needs writers. Squads of writers. Great thing about Hollywood. Nobody doubts that the writers are just cannon-fodder. Neither do I. Love the whole idea.'

'You're just being perverse.'

78

'No, it's a genuine longing. Beneath it all, desire of oblivion runs.'

'You don't want to be treated like that.'

'You mistake me. I want to do the treating. Direct a big movie. Not like my polite written-and-directed-by art-house nice little features. A great big monster movie with a chain-gang of writers. Throw us out here, Eric. It's only a few yards.'

'Edie Adams and Natalie Wood,' said Eric as he got out to open the door with his hook.

'*Love With the Proper Stranger*,' said Chance after a slight pause for pretended thought. 'Can you pick Dr Court up at three o'clock and take him home? Is that where you'll be wanting to go, Joel?'

'Yes.' Home.

'Eric's a Steve McQueen expert,' said Chance as we walked up past Moss Bros to the top of Garrick Street. 'Won't see a movie that hasn't got Steve McQueen in it. Makes it a cinch to play Stars with him.'

'A chauffeur without a hand is a real attention-getter,' I ventured. 'How did he lose it?'

'Lost it being a chauffeur, as a matter of fact. Crash killed his employer outright. But he's got the enormous advantage of a Disabled Driver's Licence. Means I can park anywhere. Park in front of Buckingham Palace if I want to.'

'That's brilliant.'

'Learned the trick from Adam. Adam Faith. Think it was David, David Merrick, who said that being driven around was the only point of having money in New York.' Chance gave his minimalist wave to the bearded man guarding the steps of the club. 'While since I've been here. Nice and quiet. Usually I'm at the Groucho but I've got so many of the young guys gunning for me I feel like Wyatt Earp. Better here. Scarcely anyone under eighty. Worst can happen you bump into Bulwer-Lytton or somebody. Hello Robin.'

Somewhat contrary to Chance's billing of the show, the Coffee Room gave the impression that all the BBC and ITN news and current affairs programmes had pooled their leading on-screen personnel in order to receive a delegation of the country's most prominent newspaper editors, literary figures and political theorists. It was a senatorial display, an effect reinforced by the total absence of seated women, although a few females hurrying about dressed as waitresses dimly suggested that the human race had some sexual means of reproducing itself.

'Mainly lawyers and publishers,' said Chance, against the evidence of my senses. 'Actors only come in late at night after the show.' He gave a little wave to Donald Sinden. 'Recommend the potted shrimps to start.'

We were at a small side-table between windows. As if he were a spymaster keeping an appointment with his best agent at a rendezvous remote from any overhearing ear, Chance, pausing only to transmit our orders to the waitress, adopted the tone in which deadly secrets are revealed.

'Good place to talk, this. Only thing you're allowed to do except eat. If you produce a piece of paper and pencil they throw you out.'

'Why is that?'

'Club rule. Garrick must have hated writers. On the rare occasions when I can't get out of a business lunch I usually have it down at Chewton Glen. But talking to my old wing-man is more important than business.'

'You wish to unburden yourself?' I asked, suddenly as frightened as a man at his own execution. I thought he was going to ask me to move on. I couldn't have faced that.

'Be surprised how I miss the opportunity to come clean. Never saw you as often as I wanted to, but when I did I could always spill the beans. Mainly because you've got your own life that doesn't compete with mine.'

'It sure as Hell doesn't.'

'That's temporary. You're off balance. You'll recover. But with all my Eng Lit friends – I mean my English literary friends – I've run out of road. They frown on the way I diversify. Frown *quite genuinely*.' He made it clear by the way he emphasised these last two words that he had taken the possibility of uncontrollable envy into account, but had generously dismissed it. His sense of humour never vanished, but when his conceit exceeded it he scared me.

'Trouble is,' he went on, 'that makes me fair game. Plus the general idea that I'm too big to hurt. Every little supposedly revealing statement gets seized upon and held up to ridicule. Your friends make fun of you behind your back, fine. What else are friends for? But they do it when *their* friends are listening, and the friends tell acquaintances, and the acquaintances tell William Hickey. If my dearest friend among my fellow-novelists asks how many copies my last book sold, and I reluctantly tell him – arm up behind my back, like this – I read next day that I've been boasting about my sales figures. Means I can't say *anything*.'

'But that's the price of fame, isn't it?' I suggested compassionately, somehow reminding myself of Esther Rantzen. 'Didn't Robert Redford say that when a man is famous beyond a certain point, he can't say anything right?'

'He was right, but I'd be mad to say so to anyone except you. AUSSIE LOUDMOUTH COMPLAINS OF FAME. *Compares himself to Hollywood star.* And the journalists on the culture beat are the most trigger-happy of the lot. In almost every case they've got an unpublished novel in the bottom drawer. I haven't given an interview in five years. Haven't answered a single question. They ask me the time of day, I say No Comment. Drives them crazier than ever. One young bloke in the *Sunday Times* wrote a whole column about how I wouldn't talk to him. Said I'd fucked up my talent by going on television. That night – not the next night, *that night* – I turned on the television and there he was, doing *What the Papers Say* in a funny voice. These guys are holding *me* responsible for leading *their* fantasy lives.'

'And leaving them out.' I was stoking his self-esteem, but not without guilt. If my own ego was dangerously unprotected, his, I could now see, had constructed a defensive system of such depth that it could be distinguished from paranoia only by its being so obviously open on one flank. It was a Maginot Line whose Belgium was his sense of the ridiculous. 'I don't suppose your complicated private life helps.'

'That's the easy part.'

'Haven't they got the Mole story yet?'

'They're still coping with the Angélique story. Press is much less bother in that respect. If I look *that* lucky, nobody wants to believe my luck. But I think it just looks vague and confused.

Which it is. No story. Not a lot happening. Nothing to get a grip on.' I couldn't believe he believed this, but he said it as if he did, as if it was a viable proposition. 'Mud-slingers have to see pubic hair before they can get to work. But a low profile doesn't stop the cultural commentators. If they see you kiss your mother they start reinterpreting your entire *oeuvre*. One of the reasons why I can't get started on another novel. All those biographical speculations. Never did an interview without being asked who was who. And of course the truth is that you physically just *can't* base a character on someone in real life. The *roman à clef* is a contradiction in terms. Not because there's no key. Because there's no lock. It's a lake. Life isn't a mechanism. You can't make a scale model of it. Whole thrill of art is to compress life without scaling it down. Pack it tight into its own spaces. Couldn't stand the way talking about my work left it desecrated. Wait a sec. Wrong word. It's not a shrine. De-created. Undone. Literally deconstructed. So I stopped talking about it. Which built up the mystery. What will he do next? Has he got a secret plan? Well, I have.'

He paused to take in a mouthful of Perrier water. There had also been short pauses for food, but these had played no part in his oratorical timing, so I have not attempted to record them. This pause, however, had a rhetorical function.

'Secret plan,' he went on, 'is to get shot of the whole responsibility. Reckon I'm bankable enough by now to do a great big bad movie. No more of those little ones I write and direct in my role as the Bill Forsyth from Balmain. And I *like* Bill Forsyth. Way I *love* Preston Sturges. Civilised, literate, proportionate. But that's what I'm sick of: those things. There's something bigger, more liberating waiting for me out there. Calling me forward. Fame driving me forward like a rail gun. In the direction I've been resisting. Destiny more horrible than Hemingway's. Monstrous than Mailer's. Where the Performing Self takes over. Personality everything. Words nothing but décor. A Felliniesque mega-movie shot mute. Professional suicide?'

'Of course it would be.' I was appalled, even though his diction, more choicely Euphuistic by the moment, suggested that for this man to eschew verbality would be less like shrugging chains from his wrists than chopping off his hands.

'Good. Sick of my profession.' Putting down his fork, from whose prongs he had just subtracted a lamb's kidney with his teeth, he thoughtfully palpated the loose skin under his jowl. 'Temptation to get rid of this. Have a little tuck. Mustn't succumb. Hair transplant's enough.'

'You're having a hair transplant?'

'Already started one. See these?' He leaned forward and with the edge of his hand pulled back his wispy fringe to reveal two lines of dots in the no man's land between forehead and scalp.

'Looks like braille. Is it a secret message?'

'Plugs. Follicles taken from the neck. More to come after these settle down.'

'I can see why you run out of people to confide in.'

'Except the girls. Or at any rate except the Mole. Angélique of course is a rabid, card-carrying intellectual. If she didn't think I was André Malraux reborn she would have poisoned me by now. You like the Mole?'

'I love her.' Afraid but defiant.

'Hard not to, isn't it? Don't get her too confused. Somehow I don't fancy the idea of hitting the sack with her *and* you.'

'Same here.'

'Funny that, isn't it? Militant poof would try to convince you and me that we really fancy each other, deep down. We not only know that we don't, we know, both deep down and shallow up, that the very idea is *not all right*. Yet we also feel that for the Mole and her lovely pal Penelope it somehow *is* all right.'

'*Is* she lovely?'

'Ethereal. Makes the Mole look like Henry Cooper.'

'I'm still not sure it's all right except as a relief from us.'

'That's enough to make it as all right as it needs to be. This is a man's world, and just look at it. No wonder they adore each other. Sometimes I think I'd like to try one last novel with a whole chapter about two of them checking out each other's expensive underwear for fit, texture, sensuality. That looks delicious, darling. Can I help you? Smoothing fingertips. A dream of gentleness. Ecstasy without agony. No cut, no thrust. Peaches and cream. Dove's-wing kisses.' He pointed his knife at me to mark a transition. 'Next chapter, next flat, same time. A 100-year-old lady is being robbed, set on fire, raped and dismembered by half-a-dozen National Front Mohawks alienated by their restricted access to tertiary education. All of human life is there.'

'Sounds like you've already started it.'

'No, the book that gets everything in can't be done. Not any longer. Not by me. Lost my anonymity, and they won't let me have it back. But I wouldn't mind feeling the thrill again. Loved that feeling of fitting one technique inside another. Character quoting another character's diary that quotes another character's letter. The ellipsis here that earns a rhapsody there, the bravura passage that rips them up like a Liszt cadenza. Is it not life? Is it not the thing? Loved it. Maybe loved it too much. My face flushed when I wrote. A day away from the book was agony. The book. A box of tricks that felt like a living thing because its driving force was your feeling for life and it always came through. Your essential simplicity that shone through the complication and put you to shame. Vision you couldn't analyse because it was yours. Now I can and it isn't mine. How's your diary going?'

'Huh?' I made the noise through a plug of lemon sorbet. I would have preferred the bread and butter pudding but, like Chance, I could feel the tug of the leash by which the Mole led her masters.

'Mole dipped into it,' Chance explained. 'Stopped when she realised what it was. Girl of honour. Moral genius, in her way. Wouldn't tell me a thing about it. What *is* it about?' He had the generous look he adopted when the time came to recuperate from the serious business of talking about himself by indulging in the light relief of talking about you.

'About a man living on charity.'

'Nonsense. Can I see it?'

'I can't imagine anything more boring for you than for me to show you my diary. It would be like telling you about last night's bad dream.'

'Maybe it's a book trying to be born. Give it a title. Very important, titles. Sylvia Beach said that was the main reason why Hemingway was such a sensation even from early on. His titles hit you from the other side of the bookshop. *In Our Time. The Sun Also Rises. A Farewell to Arms.*'

'*Green Hills of Africa*,' I insisted, 'is the best one. No. *Across the River and Into the Trees* is the best one. Worst book. Best title.'

'Some of the short stories are even better,' said Chance. '"Hills Like White Elephants." "A Clean, Well-lighted Place." "A Way You'll Never Be."'

'"God Rest You Merry, Gentlemen",' I contributed.

'Yes,' said Chance. 'He puts the comma in there to tell you, first time you ever thought of it, that the "merry" is an adverb and not an adjective. Makes you re-examine the phrase. Lights it up. "Up in Michigan." "Big Two-hearted River."'

'"The Snows of Kilimanjaro",' I pronounced, definitively. Smiling at each other in shared, purely impersonal pleasure, we paused in silence for the time it would have taken a shotgun blast to stop ringing in our ears.

'Mishima's titles are good in translation,' Chance went on. '*The Sailor Who Fell from Grace with the Sea*.'

'There's the title of my diary.'

'Where?'

'*The Failure Who Fell from Grace with the Sky*.'

'This thing about the star's got you down even worse than being thrown out, hasn't it?' It sounded enough like an invitation for me to tell him the whole story, which I did for the rest of the event, meaning it was my turn to watch *him* eat. But as he did so he gave frequent signs of listening, to indicate that I wasn't wasting my time. He didn't know much about cosmology, but he knew what he liked. He liked the words. Sometimes he would stop me and make me say something again. Light curve. Ionisation zone. Instability strip. Deep minima. With many interruptions my story got itself told, and reached the usual conclusion: Veronica was the wrong person to make such a discovery because she had done it without love.

'Maybe that's what made her the right one,' Chance said upon reflection. Upon insufficient reflection, I thought, and with unforgivable frivolity, if not the deliberate aim to wound.

'How so?' I asked, and he saw my anger.

'Forgive me. Thinking of myself, as usual. Just thinking of something I once heard Eugenio say. Eugenio Montale. *It isn't the man who wants to who continues the tradition, but the man who can: and sometimes he's the man who knows least about it.* Often occurred to me even when I was mad keen to write, and nowadays I can't get it out of my head. Maybe I like it all too much. Know too much about it. *Chi lo può.* The man who can do it. He should travel light.'

'You're completely contradicting what you said at dinner that night,' I protested sullenly, still stung.

'No. Just turning the coin over. Didn't mean to get your goat.'

'You didn't,' I lied. 'I just don't appreciate the implication that Veronica's total lack of insight is somehow a proof of genius. Science doesn't work like that.'

'Neither does art,' said Chance, putting his crumpled napkin beside his half-empty cup of coffee and signalling for the bill. 'But the closer an artist is to the centre of things, the less insight he needs. Rodin let Rilke do the thinking. Rodin never thought about anything except lunch. Which he thought of briefly before lunch and stopped thinking of during.'

'Mine was excellent. Once again I am indebted.'

'Don't be mawkish. Try and feel better about yourself. Marriages get hiccups. Careers have setbacks. No tragedy.'

'Your two cars are here, Mr Jenolan,' said the waitress who brought the bill.

Kingsley Amis was the centre of a group at the head of the long common table. On our way out, Chance stooped beside him and said, 'Spencer Tracey and Katharine Hepburn.'

'Don't be ridiculous.'

'And Charles Buchinski.'

'No idea, of course. Obviously a trick.'

'*Pat and Mike.*'

'All right. Who was Charles Buchinski?'

'Changed his name later to Charles Bronson.'

'Get out.'

At the foot of the steps, two cars were waiting, as advertised. The sun was out for once, making Eric's hook sparkle as he leant back against the Granada's roof. His silver-rimmed dark glasses should have made him the centre of attention, but one's glance swerved away immediately to the other car, a pink E-type Jaguar two-seater looking so factory-fresh that the brilliant chromium wire wheels threatened to strobe while standing still. It must have been a replica, or else a complete rebuild. If the latter, it would have had its first heyday at about the time its driver was undergoing toilet training. She was almost certainly a very beautiful girl but her make-up, hairstyle and jewellery made it hard to tell. She looked as if a peacock torn apart by chain shot had spattered itself all over a frogman. Chance in all seriousness introduced this apparition as Presley Schaufenster.

'That's a snazzy car,' I said.

'She bought it in Santa Monica,' said Chance, circumnavigating its long nose. 'Presley is the most fantastic designer since William Cameron Menzies and she will now take me to her new studio in Docklands, which you'll see at a later stage.'

'Are you an American?' I asked, because she was looking up at me and I wanted to make her purple mouth move so as to see what colour it was inside.

'She never talks,' said Chance, getting in beside her. 'But she thinks in German. See you soon. *Los.*' The Jaguar's four exhaust pipes, like Pan's pipes full of water, bubbled away into the distance before I had even settled into the back of the Granada behind Eric. There was a day when I would have got into the front seat beside him, Australian-style, but I had been away a long time.

Dear Flying Eagle Brand Diary,

I had a bad dream last night. They've given me a little room of my own now, with scarcely anything in it except tea-chests full of books and a single bed with a duvet. So the Mole got her room back. But I hate duvets. I'm either too hot or too cold. This time I was too hot. It was a warm night even with the window open. My hair soaked the pillow case, leaving patterns of fossilised fern. When I got to sleep, I dreamed of trying to get to sleep. I saw myself walking naked into the Mole's room. She wasn't there. Either she was upstairs or she was away. So at my leisure I could get one of her little white G-strings out of the top drawer and look at it. What a life it led. Imagine its typical day. Then there was a thunderous knocking on the door downstairs. It should have been two flights down but I went down endlessly, as if descending the inner staircase of a castle keep. Chance and the Mole were behind a barricade of furniture, watching the door vibrate. 'They're already in the corridor,' said Chance calmly. 'We'll have to make a break for it along the balcony.' The Mole giggled. It was because I had forgotten to put on my trousers or underpants. I had everything else on, including a silk Liberty tie so smooth that the knot kept working loose. But the breeze blew around my private parts. I crossed my hands in front of them but it was awkward running along the balcony like that, so I was glad to be last, behind the Mole's lovely flashing ankles.

A bunch of them were coming the other way along the balcony. They had changed. In my dreams when I was young, they always wore the familiar black ceremonial regalia with silver insignia while they came for you with heavy weapons. The flamethrower's name said what it did. *Flammenwerfer*. Whoosh! A ghetto blaster. Now they still wore black and silver but they looked like big children with painted heads. They were decked with feathers and wampum, swathed with Inca trinkets. They didn't shoot. They just sprayed the walls and left litter. Crumpled cans of Classic Coke. Everything was ancient history to them. How could anyone be called Presley Schaufenster? What next? Mickey Maus? Goofy Kesselring? Tweetypie Seyss-Inquart? Somehow I knew that she had designed their costumes. They might have been born yesterday, but you couldn't fool me. That style was pure *Triumph des Willens* pre-Columbian post-Cheyenne Cargo Cult Punk.

We cut back to the right through an empty flat and out into the corridor, behind the bunch who were still besieging our door. They turned and ran after us. There was another bunch of them in front. Caught. Blindfolded. Wet bag thrown over my head and drawn tight at the neck. I called for help to Chance but he didn't answer. I could tell that in my dream nothing awful would happen to the Mole. No electrodes, no branding irons, no screams bubbling with blood. The dream wouldn't be as bad as reality could be. Reality was in South America or South-east Asia or the

Middle East. It was worse than you could imagine. That was its point. A dream was to help you stop imagining reality. That was *its* point. My fears were only for me. The easiest kind, really. I can remember thinking of the feeble disarray my unconscious mind must have been in, if this off-focus fantasy were all that its repressive mechanisms could come up with in order to protect it. No, she would be all right. I would be all right too. I could wake up from this any time I felt like it, so when they took off the bag I didn't find it particularly hard to hold my head up bravely, even though I was seated precariously on the rail at the front of the balcony of the Barbican Arts Centre's main theatre and the curtain was going up on a scene that could only be described as pure Hell.

The stage space was a vast cube of black night in which haloed points of luminosity diverged slowly towards me. It was a torchlight procession. A Busby Berkeley production number. Down in the stalls, Chance was bent over a producer's improvised desk, a big square of chip-board braced to the back of a row of seats. He was talking into an intercom but of course I couldn't hear him. The music, the singing, they were too voluminous. They were horribly ample, with the disproportionate heartiness of one of those numbers in *Die Meistersinger* when the guilds of the city are swept up into an ecstasy of self-identification. The chorus was belting out some sub-Brechtian song about the decline of Britain. I couldn't move because I would have fallen off. And I knew that there was worse to come. The most hellish moment of all would be when the tenor, who was prancing in a silver suit across the stage with his back towards me, turned to the auditorium, took off his sparkling top hat, and, an octave above all the others, sang. I had to get down before that happened, but with my hands tied behind me it was difficult to do so without falling. One of my guards wet my face with a damp cloth in case I tried to escape through sleep. Then the tenor turned around, took off his hat, threw his arms wide – there was a cane in his other hand – and hit a piercing high note. It was Dick Powell. Oh no! Not Dick Powell! Anyone but

him. Not the painted lips! Not the upturned nose! Not
the over-enunciated articulation that made Julie Andrews
sound like Marlon Brando! Please! Don't!

I woke up wanting to pee and rather pleased that I
hadn't done so already, considering how sharp was the
remembered smell of an oil-cloth sheet. But I woke up
sitting beside Chance in the stalls, so I was still dreaming.
The stage had gone silent. I should really wake up soon.
Should in the sense of ought to. Ought to in the sense
of must. Don't want to wet the bed. Chance was doing
something interesting. While still talking quietly into his
throat mike he was writing a letter. He didn't know that I
had already read it.

Dearest Tunnel-dweller,

If you promise not to go on being angry with me, I
promise not to get too interested in the long shapely legs
of the woman who runs the American Colony hotel, where
I wish I was staying instead of this place. But in Jerusalem
at any difficult time you have to make up your mind who
you want to be shot at by, and for the moment I think it
better to stay in a pro-Jewish hotel and be bombed by
Arabs, than in a pro-Arab one and be bombed by Jews.
Don't worry, I'm only joking. I'd be at the American
Colony if it wasn't full of a BBC TV crew making a series
about the Dead Sea Scrolls. As it is, the lady in question
meets me in her little yellow Porsche and gives me a lift
back to Jericho past the Bedouin encampments scattering
rubbish over the escarpment. We pass with a smooth roar
through the efficient Israeli army road-blocks on the way
down through the cutting to the Dead Sea. As always, the
Arabs are more aesthetic even in their squalor, but if I
were a Jew I don't suppose I'd mind looking butch either.
I'd want an M-16 of my own even if there was no road to
block. The lady sat on the bonnet of the pretty car and
took photographs while I undressed to my boxer
shorts – the ones with pink and blue stripes, très
sportif – *and cast myself into, or rather on to, the Dead*
Sea. I didn't even dent it. Just lay on top of it like a dugong

on a zinc slab. There was a lot of girlish laughter which I wish had been yours.

Try to realise I grew impatient with you only for a tiny minute, and then only because you had grown impatient with me. 'To be brutally frank,' you said, handing back the book I had given you, 'I think this is a bit past it.' Well, of course it is. It's called An Essay on Criticism *not because he hasn't heard of Alexander Pope but because he's trying to be trad. As I told you, but you didn't listen, Hough was in a Japanese POW camp from the fall of Singapore until the end of the war. Even if the book were less well-argued, less full of the clear reasoning it can't hurt a Mole to hear, it would still be appreciable for being written from the urgency of such an experience, from the earned right to defend the valuable, the need to preserve it. If you were reading history, and were equally bombarded by clever theorists, I would urge you to read the Dutch historian Peter Geyl for the same reason – because he was in Buchenwald, where he saw what history really is, where the false teaching of it can lead.*

I know that you have your work cut out just to keep up with all the books-about-books you have to read, so that you barely have time for the books they are about. I just wanted to give you a taste of some writing-about-writing that really has a reason for being there, instead of merely furthering a career. I presumed, I know. My timing was wrong. I can't be perfect. You make me want to be. Take me back into your thoughts. I, too, have my doubts and fears. Though I fear nothing so daunting as those final exams of yours which are a mere two years away, nevertheless I am not untroubled by anxiety. My new book I told you about, the thriller provisionally entitled Bad News Travels Fast, *is so badly stuck that I have had to abandon it. There is a weight on my soul that not even the joy of knowing the exact circumference of your nipples can shift. I have not forgotten how to write, but it could be that I have forgotten how to want to. (Years ago, when you were being born, when the nipples were the merest bee-stings, an Italian director called Antonioni made movies in which the leading character said things like that. Said them eventually, after a lot of walking about. At the time I smiled knowingly, unable to conceive of a writer running out of will.) Hoping this letter has made you repentant as well as jealous, I say So Long. Outside in the street I hear the toot of a yellow Porsche. (Critic: Is he outside in the street too? Would a green Porsche toot differently?) This letter is meant to be a tease, don't worry. Nobody but you gets nearer my heart than Yasser Arafat to the Knesset. Colonel Gadhafi riding a camel would come no closer to the Wailing Wall than anyone else but you to my affections . . .*

He wrote as fast as I could read, and I remember reflecting, in my dream, that this probably held true in reality. In my peripheral vision and sub-threshold hearing I had been dimly aware that one rebarbative act after another had occupied the stage: horses doing dressage to the music of James Last, a sheep-dog trial with commentary by Jeff Bridges ('Hi! I'm Jeff Bridges'), Jim Lilywhite reading from his poems, Sir Richard Attenborough receiving an award, Vanessa Redgrave singing 'We Shall Overcome'. But now the orchestra – conducted, I suddenly saw, by Leonard Berstein employing his full range of body English – erupted into a triumphant fanfare by Andrew Lloyd Webber. Dick Powell and the Busby Berkeley chorines swept back in two kick-lines hinged at either side of the proscenium arch. As in a production number for a nominated song on Academy Awards night, with additional atmospherics reminiscent of Hitler arriving in Nuremberg, down a ramp of moonlight through the constellated void came the pink E-type Jaguar driven by Presley Schaufenster with Chance in the seat beside her, smiling sideways in admiration. The Mole was sitting on the rolled-up soft top with her legs down behind the seats. She was blindfolded. She didn't know. I turned to where Chance should have been and found myself nose to nose with Veronica. She was contemptuous of me beyond all reason, just because I had made a joke about H. S. Leavitt, the woman astronomer who established, in 1912, that the periods of the Cepheid Variables in the Magellanic Clouds were related to their magnitude: the brighter the Cepheid, the longer its period. I had innocently remarked that it was no wonder a woman scientist should be good at periods. This was a fairly good joke, by dream standards – when you consider that running endlessly up a down escalator with your pants around your ankles counts as a fairly good joke, by dream standards – but Veronica wasn't having any. 'Can't you even *try* to imagine what it must have been like for her,' she snarled, 'surrounded by men like you, only worse? Men with pants?' I looked down. She was right. I still had no pants. There was no defence except in attack. 'Anyway,' I countered, '*Anyway*, it took Harlow Shapley to get the distance, because he got the absolute magnitude. *Anyway*.' Veronica shook her head. 'He *got*, as you put it, the zero point wrong by one hundred per cent.' My mouth was open to reply but it was full of spit so I had to swallow. The Jaguar had reached the front of the stage and stopped rolling. The trumpets were pointing straight up and blaring. Dick Powell was going crazy. His top C rang out like a fart in church. A man with a tray of opals leaned down from behind me and asked me to pick the real ones from the fakes. I didn't like his breath. I had never liked his breath. Death-breath. It was my father.

PART THREE

Somewhere Becoming Rain

I have just written the word 'infinite'. I have not inter-polated this adjective out of rhetorical habit; I say that it is not illogical to think that the world is infinite. Those who judge it to be limited postulate that in remote places the corridors and stairways and hexagons can conceivably come to an end – which is absurd. Those who imagine it to be without limit forget that the possible number of books does have such a limit. I venture to suggest this solution to the ancient problem: *The Library is unlimited and cyclical*. If an eternal traveller were to cross it in any direction, after centuries he would see that the same volumes were repeated in the same disorder (which, thus repeated, would be an order: the Order). My solitude is gladdened by this elegant hope.

Jorge Luis Borges, 'The Library of Babel'

I DID ONE OF THOSE DELAYED DROP WAKE-UPS WHERE you fall about 1,000 feet before the chute untangles and pops open. The bottom sheet had come adrift from the edge of the mattress and was plaited around me like a rope. The sweat on the pillow was abetted by the dribble on my chin and this time I really *did* have to pee. Mopping my head with a towel while trying to aim a stream into the bowl without noisily hitting the water was probably not a good idea but a few squares of toilet paper took care of the stray droplets. In the kitchen I opened a new plastic bottle of freshly squeezed orange juice and expertly caught most of the emergent gout in a glass. A wet J cloth eventually dealt with the rest. The diodes on the VCR machines said it was three in the morning. To make myself tired I sat down and watched CNN. They had a very good reporter in the famine countries of Africa. I had come to depend on how neatly she brushed her hair and ironed her shirts. While all around her the little children were slowly inflated by playful death until they burst like balloons, she and her production team had seen the importance of keeping to a standard. It was irrational, but that was the point. To do the right thing was the only thing left when the theories gave out. And boy, hadn't they *just*? There is no Third World: there are only the First World and the Second. The Second World is where nonsense written in the First World is believed.

You will appreciate that I was becoming a media expert by now. When Chance and the Mole were out, and frequently while they were in, I spent a lot of time writing in my diary while watching television, and more often than not I sat up doing both things half the night, using the morning as my time of rest. When the Mole was away in the country I did her the valuable service of taping the episodes of *Coronation Street* which she would miss because her father and brother always wanted to watch something else. I don't think, or didn't think at the time, that I was entirely without use. Chance subscribed to a lot of magazines and I read them all: *New York Review of Books, London Review of Books, Vogue, Tatler, Le Monde, Die*

Zeit, Scientific American, Variety. I kept up and was able to guide him on to a target. I knew it all. I let it all come to me. Having explored the Barbican to its outer bastions I rarely set foot beyond. After one daring expedition to the Clerkenwell area I decided to draw in my horns. Taking the Mole's shopping list to Safeway was already a big enough thrill for the average day. By now I was a dab hand in the supermarket. I was even able to make a small financial contribution, at the cost of being asked personal questions by the NatWest's automatic cash dispenser. MOVING HOUSE? it flashed repeatedly. NEED A MORT-GAGE? Safeway still had no cash-only counter but I had learned to check out a check-out queue for incipient cheque-book holders and attach myself to the queue with the most cash, even if it also had the most people. I knew how to hit the place just before or just after the last big late afternoon rush. Just before was best, although you didn't get any of the Royal Shakespeare Company ballet dancers. To see them, you had to be there at midday, when sometimes the cripples in their powered wheelchairs (RECYCLED FERRARI said the jolly decals) were there too. Asymmetrically bearded hydrocephalic men who talked in sobs would squeeze their hand-throttles and corner like silent go-karts so as not to lose sight of some tall, straight-limbed, loose and easy girl in a pink track suit with blue and white Puma training shoes, her pretty head the size of a grapefruit. I flattered myself that I understood the purring urgency of those ravaged boulevardiers, but only for as long as it took me to remember that I was lucky to be walking. These moral considerations, however, only arose if I was there in the morning, and usually I was recovering during that period from the exertions of a long night watching the rubble of Beirut being fought over by a different kind of bearded man. Upright, strong enough to carry a cluster of rocket grenades on his back in the same position that a standard-bearer in a Kurosawa movie carries his banner, he was the embodiment of Santayana's definition of the fanatic – the man who redoubles his effort when he has forgotten his aim. Hard viewing. So I shopped at the end of everybody else's working day. One relatively fine evening, a bulging plastic carrier-bag in each hand, I strode powerfully back through the labyrinth to find that the Mole had come home. Dressed for the street but with her shoes kicked off, she was leafing through *Harper's & Queen*. She groaned longingly at a full-page Chanel advertisement.

'Your sort of thing?' I inquired off-handedly.

'Inès de la Fressange,' moaned the stricken Mole. 'She's probably as straight as a road. What a *loss*.' The Mole leafed further through the magazine and groaned again. I sat down beside her and looked. There, spread over two pages, serpentine in black leather, *pavonazzo* feathers and silver trinkets, was Presley Schaufenster.

'She's *lovely*,' said the Mole.

'How can you tell?' I asked, thinking here was my cue.

'I've seen her without all that stuff. Chance knows her. He's probably screwing her, the swine.'

'Could you wear that?' I asked hopelessly, thinking there went my opportunity.

'Wear what? That?' she asked, pointing at the magazine.

'I meant could you *bear* that? Him screwing her?'

'As long as he told me all about it.'

'What the Hell is going *on* between you two?'

'Not a lot, to be brutally frank,' said the Mole, casting the magazine to the floor, where it hit a copy of *Vogue* and slid away. 'It winds him up that I can't forget Penelope.'

'You were going to show me her picture.'

'I was, wasn't I? Wait here.' In her stockinged feet, legs joined at the knees in the coltish way that not even a *barre* every morning can quite overcome, she ran upstairs. When she came back down she was walking, her hands clasped to her bosom, pretending to be protective of something. 'Promise you won't laugh at me.'

'Of course not. Show me.' Well primed by the advance publicity, I was expecting something spiritually rewarding, but was not prepared for such other-worldliness as this. Penelope looked like a Pre-Raphaelite commercial for herbal shampoo. The colour photograph had the misty grain of a Lartigue autochrome. She had Virginia Woolf's eyes and mouth, with a less equine nasal structure in between. She was sensitivity incarnate, a Madonna as seen at Lourdes by Bernadette, who walked home with a song in her heart, cured of asthma. 'Good heavens. She's divine.'

'Isn't she? And since she went to Cambridge she's hardly talked to me. Snooty bitch. She takes *ages* to answer a letter. And then it's only a few lines long. You should *see* what her letters used to be like. I've got them all in my college room done up with ribbon. I bet she's lost mine.'

'Were you really lovers? I mean, you know, *really*?'

'Of course.'

'What did you do?'

'Everything.'

I looked from Penelope's face in the photograph to the Mole's face outlined against the pale sky stretched like a cyclorama behind the towers. I tried to imagine those two innocent faces registering the pleasure of doing Everything. I could imagine it, but only at the cost of realising that my own psyche was half-formed, all open down one side. How little I knew about the world. The window whistled. A Pan-Am Boeing 747 was up there, full of people finding out about the world by going places. But there was another kind of travel.

'I'm going to cry,' she said, and did. It was my chance to hold her. 'I hate crying,' she said during a pause. 'My lips don't fit together. Mouth keeps sliding open.' It did, so I kissed it, trying to convince myself that I did not relish its memories. An undemanding, helpful kiss, full of comprehension and avuncular detachment. I thought I managed it quite well and Chance evidently thought so too, because he clapped spontaneously. I had assumed he was out, but he must have come home while I was shopping. He had been lying low upstairs. The Mole must have known he was home – perhaps he had come home with her – because she did not flinch or show any sign that her troubles had been added to. She conveyed the impression that she had her own business to get on with, that of drying her tears. Once again, more powerfully than ever, I felt sidelined by both of them. Not manipulated, precisely: but marginalised, definitely. What I did didn't matter. That was the general idea. The main thrust, as it were. The burden.

'Glad to see you two getting on,' said Chance, 'because Angélique has announced her arrival in two weeks precisely.

We can stage a dinner for her here and the dinner can escalate into a launch party for my doomed book. Two birds, one stone. You two can organise the catering and I'll do the inviting. Bit short notice, but they'll come.'

Chance's publisher, who had his own ideas about how and where to promote *The Rubaiyat of Omar Sharif*, was displeased at having to cancel the Groucho but pleased that he would save money on the deal. As the Mole's assistant I was given a new purpose in life. Ample in quantity but modest in range, the supermarket's resources could not cope with this challenge. Twice I had to go as far as Soho. On the second last day I went all the way to Jermyn Street, but Eric helped there, and even insisted on carrying the cheese. I was afraid he would rupture the Roquefort, gaff the Gruyère, hook a hole in the Halévy. It was a dizzy stretch of time, made more vertiginous by my suspicion, or certainty, that the *terminus ad quem* of my sojourn was now approaching. With Angélique on hand there would be no room for me. In theory this was a relief: the Mole was a moralist's nightmare, a Lulu played by Shirley Temple, a Circe in a surplice who had drawn Chance to some kind of strange destruction and would do the same for me. In practice this irregular, barely legal *ménage* was the only home I had to go to.

Also, and perhaps this was the surest proof of how adrift I was, I sensed that my love for the girl – because it was nothing less than that by now – could lead me to salvation rather than perdition. In my disappointment with my smashed career I felt that a new affirmation might be reached, if only I could share in the secret of her spontaneity, her sublime freedom from guilt. The liberal, defending complicity in a victimless crime, agonises or proselytises. The Mole simply committed it, as she might consume a natural fruit yoghurt. Twenty years before, in the age of polymorphous perversity, I had played it straight. Now I wanted to know. To find myself through yielding. To be irradiated by the revelation of the Mole's perfectly proportioned, rainwater-pure corporeal presence. Hindering my commitment to this idea, however, was not just the Americanised sociologese in which it insisted on expressing itself, but an unavoidable suspicion that I would have felt the same way if exposed to, say, the inner left thigh of Linda Lovelace. Maybe I was just horny. If so, there was not a lot I could do about it in current circumstances, even on a self-employed basis. Chance's vast abode did no more than the Lefortovo prison to cater for self-abuse. I didn't exactly have to lie there with my hands above the blanket, but there were no erotic videos that I could find and he kept copies of *Playboy* only for the film star interviews. Searching the shelves in room after room, rummaging through packed Marks and Spencer's carrier-bags standing squarely beside each other in corners, I found nothing more sensational than *Fanny Hill*, *The Delta of Venus*, *Candy, Blue Movie* and *Cécile et Jean, ou l'amour interdit*. Whatever some of its more obtuse critics might say, *Portnoy's Complaint* could not be said to count among these. Backed up by Chance, I pressed it on the Mole as an example of a genuinely funny book. (Chance and I were both still recovering from a full-length trial reading by the Mole of her forthcoming dissertation *Krapp hams it up as Hamm craps out: the function of comedy in Samuel Beckett*. Chance, having helped with the title of this effort, had lived to repent.) The Mole did her best to enter into the rich and writhing New York Jewish spirit of guilt, frustration and the cloying family, but it became increasingly clear that she had no conception of any of these things and didn't even understand the vocabulary. In the Mole's lexicon, willy and wally were strong words. So Portnoy's scatalogical exuberance left her stumped. She just didn't get it. 'What's a dork?' she asked, forehead screwed up, trying hard, failing the test, fazed. Chance explained. It became our running gag of that period. Shostakovich provided the tunes and dork jokes the light relief. The Mole marched everywhere making cracks about being careful not to slam the dork, leaving the dork on the latch, etc. When she hummed 'The Assault on Beautiful Gorky' she always let you know that Gorky's name had been suitably modified. Chance invented a book of poetry by Ted Hughes called *The Dork in the Rain*. I invented the Ibsen play about the notorious Scandinavian seducer, *John Gabriel Dorkman*. Spurred on by this last breakthrough, we all thought at once of the Sony Dorkman, although the discovery was credited to the Mole because she laughed loudest. Dork-talk went beyond being a fad, became a rage, a mind-set, an obsession. Even today, some fused circuit in the back of my brain, deep in the verbal centre, keeps plugging tediously away at the same trick. *Memed, My Dork. A Dork on the Wild Side.* Waiter, I think this wine's dorked. Why don't you two sit down and have a nice, long dork?

You can imagine how insufferable we must have been. Even in retrospect I can't judge whether I had already begun to heal or was embarked on the last, hilarious plunge into psychic disarray. In view of what was about to happen I think probably the latter, but I had made a few confident moves that suggested a renewed capacity to stay in touch with a wider social world, if only in the sense of establishing the terms of my exclusion from it. I resumed regular contact with Cambridge, for example, so that there was much less delay in receiving bad news. One item of ill tidings was that Chance had been there. Apparently he had tried to persuade Lauren that I was not all bad and would be worth taking back into the fold, given time. He hadn't told me about that visit. I wasn't so foolish as to call his going behind my back a betrayal. Perhaps I just wasn't brave enough. Drawing myself up to my full height, however, I made it clear that I was less than delighted. 'Look,' said Chance, 'I was passing through, so I called in. Mainly to say you were all right. All right?' When I asked him whether Lauren had looked worried about me, he couldn't honestly say she had. So he said it dishonestly. 'Yeah. Course she was.'

That he was lying I knew from my own researches. Benjamin, bribed with some insider tips about computer programming, paid me back by getting his mother to the phone. Yes, Chance had been very nice. So tactfully concerned with my welfare that she had invited him to dinner, where, as I might expect, he had dazzled the assembled company. Veronica Lilywhite had been particularly charmed. 'What?' I screamed. 'Veronica Lilywhite a guest in my house?' To which the answer was that it was not my house. No, not my table, not my books, not my glass, not my brass, not my wall-sized picture of that lovely archipelago of lights, the Cone nebula region in Monoceros, photographed with the 1.34-metre clear-aperture Schmidt camera at the Karl Schwarzschild Observatory, Tautenberg. Not my stars and not my stardom. Veronica was the stellar presence now. I wondered if she was dressing any better. 'Is she dressing any better?' I asked.

'She looked charming.'

'Ankle-strap clogs now, is it?'

'Manolo Blahnik gold-tipped court shoes. A bit OTT maybe, but I'm working on her.'

'You're grooming her, are you?'

'Helping.'

'What do you do together? Everything?'

'What do you mean?'

'I mean are you in bed with her literally as well as metaphorically?'

'You're sick, Joel.'

If I was, I didn't feel it. I felt as if my small boat, deprived by storms of its rudder, oars and jury-rigged sail, was at least, at last, connected to the current. I had begun to fancy myself as a vagabond. The self-appraisal was reinforced by news from the faculty that I could indeed regard myself as being on sabbatical, provided I realised that the sabbatical was unpaid and might well modulate into an indefinite period when my assistant lectureship would not necessarily be succeeded by a lectureship. Not, the voice went on, that this would be a professional catastrophe. My media fame, with all of its attendant rewards, doubtless outweighed all such considerations. Meanwhile a medical examination was recommended. I promised to consider this. It's my standard way of rejecting advice. 'I'll certainly consider it' is shorthand for 'I'll certainly consider it a gross impertinence.' Another good one is 'There's something in what you say.' Yes, and the something is a tall, conical, steaming pile of horseshit.

The television people, on the other hand, were glad for my sake that I had such a secure academic base, because the outlook for another series was dim, owing to financial pressure. Single programmes, specials, guest spots: obviously I would be the first choice for those. Any time a probe grazed a planet's moon I could count on being there on screen to help drum up excitement about the enhanced pictures. Dig that rill. Cop that crater. But there would be no contract. No more being thrown together at Television Centre for months on end with the pretty researcher in crumpled-look overalls. Well, none of that mattered now. What I had felt for Gael had been mere passion, the wanting of her body. I wanted the Mole's soul. To be appreciated through her body, of course, but let there be no doubt about the object: her essence. Joel's goal was the Mole's *soul*. How generous of me not to be dismissive of Chance's casual involvement with the *fons et origo* of my euphoria! On the way back from Soho with two heavy carrier-bags of delicacies, the Mole and I stopped off at her little room in Bloomsbury. It had a window on a brick wall, was only twice as long as she was, and across its width she could touch both walls at once with her outstretched hands. But it was really neat. Not in Lauren's erstwhile sense of 'real neat' but in the English sense of really *neat*. Postcards, photographs and old ski passes were arranged on her pinboard with a keen eye to spacing and proportion. Her books shone. In pride of place along the back of the desk were her poetry texts, with Milton on the left and Hopkins on the right. Of the many portrait postcards and photographs on the mantelpiece, the most salient, framed in antique *art nouveau* silver against the big mirror's lower rail, was, as one might have expected, a study of Penelope which suggested that Gustave Moreau had decided to outdo Bernini in capturing Saint Teresa at the climax of spiritual ecstasy. Flanking this centrepiece, like the wings of a triptych, were two postcards occupied by great ladies of the past whose representations obviously constituted a double star.

'I recognise Mme de Staël,' I said. 'Who's the other one?'

'Mme Recamier. Isn't she smashing? They loved each other for a long time.'

'Didn't Benjamin Constant get them both?'

'He was a wimp. They were better off without him. They were faithful.'

'Is that the big rule?'

'To be faithful? Yes. What do you think of Ambrose?' She was pointing at the photograph of a haggard young man with scruffy hair and a half-shave.

'Is he a terrorist?'

'My boyfriend.'

'*What?*'

'Don't be shocked. He's not really. Just my Platonic admirer. Although he wants more, of course.'

'Of course.'

'Don't tease. He's my fellow-student and graceless escort.

I'm trying to civilise him. He's not presentable. That's why I keep him dark. Chance thinks that Ambrose is the one I'll marry.'

'Does he?' Does he *indeed*, I could have said. 'Doesn't that strike you as a bit cold and calculating?' I wasn't *really* trying to drive a wedge.

'Chance says that he doesn't want to disturb the normal rhythm of my life. But he has to admit that mine isn't a very normal life, doesn't he? Now help me choose my dress for the big night.'

There were only two to choose from and she didn't undress to try them on, just held them in front of her. So it was hardly an invitation to make a serious pass. I was a big brother, if not an old uncle. But I got a kiss. Emboldened by the discrepancy between the talk of faithfulness and the fact that she was betraying Penelope with Chance and quite possibly about to betray Chance with Ambrose, while Chance was betraying her with Angélique and quite possibly betraying both of them with Presley Schaufenster, I figured that I had *something* coming. She was still clasping the second dress in front of her, so I handicapped myself equally by keeping my hands behind my back. Two pairs of lips met in space. Sheer good taste. Yet a distinct step up from the purely understanding kiss of ten days before. Two kisses inside a fortnight: I was definitely on the road to dissipation. This was the high life.

'I want you,' I said, and knew instantly that it was the wrong thing to say: a deal-breaker, a mood-wrecker. Perhaps I should have said, 'Let's fuck.' Except that when you say that, it turns out you should have said, 'I want you.' The fact is, that if it still depends on saying the right thing, you'll say the wrong thing. The Mole wrinkled her forehead as if the question was too hard. I answered it for her. 'I'm sorry. It just popped out. Foolish talk. Foolish dork, in fact.'

'Don't be sorry. I'm flattered. Only I'm not sure I want to *be* wanted just now, to be brutally frank. You understand?'

'Life must be a bit crowded.'

'This dress?'

'I think they're both too dressy. It's not a ball, it's dinner. I like the basic black you wore the night we met.'

So the excitement was over for that day, except for the mint chocolate chip Cornetto each that we ate in the cab on the way home. Typically I finished mine in a hurry while she savoured hers. 'In Australia,' I said, 'we have a tradition that the man wolfs the whole of his Cornetto and then the woman gives him her crunchy bit as well.' She pretended to fall for it. I think it was my consolation prize.

'Have to grasp,' said Chance on the eve of the big event, 'that the Mole is a *good* girl. Not promiscuous. Serious. *Engagée*.' We were on the balcony at dusk, with poised daiquiris. The moon and the evening star, like a modern, anachronistic illustration to James Elroy Flecker, were on display between the sawtooth towers. That many heavenly bodies I could cope with. People on the walkways were hurrying towards culture.

'Not promiscuous?' I didn't mean it to sound ironic.

'Nope.'

'Is that the big rule?'

'Of what?'

'Of the game. *La règle du jeu*. Plurality but no promiscuity.'

'Yep. Specially with so many bugs about. Angélique has got exactly one bloke over there and he's faithful to her like a dog. Apart from his wife, of course.'

'Of course.'

'He's a white-haired technocrat sports fiend called Jean-Louis Cravache. Shoves fuel rods into reactors. Writes books about catastrophe theory and the attainment of Nirvana. Won the World's Freestyle Skiing Championship for Middle-aged Men. No time for any hanky-panky.'

'Is that his picture on your board?'

'That's the one. A drongo, but dependable.'

'But it doesn't matter what the girls do with each other?'

'Course not. No bugs. Victimless crime.'

'Aren't *we* the victims?'

'Not even metaphorically. Victims are sick or dead. World's full of victims. Victims in heaps. Hecatombs. No mistaking them. They swell up. They cry for years because they can't forget what those men did to them. They get dug up with their skulls still screaming. Victims of real crimes. Enough of them to make the victimless crime a positive virtue.'

'You believe that?'

'By now I believe in nothing else. But it's a *private* virtue. Twenty years ago, men preached pleasure. Ten years ago, women preached justice. Now the preaching's over, thank Christ. On our own, fumbling in the dark, we seek a *modus vivendi*.'

'On our *own*?'

'With each other.' He had the grace to smile. 'Hey, there's the phantom runner.'

Down there in the parklet beside the ornamental lake, the lone figure of Clive James plumply circulated, identifiable by the grey track suit and the extravagant slowness peculiar to those who have mastered the diffcult art of running at walking pace. Some ducks were looking at him. They were not impressed.

'Have you invited him?'

'Not to dinner. He'll come in later with everybody else. Look at him go. The Widmerpool from Woolloomooloo.' We raised our drinks to him in the gathering dark.

Preparations were well in hand by the time Angélique arrived in the early afternoon of the next day. We were on the point of taking a light working lunch when Eric rang from the airport to say that the plane was late. We were drinking coffee among the crumbs when he rang again to say that he was driving her up the ramp. Chance went down to meet her, so she had finished kissing him by the time they got to us. That left her free to start kissing the Mole. I only got my hand shaken, but it was done as if I were François Truffaut lying in his coffin and this was her last chance to convey her artistic respect.

'So,' she announced, nodding in agreement with herself, her expectations confirmed. 'It is the great Joel. The man of science. Yet the face of a poet.' Even though she was so busy being wonderful, she still looked wonderful, in her no-need-for-make-up make-up and her roughing-it travel clothes of designer denim.

'We've met before,' I tried to remind her.

'I should have realised. How else could it be that Chance feels so close to you, so like a brother?'

Eric had finished piling luggage in the lobby and had gone back for more. Among the matched bags was a basket. Angélique sprang to it, crouched with her hands beside her face, fingers extended, as if miming the concept of *embarras de richesse*, and straightened up with a stack of glossy books.

'These you must read.' She was addressing us generally. 'It is good to be among readers. In France we read only to discuss. It is you English who read. Silently. Profoundly.'

'Don't you want to go upstairs or anything?' asked Chance, bringing in an extra chair from the balcony. but she joined us immediately at the table, passing out books as if they were hymnals.

'This you will adore,' she told Chance. It was *Les Noces barbares* by Yann Queffélec. 'Yann himself has given it to me. He is very solemn. He has never danced. But he admires my work. Or perhaps he is a little in love. Do you think this is possible?'

'Probable,' said Chance, who was well used to helping Angélique appreciate the universality of her own appeal. 'Those hairy uncompromising types are the ones who fall hardest when they meet their first set of silk underwear.'

'Bernard finds him very difficult,' said Angélique, adding, for my benefit and possibly the Mole's also, 'that is Bernard Pivot of *Apostrophes*. On the television we discuss the books.'

'Until we're blue in the face,' said Chance.

'And this one is so lovely, so amusing,' Angélique raved on, having profited from the interruption to draw breath. 'For you, I think, Antonia.' The book was *Mes Nuits sont plus belles que vos jours*, by Raphaele Billetdoux. 'She is very beautiful, this girl. The hair as the punk. I have shown her a few things about clothes, but not much. She has *so* much style. Karl adores her. Also Yves, Claude, Thierry . . . '

Playing up to the men and patronising the Mole, Angélique gushed continuously throughout the afternoon. When the helpers arrived – Di and Fergie were two robust girls of good family who wore matching butcher's aprons – Angélique included them in her audience. To begin with they were so impressed they could hardly whip dip, but after not very long their large eyes glazed over like quails in aspic. As evening neared, Angélique and the Mole disappeared upstairs to bathe, pamper and dress. All the bathrooms were occupied for hours. When they reappeared, it was a beauty contest which Angélique won for sheer dazzle and the Mole for dewy freshness. I suppose if I had looked closely I would have seen that the actress had the clear skin and the classic features. The Mole was not past the odd spot, and her nose, on her own admission, was an afterthought. But Angélique I found hard to see for the presentation. Simplicity having been achieved, it had been chained into position with jewels. The flawless throat was underlined by a necklace that made the Mole's earrings and bracelet look like objects for pity, an emotion which Angélique did her formidable best to articulate.

'Did Chance give you this?' asked Angélique.

'Yes,' said the Mole with shy pride. 'It's Cartier. It's the best thing I've ever had.'

'You must tell him to be a *little* more daring. Joel, *you* must tell him.' Chance was in a cupboard somewhere digging out crates of champagne, so I started to say that I would tell him later, but Angélique wasn't listening. I, however, was listening to her. There wasn't much choice. How had Chabrol kept her quiet during all those mysterious long close-ups? He must have held a gun on her from off-camera.

'This is by Timothy Koh Choon Bey of Singapore. Almost my best but I have others. Do you know Terewan Techapongvorachai from Thailand? I have his necklace of gold, diamond, crystal and, what is it, onyx? Also Makiko Takahashi of Japan, his brooch of emeralds and rainbow silk. I wear it on my black velvet hat, big like a wheel. This size. Right out here. There are many wonderful Japanese.' Her hands, tapered for ever like Makarova's, conjured all the wonderful Japanese with a gesture big enough to include sumo wrestlers, kamikaze pilots and war criminals. 'Timohiro Asayama, you know him? He makes the watch as the bangle. And of course in Paris there are always Kenzo, Issye and Kansai, old friends by now since many years. How do you say *vieux chapeau*?'

'We say *vieux chapeau*,' said the Mole, with great presence of mind, I thought.

'Yes, you say it in French,' said Angélique, who, knowing everything, could not be startled by an item of information, but only, at most, be mildly surprised by the need to be reminded of something she knew already. 'It is strange how you do that.'

The strangeness didn't slow her down. She was still rattling away, with the Mole sending me arched eyebrows of fellow-suffering conviviality behind her back, when the other dinner guests began to arrive. Conspiring with the Mole helped to keep me going through the introductions. The guests were a daunting bunch. In Cambridge, brains and *chic* tended to be mutually exclusive, but apparently in London you were supposed to have both. I had borrowed a velvet bow tie from Chance to go with my summer suit, but I felt a bit underdressed. Chance's agent, Joni Dankworth, was in Angélique's class for grooming and had a famous novelist husband whom I won't name, out of revenge for his books, to which he gives multiple endings. If he can't be clear about what he's doing, why should I be clear about who he is? Only a few minutes behind those two, Monty Forbes, the homosexual painter, arrived, billed by Chance as one of the three best-read men in London. Leaning on Monty's arm, a brave posture in view of the current afraid-of-Aids climate, was the recently most talked-about young American *feuilletoniste*, Shir Horowitz. Variously described as an updated Anita Loos or the next Elaine May, she wore a tweed jacket with her dungarees and could not be called glamorous, but she had her own visual style. Tiny but tough, she looked like the top half of Lee Marvin.

Chance's publisher, Nimrod Plooey, was a poet in his own right. In that field he had, by far, a bigger reputation than Chance himself. Through the unmistakable, indeed inexorable, originality of his similes, Nimrod Plooey had overcome the handicap of a name which some critics had rated as the most unpoetic for a poet to burden himself with since W. D. Snodgrass. With his Tolstoyan beard and penchant for peasant garb – always an embroidered shirt outside the pants with a belt over the shirt – he looked so Russian that you wondered why Joseph Brodsky bothered to keep up the pretence. As far as the literary world was concerned, Plooey had clout where it counted – i.e., outside the literary world. He rammed home his prestige by appearing on big occasions, such as tonight, with Eva Brownlow, a glossy magazine editor who had been a coming young writer herself before moving out, as she put it, into the fast lane. She signalled her presence in the fast lane by dressing at least as well as her models and much more expensively.

Although blessed with a sumptuous figure, she had some reason to cover it up with care. Plooey wrote poems describing Eva's nether regions. His wife, when she read these in Eva's magazine, greeted them with relief, since previously it had been her own private parts which had been the subject of her husband's inexhaustible powers of comparison. Minus his genius, Plooey would have been lynched long before. But his brilliance obliged the literary world to treat him as a singleton, and so he behaved on this night, from the moment his hair-rimmed head, bifocally enlarged eyes, belted calico shirt, baggy trousers and knee-length boots appeared in the lobby behind everybody else but somehow demanding attention as if in front. Everyone complained about how hard the place had been to find. It was just that Nimrod Plooey complained loudest and longest, even though he started last.

'I couldn't *believe* how lost we got,' said Monty Forbes. 'I've been here before and I *still* couldn't identify *anything*.'

'Yeah,' muttered Shir Horowitz. 'Wild. Guggenheim Museum full of lost people that works of art come and visit, you know?'

'Darling,' said Joni Dankworth to Angélique as they clinched. 'Congratulations on being here at all. You must think you're still at the airport.'

'*So* original,' said Eva Brownlow. '*Nobody* lives like this in New York.'

'Nobody lives like this in London,' said Joni Dankworth's unnamed novelist husband. Or perhaps he said something else.

'Nobody lives here *at all*,' shouted Nimrod Plooey. 'Including us. We're dead. We died on the way here. It's a bomb shelter by Kenzo Tange. It's a holiday home for Edward Teller. It's a wet dream by Otto Wagner. It's a dry come by *Richard* Wagner. What a labyrinth! Borges would have boggled. Ariadne would have lost the thread. We passed Lord Lucan in the corridor.'

'He's sharing a flat with Martin Bormann,' said Chance, trying to damp Plooey down.

'Who *built* this place?' asked Plooey, as a man will who has already rehearsed the answer on the stairs. 'The Todt Organisation? The A. E. van Vogt Organisation?' He crossed to the windows and stared dramatically out, hands on hips, at the

112

towers with their long vertical rows of horizontal balconies notching the sky. 'Aeroplane combs,' he pronounced.

After half an hour of champagne during which Plooey talked for twenty-nine minutes, we all sat down. The Mole and I were at one end of the table and Chance and Angélique were at the other, so that I was opposite Chance and the Mole opposite Angélique. Down the outside of the table, facing into the room, were Joni Dankworth on my right, then Plooey, and then Eva Brownlow on Chance's left. Down the inside, facing the glass wall, were Monty Forbes on the Mole's left, then Shir Horowitz, and then the unnamed novelist on Angélique's right. Di and Fergie, pronounced by everyone to be absolutely marvellous, did the fetching and carrying, so there was no need for those dining to stop talking, except to eat, which the more loquacious did only sparingly. In the early stages everybody spoke politely to his or her immediate companions. Since I already knew the Mole well, I left her to tell Monty Forbes about Amanda and Robert Grill-it – we had agreed that this would be a good topic for her to start off on – while I tentatively consulted Joni Dankworth about Chance's flirtation with the idea of downgrading his literary output.

'He mustn't even *think* of it,' she said. 'But it won't happen.'

'Why mustn't he think of it?'

'You can't imagine what his pulling power is like. Not even this book of poems will manage to fail. Even though he's done nothing to push it except throw this party, and he's only done that for fun.'

'Perhaps he's tired of having it too easy.'

'Well, Rod Plooey isn't tired of having it too easy, let me tell you. That's why he's here tonight and giving his full publishing genius performance. As an artist, Rod's in favour of Chance following any whim that suits. As a businessman, the very *idea* of losing Chance Jenolan's contribution to the bottom line is enough to make Nimrod Plooey's hair turn straight overnight.'

I looked. Plooey's hair was certainly very curly. You could tell that, even though his head was moving all the time: now plunging forward towards the *vichyssoise*, now thrown back so that he could laugh at the ceiling, now shaken from side to side in a mimed negation of one of his own fantasies. This last manoeuvre left his spectacles dislodged, which made everyone at that end of the table laugh except Eva Brownlow. She smiled tolerantly: i.e., intolerantly. With a reputation for New York cool to protect, she was sitting next to a dangerous source of destabilisation. On the other hand, he was very famous. It must have been difficult for her, but Chance was beside her to smooth things over. Eva Brownlow knew exactly where she was with Chance, you could tell. Was she on the list of his old flames? I muttered the question to the Mole and received the answer 'Snooty bitch', which I took to mean yes.

The Mole went immediately back to telling Monty all about the *nouveau roman*. Angélique overheard their colloquy from the other end of the table and joined in. General conversation thus began rather early. While in no wise resistant to the charms of Joni Dankworth, I was relieved by this. I had always preferred a whole table talking. Split up into isolated units of *politesse*, it wastes energy. When all contribute, even if the topic is only nominal, a synergy is generated which becomes, in the course of time, the real subject, as if everyone present has recognised that to keep it going is the real object. The participants have to be well cast, of course. It doesn't hurt if a few of them just listen. Listeners can even be in the majority. But the talkers must not get in each other's road. Usually it takes a good hostess to sort them out. This was one of the rare occasions when four monologists in world class – Angélique, Monty Forbes, Chance and Plooey – were all able to bang away at once without the whole system overheating. Observing, I decided that it was Chance, through the feminine side of his nature, who made this possible. The hostess in him stopped him from going on too long and made sure none of the other egomaniacs – I suppose I was the fifth – did either. He enjoyed the event too much to let it ruin itself.

Angélique started off by saying how well she knew Robbe-Grillet personally. 'Always I am telling Alain to write another *L'Année dernière à Marienbad* just for me, not? It would please me so much to stand there in a mysterious manner on the marble staircase like Delphine.'

'Saying nothing,' said Chance.

'No, no,' said Angélique, not quite getting it. 'He is eloquent, Alain. It is just that he is, what is it . . . '

'Inadequate?'

'Taciturn. Laconic? What do I mean, Joel?'

'Terse.'

'Terse! Exactly. He is terse.'

'I've just been reading *Three Trapped Tigers* by Gabriel Cabrera Infante,' said Monty, 'and the guy's so terse I can't tell what's going on. I'm up to page 175 and I can't tell what's going *on*.'

'That's magic realism,' said Chance. 'We're not allowed to be scathing about magic realism in this house because *One Hundred Queers Gain Altitude* is Antonia's favourite book.'

'It . . . ' began the Mole, but was beaten to the draw.

'Márquez I know well,' said Angélique. 'He has told me . . . '

'Bananas!' shouted Plooey. 'It's a variation on the Bananas school of writing.'

'OK, Rod,' said Chance, with the air of a matador twitching his cape for the first time at an enormous animal that will take him several hours to kill. 'What's the Bananas school of writing?'

'Women writers who start off every novel in the first person by coming home from the baby-minder to work on their new novel and they find a puce hippopotamus in the bathroom. The hippopotamus says . . . '

'Which women writers?' asked Eva Brownlow.

'Doesn't matter. The hippopotamus says, "Don't be afraid . . . "'

'Why does it say that?' asked Eva Brownlow.

'Because,' said Shir Horowitz, 'if this was a Kafka story it'd be a cockroach.' Everyone except Eva Brownlow laughed, although I noticed that the unnamed novelist did not laugh aloud. He made a laughing mouth and did a laughing shudder, but it was all unvocalised.

'Your husband's the strong silent type,' I said sideways.

'He's gathering material.'

There was a lot to gather. Long before the after-dinner guests arrived, it was already a party. Nimrod Plooey would have danced on the table if Di and Fergie had allowed it. As it was, he did a Russian folk dance in the centre of the room, while being pelted with champagne corks. The unnamed novelist threw grapes at him, an embellishment which the host, I think, regarded as *lèse-majesté*, against himself if not his publisher. But Chance did not show anger, or anything except delight in the moment. Earlier, I had naively thought that he was enjoying a night off. Now I realised that he was staging a production.

The impression was confirmed when the after-dinner guests began to show up. I'm afraid my memory of events, though precise in detail, becomes structurally impressionistic after this point. Naturally I had drunk too much. It dimly occurred to me that I had been drinking too much for weeks. Pouring some more champagne in order to quell this thought, I played twin wallflower to Monty Forbes as the new arrivals poured in. Most of them had come on from dinner parties at which they had been stars. They were still stars, but they had changed clusters. Some of them I recognised and the others were identified for me by Monty, who knew everyone.

'Where did you find Shir Thingowitz?' I asked through the eruption of the entryphone buzzer.

'Horowitz. Isn't she a bulldozer? I got her here to see Angélique. The sort of thing she dreams of. Here they come.'

The bespectacled and bedraggled young novelist David Bentley arrived, with the scholar Charlotte Windhover. Monty called them a typical London couple. 'Her second husband and his second mother.'

'We got lost,' said David Bentley.

'And *we've* been here before,' said Charlotte Windhover, who turned out to be one of the Mole's teachers. I was glad to see teacher and pupil talking to each other. I was feeling very protective towards the Mole, what with Angélique on the scene, not to mention Shir Horowitz. From whom was my little girl safe? Perhaps, for the moment, from Nicholas Crane, who was swept into the room on the tidal wave of triumph generated by his huge new hit book, entitled *Huge New Hit Book*. On his arm was the effulgent, visibly pregnant Sally Draycott, soon to be back on our screens after two seasons of fronting arts documentaries for an American cable enterprise that had rewarded her for her hard work by going bust. 'Holy shit,' said Nicholas, kissing Chance warmly. 'We got lost *again*.' I was glad to see that Chance's return kiss was less demonstrative.

116

'How's the passenger?' he asked Sally, giving her, gratifyingly to my mind, a rather more physically abandoned welcome than he had just given Nicholas. He hadn't *completely* succumbed to local habits. Angélique fell on Sally with cries of love which seemed to startle their recipient. A less honest woman than Sally would have been glad to go along with the pretence that they knew each other extremely well. As it was, Sally's smile was somewhat strained. Perhaps Angélique had bumped the baby.

By now, however, any embarrassments went unnoticed. There was just too much traffic. A handsomely dissolute man in a wine-stained white suit arrived. He had green skin. Monty told me that this was Colin Thinwall, Chance's ambiguously sexual crony from his alternative existence as a Grub Street *literatus*. Every Friday when he was in England, apparently, Chance dined at Foscari's in Fitzrovia, where he was still categorised among the Australian poets at a table monopolised by the influential literary cabal known as the Dregs. The rest of the Dregs now came trooping in. Literary editors on the verge of retirement arrived with their actress daughters on the verge of stardom. There were female TV producers who looked like models, models who looked like juvenile delinquents, juvenile delinquents who had formed a dance group. Everyone was there except the kind of culture-circuit journalists that Plooey would have most liked to see. But there was some publicity value in Chance's not wanting to see them. Yes, Plooey told the world at large, that could be an angle.

The show's gathering momentum was almost stopped by the unaccompanied entrance of Presley Schaufenster. Stripped of black rubber and silver insignia, clad only in some short ruched white slip arrangement and a pair of high heels that seemed to have no shoes attached, her outrageous beauty was on unimpeded display. Her lightly tanned body looked to be fashioned from some unexpanding, uncontracting, unimpressionable material. Monobloc hot-cast carbon? Her hair was pulled back in lacquered black flames to reveal a severely classical face which would have been fearful enough in its symmetry even without whatever it was she had done to her eyes. These shone with little red white and blue roundels where the corneas should have been. The effect was hypnotic. 'Fluorescent contact lenses,' said the Mole. 'What a tart.'

'She looks like a Spitfire!' screamed Nimrod Plooey, just as Peter C. Bartelski walked in. That sensitive scholar, thinking that the publisher meant him, turned on his Cuban heel and walked out, but thought better of it and walked in again. It was a long way back to Cambridge and this was the place to be.

Fuelled by champagne, the party spilled out on to the balcony and all the way up the stairs to the gymnasium, whence it spread out on to the other balcony, overlooking the illuminated city. Chance's hideout filled up with people as if a mass of star-making material had been released through a time-tunnel into an empty stretch of space. I went with it, lurching helpfully from group to group, asking people if there was anything they wanted, although it must have been clear that I was beyond helping, indeed beyond help. I heard all kinds of things, though.

'Why is it called *The Rubaiyat of Omar Sharif*?'

'Chance likes Omar.'

'Does Omar like the book?'

'Must do. He'll be here, later. He's playing bridge at the Clermont.'

Chance was on the top balcony giving a lecture. People who had been sitting talking on the keep-fit and weight-training equipment drifted out to listen. 'Down there,' he pointed, 'is where Australia started. A mile along the Mile End Road. Where Captain Cook lived while he was waiting for a ship.'

'He's got a lot to answer for,' said Colin Thinwall.

'And the first bomb of World War II fell just over there. And Grub Street ran right under there. Milton's buried just over there, under that church.'

'Milton who?'

'Milton Friedman.'

Back downstairs again, I found Shir Horowitz pumping Di and Fergie about life in Verbier.

'And one of the chaps calls out "Dead ant!" . . . ' said Di.

' . . . and you have to throw yourself on your back in the snow . . . ' said Fergie.

' . . . with your poles and skis in the air . . . ' said Di.

'And then the guy fucks you?' asked Shir Horowitz. She had

already been to Ascot and Wimbledon but this was valuable material.

For a while I helped carry things upstairs but I overdid it and the Mole made me carry some of them down again. I overdid that too and was pensioned off. Monty talked to me. I could always depend on good old Monty.

'What do you think of the Kraut's eyes?' he asked. Presley Schaufenster was being mobbed nearby.

'Can she *see* through those things?'

'No way of finding out,' said Monty. 'She can't talk. Do you remember the Princess of Nassau in Proust?'

'Yes. She had mauve eyes like astronomical clocks cut in opal.'

'They tell me your father's got the best private library in Sydney,' said Monty, who had a famous private library of his own.

'I wouldn't say best. But it was certainly big. Too much for me. Main reason I became a scientist, I expect.'

'Chance has got some marvellous books here but they're all getting kicked to pieces lying around on the floor like this. I hate to see it.'

'Dad used to polish his.'

'How did he get them there?'

I was still answering the question when we were joined by the grim figure of Shir Horowitz. Monty sidled off, the traitor. 'How does the streetwise New Yorker find our provincial gathering?' I asked *de haut en bas*, an angle which her abbreviated stature made easy.

'Nice try, but I was born and raised in the Texas Panhandle. Town called Muleshoe.'

'Does a lot happen in Muleshoe?'

'My uncle once threw a monkey wrench clear over a grain elevator. Made the front page of the *Lubbock Avalanche Courier*.'

'Lubbock. Isn't that where Buddy Holly came from?'

'Well,' she said wearily, 'he sure as fuck didn't come from Muleshoe. You think you could introduce me to that chick with the RAF eyes and the terrific ass? You know, give me a build-up?'

119

'Sure.' My acquaintance with Presley Schaufenster was slight, but I effected the introduction with some assurance. After all, I lived there. Yes, I felt very much at home. Any bottle with half an inch of wine in it I cleared away after upending it over my glass.

'I've just realised,' said Chance as we passed each other on the stairs, 'that the best title isn't by Hemingway at all.'

'What is it?'

'*As I Lay Dying*, by William Dorkner.'

I overheard David Bentley telling Nicholas Crane that he, David, had just been fired from writing the script of Chance's epic movie. I hadn't realised that the project had got to the stage of being written. So that was where Chance got to during the day. Then I overheard Nicholas telling David that he, Nicholas, had just signed a contract to rewrite the script of Chance's epic movie. So the project had already got a stage further. This was confusing. Feeling like someone who knew nothing, I sat down on the stairs next to Clive James, who was looking rather out of it. I hadn't seen him arrive and he didn't seem to know who I was, but we got on. We had a good vantage point from which to see over the heads of the crowd. Nimrod Plooey was dancing on the dinner table. He was actually quite good.

'Look at those two there,' said Clive James, nodding towards Di and Fergie, who were clapping time as Plooey leapt and spun. 'Salt of the earth. Well brought up. No thought in their heads except to give their lives for an ideal. Hand-maidens. Ladies in waiting. Once they would have served royalty. And you know what?'

'What?'

'They're *still* serving royalty. The media moguls are the new royalty. Apart from that, no change.'

'Are you envious?' I was being frank. It was easy. He had a drink in each hand.

'Not really. Bit pissed off.'

'At what?'

'I didn't get a crack at writing Chance's movie.'

'Hang in there. It still might come your way.'

Feeling like someone who knew a thing or two, I lurched off to join the Mole in the group around Plooey. Back at floor level now, with sweat dripping from his beard, he was giving an outline of his ideas on how the Arts Council should bring poetry to the people.

'Air drops!' he shouted. 'You have to imagine these poor benighted peasants on the fells or the moors or whatever it is, and they're looking up at the sky as a Lockheed Hercules comes roaring out of the sun with its back door open, and then out come the poets one after the other! Ted Hughes! Seamus Heaney! Geoffrey Hill! The parachutes snap open and they're already reciting through loud-hailers . . . '

The Mole let me hold her hand through some of this and then introduced me to her allegedly Platonic boyfriend Ambrose. He looked like his photograph except even more sullen.

'Thanks for asking me,' he said, 'but I'm off back to the squat. I can't stand all this.'

'All what?' asked the Mole, hot and bothered.

'Everything,' he said, with a comprehensive gesture that took in everything. 'This bloody awful Swatch commercial you call a party.' Did he know what the Mole and Penelope meant by Everything? If he did, it probably mattered less to him than the mere sight of people who had money to spend. How well I knew him. No I didn't. *I* had always been a star student: money from home, top scholarships all the way, jobs to burn. Until the jobs burned.

Ambrose pushed off towards the door. The Mole, her lips manifestly not fitting together, made her way, like a salmon climbing rapids, quickly upstairs towards one of the bathrooms, which she reached before I could get to her. I waited outside but needed a bathroom myself. When I returned she had gone back downstairs and was talking to Chance. So I went back up to the top balcony just in time to be accosted by Shir Horowitz. '*Fräulein* Weirdeyes can't say a fucking word,' she grunted, 'and *you* are an *asshole*.'

'What did you do with her?'

'I handed her over to that French radio station we were at dinner with. They're made for each other. Is she yours?'

'Who? Angélique? Christ, no.'

'I meant the teenager with the fabulous tits.'

'Yes, she's mine.' The Mole had appeared and wiggled her

fingers at me as if she was. Then she turned around and went downstairs again. I started to follow her but got lost on the way. Eric was standing in the kitchen with his hook around a beer. 'Steve McQueen and James Coburn,' he said.

'*The Magnificent Seven*.'

'Har! And Charles Bronson.'

'It's still *The Magnificent Seven*.'

'And James Garner.'

'It's . . . Oh. Ah. Oh yes. *The Great Escape*.'

'I always get them with that one. Got the governor with that one once.'

I left him leading a hook-to-mouth existence. At least I hadn't said, 'on the other hand', or used any other wounding expression. Sensitive to Eric's feelings, or perhaps cravenly keen to avoid embarrassment, I always exercised a strict self-censorship over what I said to him. The most effective method was to keep the conversation short. Half a bottle of champagne ambushed me. I fought my way out of the trap but my legs could do no more than help my mind wander. Speech arrived at my ear but I couldn't pinpoint the mouth it came from.

'Have you heard that Christopher Booker's new novel is up for the Brookner Prize?'

'The facts of the TV-am thing are very simple. The guys fucked up and the girls carried the can.'

'Nobody in New York lives like this. I want Bruce to take some pictures of it.'

'Elena's idea of roughing it is pheasant sandwiches.'

'Have you heard that E. O. Parrott has written a book about Flaubert? Guess what it's called.'

'Günter Grass I know very well. *So* much of a man. Also Enzensburger is a close friend . . . '

'Plooey tried to write a poem about his own bum but the shaving mirror kept fogging up.'

'Rock Hudson and Ernest Borgnine.'

'No bid.'

'And Patrick McGoohan.'

'*Ice Station Zebra*.'

'The facts about unemployment are very simple. The jobs

aren't coming back. Every robot creates twelve jobs and destroys twenty-five. Net loss of thirteen.'

'So what will people *do* if they're unskilled and they've got no creative talent?'

'They will become Channel 4 commissioning editors.'

'I'm a *spectateur engagé*. Raymond Aron said that. I wish I'd said it.'

'Yeah. You could have said it in English.'

'*Touché.*'

'Rock Hudson and Rod Taylor.'

'No bid.'

'And Mercedes McCambridge.'

'Mercedes McCambridge? Sounds like a well-educated Scotsman in a sports car. No bid.'

'And James D . . . '

'*Giant.*'

'Nobody can play this game unless they've spent their whole lives in the dark. Isn't there another game?'

'Famous People of Humble Origins.'

'How do you play?'

'It's a cinch. Robert Taylor made clothes. Watt Tyler laid tiles. Like that. Nick starts.'

'I give up.'

'No, I meant Nick will start. Nick, you start.'

'Rab Butler.'

'Mark Boxer.'

'Eldridge Cleaver.'

'Raymond Chandler.'

'Jane Fonda.'

'Challenge!'

'Her grandfather ran a *fondue* restaurant.'

'Who *is* that bloke?'

'Some kind of scientist. One of Chance's tame . . . Whoops.'

'If she can't get the right table at Elaine's, she won't go. She won't eat at the Russian Tea Room on the wrong day. She's going to starve to death, that girl.'

'Karl, Jonathan, can I prise you apart?'

'No.'

'Australian men look like Mel Gibson as a compensation for thinking like John Newcombe.'

'*You* don't look like Mel Gibson.'

'I've been here too long.'

'He's calling it *From "Duel in the Sun" to "Jewel in the Crown": a Study in Semiotic Imperialism.*'

'What does *he* know about semiotics?'

'Same as he knows about imperialism.'

'I have met this marvellous German girl. She does not interrupt. I think that is so important, not?'

'Mm? Oh yes. Absolutely.'

'Do you know what Auden wanted to call his autobiography?'

'No.'

'*Reflections on a Marine's Penis.* We had to stop him.'

Long after midnight, Omar Sharif finally arrived and was ceremonially presented with a copy of the book. Nimrod Plooey did not underplay the scene. The Mole looked safe enough, talking to the unnamed novelist. I could tell by how she was drawing little circles in the air that she was telling him her theories about self-reflexivity. They would go over big with him. He wrote the same sort of novels himself. Come to think of it, his appearance had changed. He had grown shorter and his hair was a different colour. Hadn't he been wearing brogues before? Now he was wearing loafers. Perhaps he was someone else. Or perhaps I was. I was feeling very odd.

Everything would be all right again if I could just be with the Mole. So I went to wait for her in her bed. She never joined me. I slept without dreaming, or without remembering I had dreamed, and woke up with no sense of time having elapsed, just an awareness that everything had changed. I went downstairs and there was nobody there. The rubbish had been tidied away and all the glasses washed. Once again Di and Fergie had been absolutely marvellous. After a long swig of tap water I went back upstairs. On the floor above mine I heard Angélique's voice coming from Chance's room. 'That is heaven, darling. That is *completely* heaven. Make more of a circle with the fingertip.' Then I heard the Mole's voice. 'Like this? Do you like that?' Angélique groaned.

Chance's door was open as if I was meant to look in. If it

hadn't been I would probably have kicked it down or just stuck my head through it. I had to see this. Was he between them? But it was worse. I could see him sitting there alone, softly lit in his blue silk dressing-gown, in a chair by the drawn curtains. From the direction of his smiling gaze I could tell that the two women were on the bed to the left of the door. He was watching them. Angélique cried, 'Yes! Oh yes!' The Mole groaned in sympathetic ecstasy. Betrayed, raging, I took the fatal step further into the room and turned towards them, the breath already drawn with which I would call my darling girl a little liar and two-faced dyke bitch.

She was rubbing cold cream into Angélique's face. Angélique was sprawled in silk with her head in the Mole's lap. The Mole was in a girlish night-shirt, her own face glowing moistly. Angélique must have already given her the same treatment. Hating their intimacy for its chasteness, suddenly too short of evidence to stage a scene, I was caught flat-footed.

'You look as if you've seen a ghost,' said the Mole.

'You look like one with that stuff on,' I said, with a misplaced accusatory tone. A feeble thing said forcefully, it was a lapse which Chance immediately picked up.

'What did you think they were up to?'

'About page 164 of the *Kama Sutra*, by the sound of it. I'm going to bed now.'

'Thought you already had.' He always let you know that he had spotted your discomfort. It was an old trick of his.

'Can I have my bed back now?' asked the Mole.

'Sorry about that. I just collapsed into the first one I could find.'

I saw Angélique smiling at Chance and I knew that he must be smiling back, so I said good night without looking at him, nodded curtly to the room in general, and went down to my cell. Later on I heard the Mole's footsteps on the stairs and I thought of knocking on her door and explaining. Then I thought better of it. There was nothing to explain, except my disappointment at a missed climax. A proper scandal would have put her safely beyond me. Indeterminacy meant that my behaviour could still affect events. That made me responsible for my conduct. I tried to take comfort from being capable of so sustained an analysis.

How I longed to slip into that small bed behind her. How pleased I was at my good judgment in not trying to. Yes, I was a definite improvement over the man I had been a few hours before. Redeemed through love of this unique young woman. Was she sobbing into her pillow at how badly Chance was treating her? I stole along the dark landing and listened at her door. Yes, there were stifled whimpers. I eased open the door. More darkness. A soft mechanical buzz stopped with a click. The Mole sighed without resignation. 'Oh for God's *sake*, Joel,' she said, 'will you *please* fuck *off*.'

Chance took me to lunch at the Zippo next day. I wasn't feeling very well, but he more or less insisted. First we had to stop off at Presley Schaufenster's studio in Docklands. The Granada rolled down the ramp and headed east, with Eric at the wheel. He drove correctly, his left hand at ten o'clock and his hook at three o'clock. Uncomfortably aware that I had not made a good showing the previous night, I concentrated on such trivia. Not that there would be a scene. Not in front of Eric. It was remarkable how clean and healthy the East End looked compared with, say, Oxford Street. By the time you got to Docklands, everything was as neat as an architectural drawing. Big, crisp vertical surfaces were so empty of defilement that the eye was startled. The graffiti artists were still working their way east. The thieves, needless to say, were already here: had arrived with the builders. A small armoured door in the wall of a huge building that must once have been a warehouse swung open after Chance had tapped out a code on a set of numbered plastic keys that were revealed when he unlocked a metal plate.

'The city's replacing itself towards the estuary,' said Chance in the lift as we whined softly upwards. 'Suppose David started it really. He'd been living down here for what Di and Fergie would call yonks, but when the media started running those stories about him editing *Passage to India* in the kitchen the whole world caught on. And then Rupert did the Wapping thing and it was on for young and old. Presley had to pay quite a lot for this drum, even in Deutschmarks.'

We walked out of the lift straight into Presley Schaufenster's domicile. Dwelling. *Ambience*. *Wohnraum*. Environment. It was enormous. You could have serviced a Boeing 707 in there.

126

The arched windows, six of them one beside the other along the front and three more on the side, were of Piranesi dimensions. They faced west and south. London was out there, on the far side of a straight-edged sheet of water that looked as untouched as a glacial lake. I had already decided that Presley Schaufenster inhabited what could only be described as a Space. Through the acres of venetian blinds the light came in slices, throwing zebra stripes across long trestle tables full of photographs. Presley Schaufenster had photographs of everything and everyone. She didn't seem to have anything else. There were hundreds of books, but they were all of large dimensions, because they were books of photographs. The walls were covered with photographic collages, all done with meticulous care and, I had to admit, wit. Aluminium catwalks and stepladders on tracks gave access to the upper areas. The ceiling was one enormous, enormously elaborate montage of photographic images. Ranged in their own scaffolding construction, itself as big as the average flat, there must have been 1,000 box files, each identified only with a photograph. I could have moved in among them and settled down. I felt like doing so. It was the next world, the world without words. Truffaut had forecast it. Do you remember that scene in *Fahrenheit 451* where Montag looks at the dossier on a suspect and there is nothing in it except photographs? Now here it was. The future was with us already.

'Take a look around while I talk to Presley,' said Chance. Looking fairly normal today in a cotton shirt embroidered with a retching dragon, baggy paratrooper's pants and a pair of soft velvet shoes with long crumpled points like two ant-eaters who had raced into a wall, Presley Schaufenster was working at one of the trestle tables. Working seemed to consist of looking at photographs, picking them up and moving them about. The coloured lights had gone out of her eyes, I was relieved to see. She had a portable remote-control computer terminal in her hand, on which she was punching numbers, perhaps to enter her images in some information retrieval system, according to criteria at which one could only guess. How Chance communicated with her I didn't care to imagine. After a long trek, I reached one of the windows and looked up-river at Tower Bridge, all white and blue and shiny bright as if the Americans already owned it. I was there for a long time, waiting for the bridge to open, but it didn't. Perhaps it never did any more. Painted shut. Polished and broken. I wandered back to one of the trestle tables and looked at a lot of people thinking. You could tell they were thinking because they had one hand to their forehead or cupping their chin. One of them was Einstein. Another was Ronald Reagan. The look of the thing was all that mattered.

'She's working on the look of my movie,' said Chance when he at last joined me. 'Got extraordinary eyes.'

'So I noticed.'

'Yeah. Weird, that, wasn't it? Never would have thought of that myself.'

'How did she get into this?'

'Her grandfather was a cameraman at the siege of Leningrad. Carried the first Arriflex into battle. Most amazing collection of war photos. Basis of her archive. We're putting them in the picture.'

'What about the people? Who's in it?'

'Still casting it.'

'What *sort* of film is it? Are we allowed to know?'

'No secret. Just can't describe it. Sort of synthesis. *Ring and the Book* but without the Renaissance setting or any of the characters. Or the story. Or the verse, of course. Very tricky. Keep having to change writers.'

'I can't wait,' I said, although I could have waited for ever. Either he was going mad or I was. But he solved that one for me.

'Been a bit worried about you these last few days. Maybe you should get away from us for a while. Talk about it at lunch. Let's go down the other way and you can see the gadgets.'

The other way was a wooden staircase with high-tech pipe banisters in a well of re-pointed black bricks like caked soot. It led to a space below, which was possibly even larger than the space above. The gadgets seemed to be one of each of every desirable object produced in Britain since the Second World War. The Vickers Viscount airliner was absent, but otherwise Presley didn't seem to have missed any tricks. Her pink Jaguar was one of half a dozen cars present. There was a leaf-green Armstrong Siddeley Sapphire, a sapphire Sunbeam Alpine, a crimson-lake

Riley roadster, a matt-black Bristol 404 and a pearl-grey Alvis Grey Lady. On a long dais, there was a platoon of shop-window mannequins dressed, painted, pierced and plumed as neo-post-punk fashion plates, death-like down to the smallest detail of nose-ring and knuckle-duster. Palaeolithically out of place in the same line-up, a cinema foyer life-size cut-out of Diana Dors smiled like the grille of a Cadillac Allard. In sharp contrast again, two unsmiling blond young men who looked like *Hitler Jugend* tank commanders were loading an LE Velócette silent motorcycle into the back of an antique Dormobile. Fussily guarding their black overalls from any hint of oil, they addressed each other in the clipped, strained accents of an access television programme for Young People. Where had they come from? They looked as if they should have been killed in Normandy forty years ago, sounded as if they were born on an estate that was still being built. Everything was moving past me. I paused beside a red telephone booth with a black telephone inside that featured buttons marked A and B. Its paintwork wasn't even chipped. Outside in the real England the latest telephone booths, machined from a single block of tungsten, had a life expectancy of about thirty minutes before they were attacked with cold chisels and plastic explosives.

'Uncanny, isn't it?' asked Chance, not expecting an answer. 'Her mother crawled out of the ruins of Essen. We used to go there and pulverise them. Now they come here and preserve us. Almost equally intrusive, somehow. Presley's the Bomber Harris of the Betjeman brigade. Door's over here.'

In the car, Chance talked of everything except my impending eviction. Not before the servants, bless him. Rather than shame me in front of, or at any rate behind, Eric, he talked of where we had just been. 'Ideal place to be, this. Thought seriously about living here at one point. Power boats are a bit noisy on Saturdays. But when the Stolport's running you could be in Paris in a couple of hours.'

'Why did you decide against it?'

'Came here for the *old* London.'

'The Barbican isn't the old London, for Christ's sake.'

'Built on top of where it used to be.'

'How can she afford that place?'

'TV companies want stills. Film companies rent stuff from her. She's already in profit. Only wish I could have helped her more. Would have been in for a bigger share. Bread on the water.' Then he talked of where we were going next. It transpired that he owned a piece of that, too. 'Still own a share of the Groucho. Good place. But I needed a place to lie *really* low. Few of us thought up the Zeppo. He was the Marx brother that the other Marx brothers all hated. Only thing that kept them together was how they all hated him. Nice idea. But it sounded a bit slavish. So we called it the Zippo. After the cigarette lighter. Anonymous. Solid.'

'Built-in shelter from the wind.'

'Right.'

'Can't, guv,' said Eric. 'One way.' We were in Soho.

'Drop us here if you like,' said Chance.

'Nar,' said Eric. 'Soon be there. Here. Try this one.'

'What?'

'Robert Duvall and Robert Vaughn.'

'*Bullitt*.'

'How did you know *that*? That's absolutely amazing,' said Eric, hooking the air. 'Hardly anyone knows Robert Duvall's in that.'

'*I* didn't know,' I said, truthfully. 'What did he do in it?'

'He was a cab driver,' said Eric, still shaking his head as he drew to a halt in front of an entrance so discreet you couldn't tell what it was. 'Just incredible. Straight on to it.'

'Stick close behind me,' said Chance as we were shown into the dining room of the club, 'or you'll fall over a chair.' He was right. Care had been taken to eliminate all light not strictly necessary for the purposes of eating and drinking.

'Do you want the braille menu?' he asked when we were seated.

'No. I'm getting used to it.' As my eyes adjusted I noticed that Di and Fergie were the waitresses. Media people murmured to one another across tables in the half-light. Not media personalities. Media people. The people who employed the personalities.

'The Los Angeles equivalent of this place,' said Chance, 'is a windowless Nissen hut in the middle of a three-acre car park full of Mercedes runabouts. This serves the same purpose better.'

'The purpose being?'

'Paranoia control. Everybody here genuinely likes the darkness. Craves anonymity like a drug. Especially me. Got to the stage when I can't bear it if even *I* know what I'm doing.' After ordering two flutes of champagne, he returned to the same theme. 'Comes a point when you can't read about yourself without feeling pieces are being bitten out of you. Rilke said fame was the sum total of all the misunderstandings that could gather around one name. Pity about that rhyme: fame, name. Ruins a good aphorism. Doesn't happen in German, of course. *Rhum, Name.* Good gimmick for a novel. Author gets so sick of his image that he puts it into the book as a character. So the character with his own name is the one least like him. Listen.'

I thought for a moment that he wanted me to test the quality of the whispering silence. Then I realised that he was changing the subject. Broaching the real subject. Over the first drinks and the cold soup it was thoroughly aired. Unilaterally, I need hardly add. Not that I had much to contribute except assent.

Chance had gathered that the Mole was confused. No, she hadn't complained. He had dragged it out of her. But she didn't want to feel responsible for my mental welfare. She cared about me too much for that. (When I suggested that this was tantamount to saying she didn't care enough, Chance told me not to be so touchy.) She wanted to be free. Above all, she didn't want to be disapproved of. (When I said that I didn't disapprove of her, Chance replied that she *felt* I did.) Anyway, the Mole would soon be leaving for Lausanne, there to spend three weeks or so helping out at her old finishing school. Meanwhile, Chance's flat in Biarritz was without a tenant and needed to be sat. Normally he would be down there at this time but preparations for the movie had reached a critical stage. He needed the Barbican to brood in. He would be hard to live with even if Angélique wasn't there. I could be useful by going down to Biarritz and looking after things. A plane ticket would be immediately forthcoming. The whole place was crumbling into the sea but it was an ideal existence down there. Couldn't be more out of the swim. There were no human hazards except his old friend and rival Jean-Louis Cravache, technocrat, surfer, sailor, dancer, mystical philosopher and

131

lover to Angélique. I should watch out for that bastard. Other-wise it was sun, sand and pretty girls to look at. Not meretricious pretty girls as on the Côte d'Azure. These were well brought-up pretty girls of good family and modest means. French equivalent of the Mole. 'Do you good,' said Chance, in what I could tell was his peroration, 'to realise she's not unique. Help you realise how unique she is.'

'I don't get it.'

'You adore that perfect body. Watching a hundred other perfect bodies bouncing up and down might wean you off mere lust and on to a proper appreciation of her salient individual characteristic.'

'Which is?'

'Already told you a million times,' said Chance as he ad-dressed himself to the main course. 'Mole is a *good* girl.'

Chance had ordered breast of duck with ginger and I the medallions of beef. Both of us had been given circular works of art in which the ceramic component predominated. There was hardly any food on either plate. Just fan-shaped arrangements of slivers and segments.

'Savour it,' said Chance. 'You're eating a concept. There's a Japanese cook out there called Yamamoto. The admiral's great-grand-nephew. Studied in Paris. This is what happens when *nouvelle cuisine* meets *sushi*.'

'I'm going to be hungry at the end of this,' I said, lying. Nothing in my head could challenge the case he had made but my stomach felt miserable.

'People have died of malnutrition in here,' mumbled Chance around a tiny mouthful. 'But they died elegantly.'

We talked of other things over the dessert and the coffee. My dessert looked as if a sick sparrow had laid two chocolate eggs from the top of a ladder. A single strawberry had been added. Getting hungrier as I ate these iron rations, I topped up with more of the *petits fours* than the Mole would have approved of, but that didn't matter now, did it? Conversation was a bit restricted. Not wanting to talk about my career, wanting still less to talk about women, I fell back on talking about old times. Whatever hap-pened to so-and-so? I could see the answer in Chance's eyes: the same thing that's happening to you, only with them it happened earlier. He looked impatient. He hated talking about the past. He was like a shark, always moving forward. Having fed, we nosed away between the tables as if they were palely glowing outcrops of a reef in the sea at night. Eva Brownlow looked up.

'Chance, it was *fun*. Bruce wants to do some pictures. Nobody in New York lives like that. I've already talked to him about it.'

'Lovely to see you there,' said Chance, looking at Eva's companion. I looked too. In that light you couldn't be sure, but the visible evidence suggested that she was extraordinarily handsome, rather along the lines of those Argentinian tennis players. Boyish but girlish.

'Imogen,' said Eva, 'can I introduce you to Chance Jenolan? Chance, this is Imogen Cambio-Wechsel Todotiempo.' Eva didn't give me a mention. Either she had run out of breath or she couldn't see me in the dark.

'Hello Moggy,' said Chance. 'You've grown up. Meet my friend Joel Court.'

'Hello,' said Imogen Cambio-Wechsel Todotiempo.

'Hello,' I said, out of it; although not as put out as Eva, who had played an ace and seen it go for nothing.

'I didn't know you two knew each other,' said Eva, with pique ill-concealed even by the dark. She was probably more diplomatic behind her desk.

'When I was her mother's house-guest in the Veneto,' said Chance, 'Moggy used to make me push her around in a miniature Ferrari. Had a little engine in it but she pretended it was broken. Natural actress.' Suddenly he didn't mind talking about old times. For a while I feared that we might linger. I didn't want to be faced with any more evidence that his life contained so many personable women he had become immune to their disturbing magic. Luckily he had somewhere to go.

Eric was driving Chance to Shepperton, or perhaps Bad Gastein. So I walked home. To quell panic I did this in easy stages, starting with a detour via the National Gallery. I hadn't been there for a long time. It was full of things I didn't want to see. There was an astronomical instrument in Holbein's 'Ambassadors'. I didn't want to see that. Tintoretto's girlfriend was squirting the milky way out of her tit. I definitely didn't want to see that. Less predictably, I didn't want to see the dimpled yet firm, polite yet provocative arse of the Rokeby Venus. Velázquez, notoriously a prude, had somehow managed to forecast, along with her primping self-regard, the exact physical proportions of our polysexual little strumpet, right down to the twin dimples at the base of her spine. It took a Vermeer virginals player to cool my anger. There was no slighting *her*. She looked out of the canvas with the resignation of a good Delft bourgeois housewife prepared in advance for the challenge of sitting to a painter whose work rate was one portrait per decade. She had nothing but time.

The afternoon was hot enough for me to take my jacket off and carry it slung over my shoulder as I walked home along the Strand, down Fleet Street and up Ludgate Hill: the royal route to marriage. In Fleet Street I saw a man whom I took to be a journalist on his way back from lunch to the office, although he could have been a man with locomotor ataxia whose walking frame had been snatched from his trembling hands. He was wondering how to get from the footpath to the street. The vertical difference was three inches but he looked at it as if he were standing on the rim of a chimney. If he didn't make the leap soon, his office would be gone: Fleet Street was in the process of dispersing itself all over the city, a Gondwanaland transformed into wandering tectonic plates. I wondered how I could help him. I wondered how he could help me. At least I'm sober, I thought, almost stepping under a car. In front of St Paul's, a coach-load of Japanese were already in position for the next royal wedding, more than a year away at a conservative estimate. A Japanese emporium had opened up in St Paul's Yard. There was a Japanese bookshop. It was a little stretch of the Ginza away from home.

Home. Murphy's word. Play it again, Sam. What a sense of humour. Packing should have taken ten minutes but I dragged it out to twenty. On CNN they were dying in Beirut. It looked easier than living in Beirut. The high-rise apartment blocks had acquired extra, ragged windows in odd places, so that the camera could zoom in and see people just sitting there in space. You could see somebody's feet through one hole and then through another hole you could see the head and shoulders of the person he was talking to. It was all elliptical, like a work of fiction, except that the chosen details were irrelevant to any theme save randomness. There's always someone worse off than you are. Does that make you feel better? Nothing could make me feel better, except that lovely key crunching in the lock, followed by the triumphant trill of the home-come Mole. 'Hello! I'll put this stuff away and have a widdle and then we can go for a walk. Isn't it a lovely day?'

But it didn't happen. She never arrived. The hot afternoon became the muggy evening. Vaguely I remembered that Angélique would be somewhere else. But there had been no mention of our little darling's possible absence. All alone in the place from which I was getting thrown out owing to lack of *Lebensraum*, I built miniature Beirut apartment blocks out of ice-cubes, filled their interstices with fluid, and stared out over them at the towers of the Barbican. Down there on the walkways, people were arriving for their date with Gwen John, who had loved Rodin too well. They were hours early for their tryst with Hamlet. In the Arts Centre they circulated from level to level, gathering in front of the jazz quartet, dispersing during the bass solo, breathing subsidised air braced with art ions. Culture had become universal. At the poolside tables of the cafeteria, Young People threw their plastic cups to join the lilies. Coke cans bobbed until they filled, then tilted upright and floated with only their top rims gleaming above the water: contact mines for ducks. I put down the field glasses long before dusk. It was never dusk. Daylight dragged on. There was a Lean Cuisine in the freezing compartment. Chicken *à l'orange*, my favourite. The scissors must have been blunt. I had to hack at the plastic bag and got sauce all over the blades. Several hundred compact discs and twice as many tapes held nothing I wanted to hear. The best thing on television was a documentary about North Vietnamese boat people in New Orleans who were being persecuted by the Ku-Klux-Klan. Terrific. When Chance rang, it was like the door opening on an isolation cell.

'There'll be a ticket waiting for you on the Air France desk,' he said among other things. 'Don't forget your passport.'

'I won't,' I said. 'Where is she?'

'Angélique? French Embassy ball.'

'No. The other one. You know the one I mean.'

135

'Staying at home for a few days before she goes to Switzerland.'

'Can I call her there to say goodbye?'

'No, don't do that. Too confusing. Give her a buzz at Olympia tomorrow.'

'What's she doing *there*?'

'Earning three days' pin money at the Personal Computer exhibition. Call her on the Ultrasopht stand.' He spelled it out.

'Ultrasopht. Sounds like ice-cream.'

'Here's the number.'

Feeling better after that, or less desperate, I read all her letters from Chance over again. I had a real binge with them. There was some of her underwear I gave what for as well. And I found that machine. It wasn't in her room. It was in among Angélique's kit-bag of high-class toiletries. It was lurking in there like a blind torch. The Mole must have borrowed it for the night. I felt relieved. Not an habitual user. Just occasionally, for kicks. I twisted the base of the object and a kick is what it gave me. It was like a mild electric shock. A high-frequency buzz that I could feel in my teeth. You little bastard, I said to that machine. Leave my girl alone or I'll get the boys on to you. Then I dropped the thing, still buzzing, into Angélique's all-absorbing reticule and went back downstairs to pour myself the last drink of the night. It was a Mies van der Rohe masterpiece. Less is more, but not as much as more is. There was scarcely any hope of drinking it. I moved into it, slipping in water-slides of liquor down its icy inclined planes. I could just tell that I was the only man of my age in the whole of English history listening alone to Sade singing 'Smooth Operator'. So I stopped her. Pushed down the silver tab and choked her off. Channel 4 had torture in Uruguay. Tupamaros talked about their season in Hell. Feeling bad about feeling miserable, I put on a video of *The Band Wagon*, zipped through it until I found 'The Girl Hunt', and watched it over and over until I nodded off with the remote control still in my hand. The sluggish suggestion of a breeze through the open sliding glass door woke me long enough for a zig-zag wall-banging stumble upstairs and an approximate dive on to her bed, where I soaked the pillow with sweat and tears.

Next morning I felt so lousy that I laughed. My hangover was like a low ceiling that I had to hobble around under in a crouch. If I straightened up I hit it. When I called Cambridge to say goodbye, my own voice told me to leave a message after the beep. So I said goodbye to myself. Eric buzzed me on the entryphone when it was time to take me to the airport. He had all the details worked out but after co-operating in a long discussion about Steve McQueen I was able to persuade him that it would not hurt our schedule if we stopped off for a few minutes at Olympia. All along the footpaths from Knightsbridge to Kensington the pretty girls were out like flowers. Agreeing by means of grunts that in *Le Mans* Steve McQueen had achieved the miracle of conveying the full range of his facial expression through the eyes alone, I observed the up-market young ladies proliferating around Harrods. The Albert Memorial was the centrepiece for an international exposition of clear-skin sweethearts. Perhaps Chance was right; although the perfect bodies had to be guessed at, even through the floating summer dresses. But there were plenty of perfect faces, impeccable pairs of upper arms, unimpeachable twin-sets of delicately articulated ankles. In the sweltering, unairconditioned heat of Olympia there was more of the same. Just as naturally as the old Motor Shows at Earls Court had featured tarts tottering on high heels with swimming costumes they had to keep rescuing with a crooked finger from the crack at the back, the new high-tech exhibitions featured the kind of girl you hoped your son would meet and marry. There were Dis and Fergies all over the place, busy being marvellous. There was a Caroline looking alert on every stand, an Emma handing out pamphlets in every aisle. A few Amandas and Lucindas were actually working the machines. Visual displays altered brightly as long fingers with well-kept nails pressed sculpted keys. The figures of authority, however, were mostly male. Millionaires to a man, they weren't much older than the females, but they had the look of being in control, whereas the girls were just being marvellous. From far off, down a long aisle, I saw the Mole being marvellous on the Ultrasopht stand. She had her long light-blue cotton dress on, the one I liked best. She was greeting people, handing them pamphlets and guiding them about. As I walked towards her, some of the men on the stands waved to me. They were science-minded and had seen me on television. Evidence of my existence accumulated thinly in the form of nods. It was nothing beside the evidence that the Mole existed. She burned. She beamed. She even had a smile for me, instead of the shocked grimace I had expected.

'Hello! What are *you* doing here?'

'Chance has sent me into exile. But I thought I might say goodbye on the way.'

'We can go and have a drink. My break's just coming up. I get the first break. Don't I, Jeffrey? Can I have my break now? This is Joel.'

'Of course you can, my own lovely,' said a young man with an oiled quiff, Buddy Holly black-rimmed glasses, a Black Watch tartan zoot suit and monogrammed casuals. 'Glad to meet you, Joel. Jeffrey Chaucer's the name. Welcome to Ultrasopht Eposanal. Electronic point-of-sale analysis. They buy, we scan, you profit. That's our programme. And let me say that I love *your* programmes, Joel. You're a communicator. And at the end of the day, that's the business we're all in. Am I right?'

'Well, I'm not sure it's a b . . . '

'Look after this nut-case here. She does wonders for our image. Because at the end of the day, Joel, the customer isn't just buying the technology, he wants to know that the dealer is user-friendly too.'

'I'll look after her,' I started saying several times during the momentary pauses in his flow. But as usually happened, she looked after me. Firmly she took me to one of the biggest stands – Olivetti, as I remember it – which had a coffee bar on its roof. From up there you could look down on the whole acreage of state-of-the-art electronic commerce, human beings forming interacting groups to interact with machines which interacted at a distance. It was Interface City. Nothing could have been further from the Mole's temperament, more alien to her attainments: a fact which she realised the necessity of explaining.

'I know *nothing* about all this, so they've got me just folding bits of paper and handing them out. Jeffrey is a *total* jerk but his father knows Daddy. Look what Mummy's done to this dress. I'm so *cross*.'

'What's she done to it? I love that dress. It looks perfect.'

'She *shrunk* it.'

'She can't have. It practically scrapes the ground.'

'It does not. The waist used to be right down here. God knows
how she managed it. This isn't denim, you know. It's cotton. So
how could it shrink? It's not as if she's got much to do all day
except wash my clothes and bugger up the Porsche. But she's
turned all my bras pink and now she's shrunk *this*. How did she
do it?'

'Did you know he was giving me the push?'

'I'm going, too. It's better, anyway. I can't stand Angélique
and she takes up all the room. Thank God she's never here for
long.'

'You can't stand her but you rub cream into her.'

'Vanishing cream. It's the only way to shut her up. If she
opens her mouth I stick some goo in it. He doesn't get much
out of either of us, you know. He's sort of lost the knack.'

'Who hasn't?' This was news I would have to consider later,
always granted that I believed it. 'Can I phone you in Switzerland?'

'It wouldn't be a good idea. Madame would throw a moody.
You can write to me, though. Will you do that?'

'You won't think I'm being a pest again?'

'I've never thought that. Not for a minute. You're one of the
nicest men I've ever met. But you were making me a kind of
symbol or something. And I'm just me. Barely that, really. And
anyway I couldn't respond. Because of, you know.'

'Penelope.'

'You don't hate me for being gay, do you? I only am a little
bit.'

'I'd still think the world of you even if you were that a lot.
Anyway, I don't disapprove if it's women. I'm a bit turned off
at the idea of men. Also it seems to have got a bit fatal for them
lately. But I can't say that I disapprove even there. Especially
not here.'

'What's special about here?'

'Computers all come from an idea by Alan Turing. He was a
mathematician at Cambridge who worked out a way of decod-
ing German radio traffic. This was World War II, about three
wars before you were born . . . '

'I know about that. Don't tease.'

'Hitler almost won it. Without what Turing did, England would have had to surrender. The U-boats would have starved her out. Turing didn't win the war all on his own, but it would have been lost without him. And he was a queer. A queer boffin. Not even attractive to other homosexuals. Just an awkward poofter with a high-pitched voice. He had an awful time. It was illegal in those days and he got caught at it. They made him take medicine to straighten out his hormones and he ended up growing breasts. Not pretty ones like yours. So he killed himself.'

'The poor man. How did he do it?'

'He ate a poisoned apple. The man who saved the world. Every time I walk through King's I think of him. It's one of the reasons I love Cambridge. His memory. Some people feel that way about Wittgenstein. They go to Trinity college chapel and commune with his brass plate. PHILOSOPHANDI NOVAM VIAM MULTIS MONSTRAVIT RATIONEM EX VINCULIS ORATIONIS VINDI-CANDUM ESSE. *He showed how reason must be unchained from language.* I feel that way about Turing. He could see how everything came down to numbers. But that didn't make nature less marvellous. It made it more so. When I'm feeling down, I go for a walk through King's. Or I did. It's a while since I have.'

'Are you very down now?'

'It's not a good time in my life, Mole. But knowing you has made it better.'

'You'll like it on the beach. There are simply masses of pretty girls.'

'Yes, but *you're* my popsy.'

'How can I be your popsy? Daddy's my popsy, silly.' Sometimes she was straight out of *Jackanory*.

'Never mind. Just another word that's gone out of date. They all do, in time.'

'What did all that Latin mean?'

'What I said. He liberated reasoning from the chains of . . . '

'How is this nut-case looking after you, Joel?' asked Jeffrey Chaucer from behind my shoulder, on which his hand had descended with a squeeze of reassurance. He sat down with us, although by rights, caught full in the chest by the glare I beamed at him, he should have been thrown backwards over the balustrade with his legs in the air. 'I'm just passing through, Joel, I'm afraid,' he went on, the hand still in place, 'otherwise I would have liked nothing better than to join you for a good one-on-one thrash-through of what we're doing in your field. But there's no let-up down there. It's fantastic. And we have to stay on it. No, I don't mean you, Antonia. Come back down in your own good time. Pace yourself. Because at the end of the day, it's the whole week's work that matters. And that can take a while to assess, Joel. At the end of the day, you might not know for a year.'

'There's something in what you say.'

'Look after this madwoman now. Mind how you go, Joel. Love your programme. Glad to have met you. Look after yourself. God bless.'

'Goodbye.'

'Goodbye, he says. I like that. A man of few words. The one word that sums everything up. Precise. Love it. Antonia, look after this nut-case. He's a precious commodity.'

'I'll see you later, Jeffrey.'

For a while it seemed as if she would be seeing him later without his having gone away in the intervening period, but finally – at the end of the day, as he would have put it – he withdrew, littering the air with further blessings, farewells and injunctions to have a nice one. Frittering away the short sweet time with my popsy. We sat for a while in the wreckage of our conversation. We parted at the foot of the blue-carpeted plywood stairs.

'Look after yourself,' I said, putting my hand on her shoulder.

'Mind how you go,' she said. 'And don't forget to use a lot of blocker the first day. Even if the sun isn't out. Really cake it on. Do you promise?'

'Don't worry. Bronzed Aussies never burn. I hope you're getting some loot out of Jeffrey. At the end of the day.'

'I know he's a bit naff but he's very clever. It's a bit depressing really. They all *understand* it. I mean, I can stand *you* understanding it, but they're all *my* age. I'm just going to get a not very good degree in English and what will I do? What am I *for*? I'll be washed up. I wish I was technical like you.'

'You can be technical like me and still be washed up, believe me.'

'Now you're depressing me worse.'

'I have to get going. Is it all right to miss you?'

'Yes. I want to be missed.'

So I walked away from her along the blue carpet of the aisle, applauded by VDUs full of information I didn't want. It should have felt like progress towards rehabilitation. I had made a fool of myself with her, yet without losing her friendship. By my standards, that was a breakthrough. It still felt like a breakdown. Eric looked put out, but he made up enough time on the M4 to feel cheerful again before we reached Terminal 2, where he handed me my final defeat.

'Robert Redford and Katherine Ross,' he said, hefting my hold-all from the boot of the car.

'Here,' I said, 'let me lend you a . . . It can't be *Butch Cassidy and the Sundance Kid*. Steve McQueen isn't in that. Deal me another.'

'And Barry Sullivan.'

'I give up.'

'*Tell Them Willy Boy is Here*.'

'Steve McQueen isn't in that!' I protested loudly.

'*Course* not!' laughed Eric, the happiest of men. 'I got the governor with that one as well.'

'You've widened your range, Eric.'

'Yeah. You've got to know how to mix the serves. Got to be a bit of a John McEnroe. Take care of yourself, now. Mind how you go.'

The ticket to Biarritz was business-class, with an open return. They were sending me out in style. The Caravelle was only two hours late getting away, because Düsseldorf airport fielded the general alarm in time to pick up Mr Nagoya at the immigration desk. Mr Nagoya, a Toshiba executive, had checked his baggage on to our flight, walked unchallenged through the wrong gate, and left us with one passenger too few, so that all our luggage had to be unloaded on to the concrete and checked for bombs while he headed for Germany, where he arrived under the impression that it was France. Many of our passengers cursed the chief cabin steward for having so officiously counted heads, but I did not. I didn't really want to leave anyway.

PART FOUR

Jailbait Teriyaki

But he knew the happiness of watching. Nature had told him of it. No eye could be clearer or brighter than the eye that had nothing to create, nothing to do but gaze. The invisible horizon beyond which the conscious eye could not penetrate was far more remote than the visible horizon. And all manner of entities appeared in regions visible and accessible to consciousness. Sea, ships, clouds, peninsulas, lightning, the sun, the moon, the myriads of stars. If seeing is a meeting between eye and being, which is to say between being and being, then it must be the facing mirrors of two beings. No, it was more. Seeing went beyond being, to take wings like a bird.

Yukio Mishima, *The Decay of the Angel*

ARRIVING AT BIARRITZ IN THE LATE AFTERNOON, I found it impossible not to feel better. In that context, the sunlight struck me as relevant. All the arrangements went smoothly. As instructed, I asked the taxi driver to take me to Le Sable d'Or, and he took me there instead of to the local Saab dealer, a mistake which my accent might normally have been expected to bring about. Le Sable d'Or was a charming restaurant perched on the cliff top above the Côte des Basques. Chance had said it was a good place to eat and that I should treat it as my dining room. The proprietress was a lady of advanced years who had been born and brought up in San Sebastian and had the lustrous eyes to prove it. After an adult lifetime spent in Biarritz, her spoken Spanish had lost all of its endings except those that helped to make her French unintelligible, so she sounded a bit like me. We got on famously from the start. When I asked her for the key to Chance's flat she smiled nicely. When I mimed the same request she caught on. I was introduced to one of the waitresses who was also her stepdaughter and doubled, or tripled, as Chance's char. Madame detailed the stepdaughter to show me the way. The block of flats was only fifty yards away along the same cliff top. The stepdaughter, whose name was either Marie or Maria, showed me how to work the lift and didn't complain when I put my bag down on her foot. She tried to unpack it when we got inside the flat but I shoved her out, closed the door behind me, and went over to the balcony, where I dared the view to impress me. It was a wow.

Five floors up in a building whose base was already a long way up from the beach, I looked straight out on nothing except sea and sky. The sky was more white than blue and the sea more blue than green. If not for the colour, you would have said that the Atlantic was doing an imitation of the Pacific. It should have been a more serious green, but otherwise I could have been looking at three lines of breakers rolling in at Cronulla. Out beyond the third line, surfers on potato-chip boards waited in clusters for a wave worth the effort of paddling back again afterwards to where they already were. Further out, windsurfers wrestled their sails to find a breath of moving air. Skeletal catamarans, with sails lit through like pastel spectra, slowly manoeuvred in the calm or caught a wave and came scudding suddenly in. It was peace with a ragged edge. Under the still air the sea was mobile. Bodysurfers with flippers took a long lazy ride but got off early so they could go back for another trip. Greedily I weighed the odds against getting down amongst it before the light went. The sun was falling towards the horizon even as I watched. No, better wait until tomorrow. My exile would last long enough, in this unsung outpost of Chance's empire.

Compared with the Barbican fortress, Chance's Biarritz redoubt ranked only as an airborne foxhole, but it had been well tended in his absence. Though there was nothing in the refrigerator except ice-cubes, there were some interesting bottles in the drinks cabinet. With my fist around a slowly cooling glass I explored the place. There were only three main rooms but they had everything. A wall of cassettes duplicated, or more correctly predated, much of the music library in the Barbican. He seemed to buy these things prodigally, although not indiscriminately. Always the best performances: the Honegger Second and Third Symphonies, for example, conducted by Karajan. Think what you like of *Das Wunder*, the ghost was with him when he recorded those. *Screen International* was present in flat stacks, up to the latest issue. Marie-Maria must have had, among her duties, the task of stripping the wrappers from rolled-up subscription copies of magazines and putting them on the right pile against the master's return. Probably he got the subscriptions as gifts, like his wines. There were a lot of books: a whole working library, dating from the days when Chance had come here for months on end to write books himself. One entire wall was given over to paperbacks of everything Simenon had written. Simenon's volumes of *mémoires intimes* were also there, along with a collection of magazines and newspaper literary sections containing interviews with the author. The special Simenon edition of *Lire* had an interview with Chance in it, recording his debt to the master. Chance might have been an intellectual gadfly but he usually worked a patch pretty thoroughly before gadding on. Only slightly less impressively, another, smaller wall case displayed everything Chance himself had written. I resolved to read it all again. There were notebooks, typewritten manuscripts, files of xeroxed letters. Rich pickings for the archaeologist – the right word, because it was clear, despite the neatness conferred by Marie-Maria, that Chance had left all this behind, dead and buried. He had shipped out. As if to rub this in, the phone rang.

'You comfortable?'

'Couldn't be more so. Where are you?'

'New York. Listen, if you want to stock up on milk and stuff you've got an hour before the supermarket closes. Turn left into the rue Gambetta and it's about a hundred yards down the hill towards the town centre. Got any money?'

'I changed some at the airport.'

'Don't be surprised if you dream a lot. The weather's changeable. Gets into your head and stirs your brains around with a spoon.'

'I do anyway.'

'Yeah? Got to go. It's all yours.'

If it was, there was no reason to take it in all at once. Leaving the town centre for another day, I went only as far as the supermarket, where my Safeway skills came in handy. After transferring some of the contents of the supermarket to my refrigerator I showered, changed and went to dinner at Le Sable d'Or, just as the sun prepared for its farewell performance. Sending its light rays the long way through the earth's atmosphere, it turned the colour of simmering plum juice. The sea turned to beaten silver, shivering like a gong struck with a soft mallet. The bands of light cloud above the horizon flooded with pink as the disc took its dive. There was no holding it. Behind the stone balustrade on the cliff's edge, the fringe of tamarisk turned a deeper green, a darker gold. Then it was a silhouette. Madame asked me if I did not think the effect was formidable. Clearly I was to be her favourite. Though the restaurant was jammed with people of all European nationalities, she would attend to me personally. Forewarned, I ordered my meal with care, pronouncing the words as clearly as possible, resorting to mime when it came to specifying the fish. From empty air I conjured a fillet of plaice which Marcel Marceau could not have made more flat. Madame brought me veal instead. Well, veal was flat too, and nobody made a mistake about the wine, which thickened my tongue like a dentist's injection. Having asked for mixed ice-cream, it was no surprise to receive a basket of fruit. Some of this I ate and the rest I took with me, back up to the fifth floor for an early night. The Comédie-Française production of *Cyrano de Bergerac* was on television. There was no twenty-four hour channel of the international horror show we call the news, so until *Soir 3* came on I had to content myself with Cyrano lending his magnificent eloquence to a fool, while Roxanne, the biggest fool of all, failed to realise that the man who talked so well in the dark was the same man who had talked so well in the daylight. Later on, it was hot enough for me to lie in bed with the window open and nothing over my bare body except a sheet. I didn't dream, but that could have been because I didn't sleep. Knowing that the Mole must have lain on the same bed many times with her legs wide apart didn't help. Out on the balcony with a drink in my hand, I did not look up, although in the light thrown up from the town the sky would not have been all that brilliant. A long way to the left, where the coastline curved outwards, the lights of Spain shone steadily. Out to sea were the red riding lights of fishing boats, where they put their nets over the side to catch veal. They put the veal in a veal-creel. Clunk clink. Another drink. Clink clunk. Another drunk.

My first day on the beach was more than I deserved. Making a gradual start, by late morning I was on my way down the cliffside *trottoir* that descended through the clumps of tamarisks by a switchback series of easy asphalt ramps, well sign-posted by mounds of fresh dogshit. Where the ramps switched direction, there were way-stations with benches. Old ladies sat with their leashed poodles. The dogs had their tongues out, gathering strength to shit again on the next stage. It was as if the *Tour de France des Chiens Merdeux* had reached a climbing section. The dog that crapped most often wore the yellow jersey. In my Hong Kong thongs I flip-flopped carefully downward. Flip-flopping through the plop. The thongs I had brought with me from England, along with my swimming costume, shorts and T-shirt. My straw hat and rattan mat had come from Chance's copious supply of beach gear, and from his book-shelves had come my volume of Julien Green's journal, *Les Années faciles*. Thinking seriously of working my diary up into something more grand, I was looking for tips.

There was a road along the sea wall with a parapet on the seaward side. The grand staircase down to the actual beach was a couple of hundred yards along to the left. It would have been an easy walk along the footpath if not for the females sunbathing on the parapet. I would like to be able to say that my imagination, warped by the glossy pornography of the everyday soft-core hard sell, received so much unadorned naturalness as a salutary shock. Indeed, the topless old ladies were not a pretty sight. But the topless young ladies were. As I flapped and flopped past them only a few inches away like a shot-up vulture making a crash landing, they ignored me in the nicest possible manner by sitting up to oil their breasts or by simply lying there with their pubic mounds, cupped by the flimsiest of bikini bottoms, swelling softly skyward like little radar blisters. Resisting the impulse to choose a pair of slightly separated young thighs and plunge my head between them, I just made it to the stairs without tripping over my tongue. An erection would have converted me into a tripod. Luckily there was no sign of such a thing. In that area I was numb as if cauterised, blasted and stunned as if struck by lightning. Too large a stimulus had obliterated desire. It was like feeding a whole power station into a curling iron.

The tide was in. From overheard conversations I deduced that there would be no beach for another hour. Its potential population was draped around the battered cement staircase, which led half-way down to the beach in one broad flight and then, before bifurcating left and right for the final descent, formed a landing, itself equipped with a parapet on which yet another row of oiled girls offered themselves to the sky. They glistened as if they had been cooked in a light sauce. Rows of under-age girls were connected by their succulent colour. Jail-bait teriyaki. I sat on the stairs and cursed myself for not having worn a pair of Chance's mirror-finish sun-glasses. Tomorrow I would, so that I could gaze my fill. I had to get enough of this.

Not enough was too much. As it was, there was nothing to do except take off my T-shirt and wait for the water to recede. Already it was only lapping at the rocks which it had previously swamped. Some sopping patches of sand intermittently appeared. A few oldsters waded away to bag a good spot by perching on a rock above it, where they would wait for the sand to dry before spreading out their gear. Eventually I did the same. I was one of the oldsters. But at heart I was still a bronzed Aussie. Scorning all protection from creams or filters, I stretched out in the deliberate quest for a mild burn. That was the way we had always done it in my childhood: burn today, brown tomorrow, don't mind if you peel. Hence the tough tone of my skin, out of practice but still well able to cope with anything that hazy sun could send down. You could tell it wasn't very intense, by the soft colours of sand and water: raw calico and faded blue denim. It was hot, but not unpleasantly so, and whenever I felt a tingle I could always submerge myself in the flat surf, walking further to it each time.

The first time, there was a girl walking towards me, leaving the sea with her translucent Dayglo pink flippers held in one hand like two shopping bags from a chic boutique, her one-piece Lycra apple-green costume simply bursting with meaningful content. The second time I was a few yards behind two topless girls above whose firm bottoms a line was drawn which could be identified as the horizontal component of a G-string only by the central knot, because the vertical component had been sucked in so decisively that it would have taken forceps to retrieve it, although I would have been willing to try with my teeth if given the opportunity. Perhaps I was already feeling better: not better in terms that any feminist study group would applaud, but better in the sense of more alive. Striving to maintain detachment, however, I was careful not to draw level with them and they waded out through the frilled swell. I didn't want to face the full, flagrant challenge of their swelling breasts, the outer curves of which could already be seen from behind when they threw up their arms to punch an avenue through the froth. At last there was a breaker that they had to dive under or else be bowled over by, and here I drew the dubious reward for my forbearance, because suddenly they had both porpoised forward and their brown bottoms flashed against the wall of white water like the Greek letter omega carved twice in marble. Two ziggurat sets of ten toes materialised for a moment and then plunged out of sight, a lost Atlantis. The same wave knocked me rolling. I let it happen. The next one I tried to catch, missed, and followed in on my feet, attacked from behind by its sycophantic friends, a walking patsy. Then I lay down, propped on one elbow, and ate a peach out of my flimsy, filmy plastic carrier-bag from the supermarket. The beach was expanding. Young men drew tennis courts with their feet. Not interested in young men, I fell asleep, to be awakened some time later by an English voice.

'You'll be sore tonight, at that rate,' it said. It was Ann Todd in *The Sound Barrier* or Virginia McKenna in *The Cruel Sea*: an English rose in a bucket of ice, wired for sound. Looking up into the hot light, I focused on a shape at odds with the emitted noise. Tall, taut and tanned, she was in her well-preserved early forties. The bare breasts held themselves up unassisted. The G-string unashamedly spilled ash-blonde hair that looked strong enough to sew on a button with.

'Nice of you to be concer . . . ' I started saying.

'Chance told us you might be showing up. I saw you on telly last time I was over. My name's Gloria Cravache. Jean-Louis and I have a house back that way.' She gestured inland. 'We'll get you to dinner, yes?'

At the water's edge, the man I recognised from Chance's pinboard was taking a catamaran apart. He and Gloria must have just arrived on it. White of hair, flat of stomach and trim of limb, he turned and waved to her, then pointed at the waves, picked up a surfboard and ran out towards them, stepping extraordinarily high. 'That would be ni . . . ' I started saying.

'Bloody Hell, he'll be there for another hour,' said Gloria, but showed no inclination to spend the time with me. She moved away towards the staircase, saying, her head only half-turned, 'We've got the number. Call you soon. Put a shirt on or you won't be able to come.'

Still feeling more hot than burned, rather enjoying how my sweat ran, I scorned her advice. I could see why Jean-Louis found Angélique such a nice change. After being interrupted

151

all the time by your wife, it must be a relief to be interrupted all the time by your mistress. Sitting up, I watched him out there in the waves, which, even though the tide was still going out, were beginning to run high. He must have sensed they would. Perhaps they always did, as a tribute to him. He was like Poseidon, except that he didn't just stand on the water, he danced. Rarely did he merely face forward on the board. His long legs were bent sideways so that his behind was between his ankles. He swivelled the board from left to right like a flopping fishtail, finished a ride by turning all the way around and flying off the wave going back the other way. Young surfers on their way to the water stopped to study him, compare notes, shake their heads. I watched fascinated for as long as fascination felt fascinating, then peevishly diverted my gaze to the pages of my book. ' . . . *voici la vérité sur ce livre: je suis tous les personnages* . . . ' Oh Christ, I thought, not you too. How about writing a book in which you *aren't* all the characters? But he had said this on 5 October, 1928, when writers were still professing to make things up, and the claim not to have done so must have seemed daringly frank. You had to admire the poor old faggot, getting something out of every day. Resolving to start work soon on the reworking of my diary, I closed the book and looked up just in time to see Jean-Louis catch a wave and stand on his hands. High up on the sea wall behind me, spontaneous applause broke out from the frieze of well-oiled nubile lovelies. Ten years younger than Jean-Louis and feeling twenty years older, I packed up my gear and headed for the stairs, the sand sucking me down as the water buoyed him up. It isn't always a question of your attitude towards the world. Quite often what counts is the world's attitude towards you. But at least I didn't *care* how I looked. I left all that to the bleached-haired young male surfers with long faded trunks and peeled-down hip-length wet-suits, raw blisters on their chests from their crustily waxed twin-fin boards. Even the middle-aged ones looked no less fit than Henri Leconte or Yannick Noah. Feeling less ridiculous than negligible, I retraced my hazardous route past the outstretched houris. They couldn't see me, but I could see them. A girl with Julie Christie's nose was oiling the back of a girl with Jane Fonda's behind. Bits and pieces of grown women were gravitating into the next generation. The girl with the oil gave the other girl's back a final stroke and then wiped her hands on her own breasts. I looked away just in time.

At dinner I mimed for the fish by pouting with my mouth and wagging my hands like fins. Already it had become evident that my burns would allow me little sleep that night. Before the meal was over I found it difficult even to stay seated. Leaning forward and tensing my legs so as to keep my back and thighs clear of the chair, I spooned ice-cream into my mouth as if its coldness would quench the fire in my skin. Madame and her family, including distant relatives, gathered around me to discuss my redness and offer remedies. Coated with various white creams, I spent the night foraging in Chance's archives. As long as I didn't turn the pages too violently I felt no more pain than I would have done if whipped with a sting ray's tail. Poised so as to present the minimum skin area to chair, couch, bed or carpet, I read the abandoned manuscript of *Bad News Travels Fast*. Chance wrote an italic hand which was legible even when he scribbled with a thick black Pentel. His working methods were easy to follow. He drafted on the right-hand pages of the folio notebook and corrected on the left-hand pages.

Bad News Travels Fast started out as a mystery story set in the world of sports car racing. It would have been an obvious pot-boiler if not for the fact that it was so obviously an obvious pot-boiler. In other words, it was a spoof: horsepower instead of horses, a Dick Francis on wheels. But it was not content to be a spoof. The book began to discuss its own genre. When he should have been investigating the death of a racing driver – had the car been sabotaged? – the hero ruminated on the difference between a straight Simenon novel and a Maigret. The private eye became a literary critic. He was immobilised by critical reflection. Thinking too precisely upon the event, he could not get back into the real world, the realm of action which alone gave him his *raison d'être*. The way Chance kept the mystery plot going while simultaneously developing the protagonist's inner conflict was a tribute to his craft. Though the whole concoction thoroughly exemplified the kind of poly-thematic, multimodal Chinese-boxes novel that drove me nuts,

Chance was incapable of writing a dull sentence, even as parody. He could imitate the cracked tone of books with titles like *The Horsepiss Discrepancy* and still generate a narrative drive, a vivacity of response to the observed world, that the lampooned author would have been glad to possess – unless, as seems likely, limitations are crucial to success in that type of writing. Guying cheapness and considering its possible merits at the same time, Chance was, or had been, engaged in a dialectical *tour de force*. But in the fifth chapter, which brought the manuscript to a premature end, the highwire act went haywire. The fifth chapter was called 'Headlights in the Forest'. At two o'clock in the morning of the second day of the Le Mans 24-Hour Race, the hero was at Le Ferme, standing behind the metal barrier at the edge of the Mulsanne Straight, just before the big cars, travelling at 230 mph plus, take the full-bore right turn known, apparently, as the Kink. But let him tell it.

If Claxton had not been alone he would have done his best not to flinch. But in the dark and unobserved he allowed his body to do at least something of what it would have liked to do. The speed had impact. It would have had that even without the noise. Far enough away, each pair of headlights began as a point source. When they separated, they were obviously a bit closer. Far sooner than you would have believed possible, or experience could get you used to, they were a lot closer, their radiance cut up by the trees into thin slices, slats from a mother-of-pearl fan. If you moved your head quickly, panning it like a camera, you could identify the car as it transformed itself from an arriving object into a departing one, the nacreous display of headlights, now decorated in its dark centre with an array of rubies, curving away to the right so that the dark trees cut across it vertically. Going that fast a few feet from your face, the car was already an injury. But the noise added insult. Claxton checked his ears in the hope that his earplugs had fallen out. They were still there. Three Porsches, two from the factory and the Joest No. 1 car, went past one behind the other on the racing line, a rocket train in a light storm.

After a while, Claxton's neck hurt. He settled for just looking up the straight past the café and watching the indiscriminate glare of the distant headlights separate into pairs of spectacles that came shrieking forward pushed by ghost faces and went out of focus past his unmoving head, a Doppler swoop in his ears and an opalescent diffusion in his peripheral vision. So he was actually watching Bannerjee's Porsche – although he didn't yet know that it was Bannerjee's Porsche – when the pair of spectacles turned into a monocle, then a ruby brooch, and then back into a pair of spectacles which were too near the barrier. The crunch could not be heard in the general uproar, but Claxton felt it in his stomach. The headlights of another car, which was already manoeuvring to get past an accident that was still happening, illuminated the wreck as it crossed the track, covering a lot of ground forwards as it did so, and clouted the opposite barrier. After that, the smash provided its own light. Spilling fire, the main component of the mess crossed the track again. Claxton saw the lime-green lightning flashes on the white undertray panels and knew it was Bannerjee. A big piece of body panelling went up in the air, caught by the glare of the flames and the headlights of the cars coming up behind. It hadn't landed before Claxton was over the barrier and running in the narrow grassed gap beside the track. The No. 1 Joest Porsche lit him up as it came by at less than 200 mph but already accelerating back up to racing speed. Claxton blinked and ran on. A marshal who was running too made a gesture towards stopping him, but . . .

But Chance lost interest. Beyond that point he couldn't make it matter. The hero tried to care about the victim and couldn't. What was worse, the author couldn't care either. He had tried. Paragraphs had been written, crossed out, rewritten and crossed out again. Then the pages went blank. I wondered what had happened. Even when he wasn't with you, when you were merely dealing with something he had touched, it was so unusual to see him at a loss.

My month alone in Biarritz fell into a rhythm after that

sleepless night. The weather changed next day. With my skin lit up like a red bulb, a clear day was the last thing I wanted, so it was good to see the sky filled in with cloud. Rain fell out of it emphatically. I established a routine which I kept to on overcast days from then on. The Bar du Haou had an unusually sayable name for a Basque establishment. Biarritz, I soon found, is full of names that not even the locals can pronounce, unless they have Basque blood. Challenged by the signboards of the Boulangerie Axolotl and the Blanchisserie Exocet, it was a relief to sit down under the striped canvas awning at one of the outside tables of the Bar du Haou and watch the world go by, which it did even while the rain sluiced down. There I would sit toying with sobriety – I dared the occasional Orangina in among the Kronenbourgs – while I fiddled with the short first draft of a long letter to the Mole, or re-read Chance's books, or, stung to action, reassembled bits of my diary in what was meant to be a more significant order. At Prisunic I had bought a big plastic-covered exercise book for this purpose. Borrowing Chance's technique, I drafted on the right-hand page only, keeping the left-hand page for notes and revisions. The book started to fill up quite quickly that way. It startled me to see how altering the order of events altered the events. My diary had been like life: things happened, but not as a consequence. My super-diary was more lively. It was the edited highlights. I was able to eliminate those long stretches in which we change, but don't seem to.

Perhaps I should do the same here. When the sun shone, I lay down in it, and what I saw over the next few weeks healed me, or at any rate what I thought about it did. But practically nothing happened. Later on in that first week I went to dinner at the Cravaches'. There were fifty other people there, all eating salmon off china plates with silver forks. A lot of the girls who looked so good on the beach in a bikini bottom or a rolled-down stretch one-piece were there to prove they looked just as wonderful when dressed for dancing. One of the girls I especially admired, a Spanish teenager whose black corneas shone like Continental coffee beans against eye-whites like poached eggs, seemed glad enough to dance with me – or, rather, dance in front of me while I did a reined-in dead-foot tremble. Far gone into sobriety by now, I had been too smart to show up drunk, and so was able to manage a pretty convincing display of avuncularity. Dignified enjoyment: that was my role. Besides, Jean-Louis all too clearly had the monopoly of middle-aged marvellousness. He danced as if John Travolta had taken lessons from Fred Astaire. Chance had told me, in one of his phone calls from various parts of the world, that Jean-Louis practised dancing in front of mirrors. His house, which only the absence of the Loire saved from being classed as a château, had plenty of mirrors everywhere, so he must have felt as if he were still practising on his own. Gloria also danced very well, but strictly as a foil. People stood back to watch Jean-Louis. They clapped their hands in time as he dipped, leapt, slid and spun. His permanent smile could have been called self-satisfied by the envious. I was the opposite of envious. I deeply, sincerely considered him just about the biggest prick I had ever met. Thus detached, I was able to see his pleased grin for what it was. He was delighted with the prodigies of which the human body was capable. It was the merest coincidence that the body in question happened to be his own. Gloria, as she had on the beach, looked bored, but only in the way that Mary Magdalene might have done if Jesus had lived to be a hundred. She had grown used to miracles.

Otherwise there was no news, especially not in the local newspaper, although as I lay in the sand on one elbow I was mildy appalled to see Jeffrey Chaucer, mine host of the Ultrasopht Eposanal stand at Olympia, staring keenly out of a story about Biarritz's already redoubtable, and soon to be revolutionary, commitment *profonde* to information technology. Despite the presence of several anomalous new hotels and high-rise blocks of flats like the one in which I was sleeping each night, the architectural fabric of the town was still mainly pitted stone, flaky plaster and crumbling cement dating back to the Empress Eugénie's heyday. Above the shop windows the façades were of timbered Basque houses or *belle-époque* pastiche follies designed to convey the holiday spirit by the frou-frou of their embellishment. But under the shop counters, the wiring all led to central computers. Biarritz was plugged up like the Pentagon. According to the newspaper, the town was already unique in the opportunities it offered the citizen to conduct banking operations from the tranquillity of home. Now, based on the electronic infrastructure already laid down, the town's nervous system would be remade. Soon, electronic point-of-sale analysis would also be the norm. M. Chaucer of England was here to co-operate with eminent French technicians. So was M. Nagoya of Japan. M. Nagoya's face, heavily bespectacled and grave with secret electronic knowledge, betrayed no sign of his having recently paid an unplanned visit to Düsseldorf. There was a paragraph about how, late at night on a date not far in the future, all the electric power in town, save that devoted to essential services, would be switched off in order to expedite the scheduled supplement to the capabilities of an electronically integrated system already unparalleled in its sophistication. Bound by the Fascist-looking collar insignia that serve the French for quotation marks, the word *hightech* featured largely. Superficially a throwback to a bygone age, Biarritz would acquire, beneath its cherished carapace, a microchip musculature, a digital nervous system. Through being remade it would be preserved.

Perhaps I was regaining my interest in the future, but from where I now sat it didn't look so bad. My favourite naiad, the one most stunningly combining long hair, big breasts, short waist and amphibian affinity with water, went stalking past me on the way to her element, her pair of translucent Dayglo pink flippers easily dependent from her right hand. On the wrist of the same arm was an iridescent pistachio digital watch. Wasn't she going to take it off? Of course not. Small boys kicked their way down the face of a dumping white wave on radiant Rip Curl Hot Squad boogie-boards. There were shapes of luminous colour everywhere, from nearby out into the far distance: small triangles of bikini bottoms, large triangles of sailboards and catamarans; ellipses of potato chip surfboards, discs of Swatch faces, Frisbees and fat soft beach tennis balls. Zinc cream for the nose was now a neat miniature pink pyramid instead of the proper white splurge I had grown up with. William Cameron Menzies had been wrong not just about the shape of things to come but about their colour. The science-fiction future, far from being monolithic and clinically white, had turned out to be a fractionated aggregate of supersaturated colours, the contents of a smashed kaleidoscope, or of one of those giant jars that fill the windows of candy stores in American shopping malls. The beaches of Biarritz, once Picasso's playground, now looked as if they belonged to Joan Miró. When you looked down from the cliffs you saw a hessian wall-painting lying on the floor, the near half unprimed, the far half stained with Reckitt's Blue, the whole thing spattered with these hard-edged patches of aching pigment, a swathe of relaxation prickling with local intensity, a daylight version of the night sky as it had once pleased me to conceive of it. It wasn't an idea I wanted to work too hard on. I was beginning to cope with the lack of pressure.

'Great place to just lie down and do fuck all, isn't it?' asked Chance proprietorially on the phone one night. 'Spanish Basque terrorists come up there to relax. You're pretty safe around there unless one of their bombs goes off while they're actually building it.'

'Can you tell which ones they are?' I asked with strained offhandedness.

'Ones on the beach with dark glasses reading Jeffrey Archer novels in Spanish translation. Place gets into your system. It's in half a dozen of my books.'

'I know. I've been reading them again.'

'I'd come back from somewhere like Tibet and start writing about poor bloody Biarritz again. The newest place to have become old. Just love the worn-outness of it. Like me. Thought I was going to keep on coming back for ever.'

'You aren't?'

'Not now. Miss it though. Love that sleepy feeling in the limbs. Takes all day to write a letter. Buying lunch becomes an epic. Mole and I had a gang down there last year. Called it Wimp Squad. Otherwise known as the B-Team or the Mild Bunch. Idea was to do nothing. At an agreed signal we surged into inaction. I wanted to call it Ziz-Cars but the Mole had never heard of *Z-Cars*, needless to say. We were awe-inspiring. Our inertia was formidable. Onlookers were astonished by how little we could do.'

'Where are you speaking from?'

'Switzerland.'

159

'Are you with her now?'

'No. She's still at school. I'm in a kind of clinic.'

'Is there something wrong?'

'Nothing they can't fix. It's a nice lay-out. *Magic Mountain* with overtones of Scott Fitzgerald. Girl doctor who ought to be called Dick Diver, if you get me.'

I got him. The *double entendre* was one of his more imitable verbal tricks. He had others that were harder to fathom. Working my way again through all his books in sequence, there was little I did not remember from before but still less that did not come up fresh. It was his way of putting things. His merest sentence was packed tight with meaning and painted shut with tone, like Technicolor Latin. How could he give up? Certainly it wasn't for lack of ideas. Among his papers I found a working notebook empty except for the first few pages, but those were full of sketched notions that betrayed no lack of conceptual energy, however appalling their want of taste.

Idea novella. Nazi middle-rank war criminal harmlessly growing old under false name. Has a stroke. Gets taken by daughter to Miami for last holiday. All hotels booked out except Fontainebleau. He thinks it's a concentration camp run by Jews. Swimming pool full of children makes him remember cess pit, etc. (Check Max Frisch, *Tagebuch*.) Electrical storm makes him think prisoners suiciding on wire. Same tone of lamentation as *Death in Venice*. Same slow drum-beat. Thinks self great man. Our unfinished task, etc. Dies fright.

Idea short story. Academic working on study of Flaubert's interest in red wine. Provisional title: *Flaubert's Claret*. Refuses to be discouraged when Peter C. Bartelski-type rival academic publishes *Flaubert's Garret: Atelier and Ivory Tower in Second Empire French Fiction*. Goes ever deeper into subject. Everything F. wrote. Everything written about him. Proust's essay. *Ce n'est pas que j'aime entre tous (sic) les livres de Flaubert, ni même le style de Flaubert*. He reads all of Proust. Henry James's review of F.'s *Correspondance*. 'Why was such a passion, in proportion to its strength, after all so sterile?' He reads all of Henry James. Grows old. Like F. he must go on verifying. Finally someone else publishes *Flaubert's Carrot: the Vegetable as Challenge to the Stylist of the Imperishable.* Shoots self, but bullet emerges slowly from barrel of gun and never quite reaches his head. Rigor mortis precedes death.

Idea story main characters made up from spare parts. Douglas Bader's legs, Sammy Davis Jr's eye, Wittgenstein's brother's arm, Van Gogh's ear, Freud's jaw, etc. Half Apollinaire's head? Whole Jayne Mansfield's? Could be fictional components also. Claire's knee. Achilles' heel. King Charles's head real *and* metaphorical. Pompey's head. How funny amputation to amputee? Ask Eric.

Idea self-destruct novel. Deconstruction bonanza. Art form wants suicide? Let it. See how self-reflexive can be. All main characters coded versions each other. Narrative insist emerge? Kill it. Personality comes through? Distort it. Whole thing self-conscious, calculated. To the roots. Whatever survives must be essential self. That whereof we cannot speak must be us. Game? Not now.

So even then he was leaving now. Nothing for him was now any more. He had thought of a book to end his life as a writer, but already he was so finished that he could not begin it. I wondered whether he had written down what had stopped him. If there was a secret document, a Saragossa manuscript, it was probably here. Here was where energy ran out. Except, I need hardly add, for Jean-Louis. I read his books too, or one of them. No doubt he was a good enough technician, but as a *philosophe* he was Teilhard de Chardin with a cocksure impertinence that was all his own. His universal theory, a sort of *omnium gatherum* of all the transcendentalisms, was soup plus cheek, soap plus chic. Decking out the mandatory Althusserian re-reading of Descartes was a diagram of something called, in English, a Force Field, with arrows leading from Magma Impulse to Individual Consciousness, etc. It was voodoo. As a tract promising the reader a perception of the All through relentless pursuit of Self-Realisation it had no more internal consistency or rigour than a hundred other silly books like it. Externally, however, it had the persuasive attribute of having been written by Jean-Louis, a man whose Self had been Realised to an extent that would have left Pico della Mirandola feeling like a builder's labourer. On the beach one day I was actually snorting with superior knowledge at one of Jean-Louis's footling diagrams when the roar of a speed-boat made me look out to the calm sea. From the speed-boat a long tow-line led up at a shallow angle to a parachute about fifty feet in the air. Jean-Louis, wearing long tight surfer's trunks, was hanging from some sort of trapeze suspended from the parachute. People on the beach clapped. The girl with the pink flippers, on her way to the sea, or on her way back, or more likely just walking about in her normal sequence of loosely adopted poses, waved to him with her free hand. Her chartreuse Lycra one-piece was rolled down to a bikini, leaving her magnificent breasts free to hang. They didn't. They stuck straight out like guns. The speed-boat cut its outboard, slowed and turned aside. Jean-Louis left the trapeze and turned a lazy, open one-and-a-half somersaults on the way down to the water. When he surfaced to applause, the only wave of the afternoon welled up and crested to bring him in. Before he had reached shore I was already on my way up the cliff *trottoir*, having called it a day. He talked bullshit, but he could back it up. Tolerating him was going to be part of my breakthrough. I didn't want to rush it.

Angélique talked bullshit too, of course. No wonder she and Jean-Louis had found each other. She arrived in the form of an electronic image. I was drowsily watching television one wet night when the screen was suddenly full of her instead of Joelle Hazard, the blonde beauty who functions as *Soir 3*'s Middle East correspondent. Perhaps I had nodded off with my finger on the remote control. Anyway, there she was: Angélique Visage, with a whole show devoted to her career. A master of ceremonies in a velvet suit, patent leather pumps and a bouffant haircut marshalled a panel of film critics in leather jackets as they choroused hosannahs in her praise between film clips from which her co-stars had evidently been edited out. Then a curtain opened, the swing-band-sized studio orchestra experienced sexual climax, and Angélique was revealed to be physically present, standing on a columnar, capitalised plinth. Although the appropriate garb would have matched that of the Winged Victory of Samothrace, Angélique had sensibly chosen a Chanel suit. She looked, I had to admit, ravishing. A set of airline-type steps glided into position under its own power and she descended to the crashing chords of what was clearly her signature tune, written for her by someone like Jaques Brel, unless the orchestra was just practising scales. *Do not leave me*, sang a tuneless voice, *do not leave me do not leave me do not leave me. For if you leave me*, it went on, *you will have left me, and I will be left alone.* The hubbub was maintained until she sat down in a semicircular banquette-cum-conversation-pit with the assembled savants. The MC handed her the same sort of microphone he and the other contributors to the symposium were already holding. They all sat there gripping these bulbous devices with attached flex, as if attending a convention to discuss the historical reasons why French television engineers had been unable to invent the radio microphone. It was a tribute to Angélique's poise that she could wag that thing in front of her mouth in a stylised manner while discussing herself with a pack of hierophants whose leading questions on the subject of her genius would have been disproportionate if addressed to Madame Curie.

But Angélique gave even better than she got. She talked of how Edwige Feuillère had influenced her Art. Arletty, too, had had a great impact on her Art. Also Michèle Morgan, particularly with the voice. Angélique's Art had positively reeled under the impact of, been saturated by the influence of, Michèle Morgan's Art of reading aloud, especially from the work of Colette. The MC cued for silence and all present listened reverently while they melted away into a black and white picture of Michèle Morgan in her prime. A voice that must have been hers – unless they were playing a trick and giving us a recitation by, say, Madame Pompidou – began speaking about a cactus rose. Dimly I recognised the narrative as a late piece by Colette, whose face, still feline in old age, was now mixed into vision. After lingering for a while, the old lady became Michèle Morgan again and then went all the way back to being Angélique, listening with genuine attention, or at least with what appeared to be that, instead of with what might normally have been expected of her – namely a show of genuine attention just bogus enough to remind you that here was no ordinary individual paying attention, but someone in the public eye coping with the paradox that while she was paying attention to the world, the world was paying attention to her. Perhaps I had been too hard on her. No, there was no perhaps about it. I had. She was lovely and gifted and worth her salary. Other women who were an even bigger pain in the arse were none of those things. I communicated this change of heart to Chance when he rang.

'Always been pretty stunning on her home ground,' he admitted. 'But you might have been thrown by the culture.'

'Whose? Hers?'

'Theirs. Centrality of it. When you see them all discussing literature on the local equivalent of *This is Your Life* it's hard to quell a pang of envy. Doesn't happen anywhere else. Certainly not here.'

'Where's that?'

'New York again. Did the *Today* show this morning. Have to do that sort of stuff here. No book shows worth a damn.'

'It must be tough.'

'Was. Jane was away.' Jane Wyman? Jane Austen? Lady Jane Grey? 'But Tom was filling in for her.' T. S. Eliot? Tom Thumb? Tom, Tom the Piper's Son? 'Don't be amazed if the Mole shows up. There's a few things going on in London, so I asked her to stay out of the picture and do some business for me down there. Think she took umbrage. Calm her down, will you?'

Honestly, I coped. In the days of waiting, which might well have gone on indefinitely, I looked forward to her arrival with pleasure, but without desperation. My long letter to her, which had never got much past page two of the rough draft, I could now safely abandon. On the mend, my soul clicked healthily like a scab touched with a fingernail. Though I could never quite convince myself that things would be even better if she failed to materialise, I persisted in enjoying my solitude. Insisted on it. Chance had sent me there that I might be cured of my madness for her. Either he had forgotten why he had exiled me in the first place, or else I had got the whole thing wrong, and he had posted me away only in order to get me out of his transplanted hair. Or then again, perhaps he was testing the cure. If so, I would pass. By the contemplation of women I had been restored. To begin with, I had ogled askance the odalisques on the wall and wondered how I could live without them. Now, although I still couldn't walk past them without looking, I was able to accept that they could exist without me. Older women no longer offended me when they bared breasts less than perfect. No saint, I was not visited by the urge to kiss their varicose veins, or dote on the liver spots that still showed through the deep tan. But I could grasp why the fact of their not mattering to me sexually should not matter to them at all. They were alive without me. Women even older, women so old that they had been alive before any grain of the sand on which they sat had replaced the grain which had once occupied that position, were knocked sideways by the wave's edge in a thalassic rough-and-tumble for which they volunteered like elephants for death. They were worse than shapeless. They were a parody of shape. Legs like bags of *moules* were spread so that the foam might rush in like a tidal bore up a river's mouth. Over they went, wrecked like the *Deutschland*. But I had begun to see them as part of the process. It is one thing to understand the process of replacement, but another to feel it. You can understand it and not want it. But to sympathise is to participate. I had the inklings of belonging. There was a beautiful mother on the beach. Such a body, which two children had stretched but not ruined as a spectacle. The stretch marks were there in her tan like sand ripples under shallow water. They were not lovely in themselves, but her two children made them so. The little boy pointed his peanut at the little girl and blew a raspberry. He was a pain in the neck who made a point of kicking sand on my towel and farting up-wind so I could get the drift. But I loved his mother from afar. Not having her wouldn't kill me. She was not alive for my sake, but for her sake and for all their sakes. Seeing how alive she was, I had possessed her sufficiently. It was generous of me, this forbearance, because when she stood up, arched her back, and walked towards the water, the build of her showed all over again how important is proportion compared to texture – even when, as in her case, *combined* with texture. Those stretch marks were on a skin like silk. Why didn't I die of lust? Because lust was keeping me alive. The same force had switched tack. Or it had spread out. Yes, that was it. Lust was getting into everything, like gravity. Not de-fused. Diffused.

The girl with pink flippers was no less enticing than she had been before. But I had begun to enjoy, on top of the way she looked, the look of what she did. Swimming as far out as the strongest men, she caught a wave in two strokes and rode far forward on its sliding façade with her head and shoulders in front of the foam. When she got off the wave she tumbled forward like a sprinting swimmer turning between laps against an invisible wall. Her bottom and the backs of her legs lifted out of the flurry. Fitted together like two pieces of an elementary jigsaw puzzle, the pink flippers swung over and slapped down as if a Disney mermaid had become angry. She was gone long enough for the transition to seem plausible when she smoothly surfaced facing the other way, into the next wave. When she slid under that, I saw the flippers edge on, a thin pink line until they opened in a casual flutter that drove her deep. All this was either sexless or it was all sex. To behold was to desire.

'It's all sex,' Chance had once told me, long ago in London. 'When they give me a Sunday lunchtime TV show I'm going to crawl into bed with a million pommy women while their husbands make the morning tea.' He had already gone down from Cambridge then. I was still up, of course, but whenever Lauren and I were in London to see a show – we saw everything together in those days – a foursome formed with Chance and his first wife, Paula. Though worldly success had not yet wrought its full damage, they were already spending a lot of time apart, which scared us. We congratulated ourselves on keeping them together for a single evening. Lauren's money came in morally useful. We established a tradition of dining at the Étoile once a month. The tradition lasted about three months, but as this world goes, anything that lasts long enough to be recognised as repetitive lingers in the memory like an old song. A custom is anything that happens twice. From the balcony I looked down at the tide going out, the waves returning in an endless series of comebacks, like Nellie Melba. *Thalassa, thalassa.* It would always be part of me, this place. I patted the door frame as if it were made of timber from my ancestral lands.

The Mole arrived to announce that Chance had sent her on a mission to sell the flat. 'He's being so strange,' she said when I met her at the airport. 'A bit beastly, really.'

'What have you got in these bags?' I grunted. It's a hard sentence to grunt unless you are trying to lift three hundred-weight.

'Books, mainly. For my long essay. I think he's changing. Penelope didn't ring me even *once.*'

Our girl wasn't happy, but we kept her busy. Chance was on the telephone every evening, mainly from Tel Aviv or Hong Kong, telling her whom to see and what to send him for signing. In her spare time during the day, I established the tradition of walking with her, when the tide permitted, all the way south under the cliffs for as far as we could go. Charlotte Windhover and her children, with her first husband in attendance in the role of servant, had a base camp on dry sand near the start of the journey. The Mole would linger to talk for a while, while I pretended to study the dribbling clay of the cliff. Then there was mainly wet sand and jetsam all the way to the next proper beach, called Milady. Just before we reached that point, however, there were two rocky salients hedging a cusp of driftwood-decorated sand where men sunbathed nude. Some of them were not content merely to sunbake. They played beach tennis, threw Frisbees, stood on their heads. The Mole did her best to avert her eyes but there was nowhere to avert them to except the sky. There were exposed virile organs everywhere. The Mole called it the Cactus Garden. One character just stood there on a rock, one hand on his bony hip while the other cradled the bowl of a smoking briar pipe on which he sucked reflectively, his majestic member descending like the lazy proboscis of a grazing elephant. Inevitably we christened him Hugues d'Orque.

Luckily the ponderous plumper of Hugues d'Orque did not react to the Mole's presence, or it would have knocked us both into the water. How Hugues's titanic tonk remained quiescent was a mystery, however, because the Mole looked pretty enough to excite the erectile tissue in a flatworm. Among her books she had found room to pack a couple of one-piece black stretch swimsuits which so fitted and flattered her dancer's body that Miss Pink Flippers looked past her sell-by date by comparison. Yes, the peach of the beach lay on the towel beside me. Who cared if they all thought I was her father? While she lay on her breasts and wrote long letters to Ambrose, or shorter, more urgent ones to Penelope, I smoothed cream into the curve of her back as if she were a sculpture I had just finished: Rodin, thinking of nothing but lunch. Tell Mademoiselle John that I am not at home. There is a satisfaction that precludes intercourse, or at any rate takes the sting out of its absence. Lying awake beside her as she dozed, I could feel the rough caress of my folded T-shirt under my cheek as if it were a poultice. The moment of happiness was like the moment of truth: I knew myself, and knew also that I was not unique. The world is not just you. Solzhenitsyn, I recalled, had spent such a moment of bliss in the Lubianka, lying on the floor of a crowded cell with his head under a bunk. He had felt the cold granite floor under his cheek and loved the world. Nor had the Mole been lying next to him: you had to give him extra points for a solo effort.

Another tradition was to bathe in music while basting the body. I was equipped with an old Walkman from Chance's junk cupboard and the Mole sported a brand new, state-of-the-art Sony Professional that he had bought her when he had an hour to kill at Changi. Deciding that Shostakovich was too heavy for the beach, we passed through the Prokofiev violin concertos – it was a toss-up between Itzhak Perlman and Shlomo Mintz – and finally arrived at a mixture of Chopin, Debussy, Ravel and Satie piano pieces, with Alison Moyet for light relief. The Mole knew a girl who had been to school with her. It was a pleasure to see that the Mole, who had never heard of Blossom Dearie and regarded even Crystal Gale as an historic figure, went suddenly mad for songs with real words. She had to admit, if pressed – and don't think that I didn't press her while rubbing the cream into her lumbar regions – that those 'no more war no more war' lyrics of Sade's perhaps erred on the side of the simplistic. When Alison Moyet sang 'Where Hides Sleep' the Mole smiled at the sky. I could always guess it was that song, and sometimes which stanza, even though no sound leaked through her earphones, as she made a little *moue* in the direction of Andromeda, mercifully hidden, like all the starry heavens, by the white light of a perfect day.

We would also, by night, after one of our traditional salad dinners by candlelight, make our traditional visit to the open-air *grand chistera* match at the *fronton* a mile away inland. Before the *chistera* match began, there was always a session of Basque folk dancing, which the Mole liked. It affected me like an all-Soviet folk-dancing show I had once sat through in the Palace of Congresses in the Kremlin, when team after team of Young People in peasant garb had come on to perform a pantomime of boy chases girl, girl runs away from boy, boy catches up with girl, girl flirts with other boys, boy retires defeated, girl beckons boy, boy returns to girl, whole team spins around rapidly in delight. The Basque version had a less riveting plot but from the Mole's angle there were compensations. While the boys in black berets were not very interesting as they hit each other's tin swords – the parallel with Morris dancing was inescapable – some of the girls were charming, with elegant hands which had survived, in proportion if not in texture, the daily round of baking *gâteau basque* or, increasingly more likely, pressing the keys on the supermarket check-out desk's electronic cash-register. Yet even the Mole had to admit that the choreography did not look very demanding. Apart from a high mid-air scissors kick which only the boys were allowed to do, the most spectacular step was a shuffle forward and a skip sideways, with hands on hips. A wimpish boy with steel-rimmed spectacles, who looked rather like Jim Lilywhite getting ready to recite, was the star skipper, eliciting learned applause from old men in berets as he hopped about in time to the sparse music emanating from another boy who blew on a pipe while beating a small drum. None of this looked hard. It was a sweet, neat little folkloric culture well worth preserving, but not to the point of letting bombs off in Madrid or training young men to withstand torture by torturing them in advance. While the Mole watched, tapping her foot, Joelle Hazard was no doubt dodging bullets in Beirut, Biarritz's riddled twin. The star skipper might look a bit more macho with an AK-47 to supplement the tin sword, but one hoped – could only hope – that it would never happen. When he at long last skipped off, I couldn't help worrying about where he had skipped to.

In sudden and vivid contrast to the dancing, the *chistera* match looked hard in every aspect, especially the ball, which men in white pyjamas flung with smooth violence from a long basket strapped to the right wrist. The ball rebounding from the high front wall of the *fronton* made a cracking report which echoed off the back wall, about 150 feet away. Sometimes the ball itself rebounded all the way to the back wall, following its own sound, only to be caught by the full-back of one of the two three-man teams and flung forward all over again. The Mole informed me that the ball did not travel quite as fast as in *cesta punta*, the indoor version of the same game, in which the players had to wear helmets or else be killed. But the indoor game was separated from the spectators by a fourth wall of strong wire netting. Outdoors, in the sweet warm night, there was nothing between us and the hurtling *pelote* except balmy air. For an admission fee of thirty francs, the hundred or so spectators sat anywhere on a three-step stone terrace along the fourth side of the floodlit court, hired cushions extra. It was advisable to keep your eye on the speeding pill, lest it terminate one of its frequent incursions into the crowd by smashing you in the teeth. Sharing the danger with the players, one found it difficult to remain unmoved. The Mole bounced up and down with excitement, like a little girl. Wait a second: she *was* a little girl. I had to admit that it was a great night out, even though the second and more important match turned out to feature, as captain of the home team, none other than Jean-Louis, who waved his basket at the Mole in what was obviously fond memory. When she told me what a wonderful guy he was I took it quite well, screaming only through flared nostrils.

Any hopes that Jean-Louis would be shown up by the local boys were soon shattered. They might have spent their whole lives mastering the basket, but our man was an all-sports fanatic who knew his physics. The crowd cheered and even the opposing team made clicking noises of approval as he whirled,

170

dived, scooped and flung. One of his cross-court whip-lash winners came fizzing straight at the Mole. She ducked just in time and I caught it neatly with the side of my head. 'He should not have put is haired in front of the *pelote*,' said Jean-Louis as he bent to kiss the Mole. 'Does he not know it is dangerous? Now we must interrupt the game.'

'Are you all right?' my darling asked me concernedly, instead of getting up to dance the tango with Jean-Louis as he clearly wanted. Ah, I thought, more power to your elbow, dearest, and less to his. Ah. Oogh. It was no use currying any sympathy apart from hers, however. It soon became obvious that any injury to a spectator was generally regarded as an interval in which to buy the children one more Orangina each. An old man in a beret and baggy pants shuffled slowly across the court and examined my wound, jabbing it with an expert thumb to make it worse. He pulled a large white handkerchief out of his trouser pocket, but instead of binding my head with it he waved it to indicate that the game might continue. Within seconds Jean-Louis was running, whirling, diving, scooping and flinging all over again, leading his team to victory. I could see Gloria in the half-light behind us, leaning against a tree, yawning so often that she no longer saw any point in covering her mouth.

My temple was still hurting when Jean-Louis's final overhead loop-shot from a backward somersault brought the evening to an end, but my eyes were working again well enough, which was lucky, because then, at that unlikely time, came the real epiphany, the emotional crisis of my spiritual recovery, the climax of my cure by the contemplation of women. Believe me, as I must believe myself, that the moment would still have come even if the Mole had not been there to kiss my sore place and make it better. Gathering its children, the small crowd streamed across the court to the exit. One pretty young mother was too expensive-looking to be local. If French she must have been from Bordeaux or perhaps even Paris, if Spanish from Madrid or Barcelona. Probably she was Spanish, her hair was so black and the white of her eyes so very white. The Mole groaned, but it was not just the woman's beauty that moved me. It was the way she held her crippled son by the hand. He was palsied. So badly was he stricken that his walk was a careening lurch, a movement not aided by an extra, windmilling gesture that he was making with his free hand. He was pretending to catch the *pelote* and throw it. He was wielding an imaginary basket. His mother smiled down at him, her night complete because she had made him happy.

'Look at that,' I said.

'She's lovely,' said the Mole.

'You'll be like that.'

'I hope I don't have to be. I couldn't cope.'

'But if you have to, you will. It's why I love you.'

Don't imagine that she let me sleep with her after that. Romance between us never came so easily. But with the night turning suddenly stormy outside, we lit candles, drank *Punt e Mes* and let Ivan Moravec loose on César Franck's *Prelude, Chorale, et Fugue*. ('The fugue is not a fugue,' sniffed Saint-Saëns, unhinged by envy.) Moravec's stamp-collector's touch with Debussy had led us on to all his other Vox and Supraphon recordings, of which Chance's shelves seemed to lack not one. I don't know why, in exchanging the Thames for the Bay of Biscay, we had replaced the cello with the piano. Perhaps it was because the sea was already scored for strings and we wanted a countervailing range of colour. 'The piano is my second self,' said Chopin. For a nightcap we unleashed Michelangeli on the Mazurkas. As was traditional, we slept in separate beds, but I was allowed to give her the Big Tickle. While she lay on her front, I stroked her minutely from the neck down, stroking her bottom pink, stroking her thighs open. Finally I got the job of human vibrator: no batteries necessary. My dubious reward was to hear her, at the instant of ecstasy, sadly cry out the name of the girl she loved. If it sounds like the biggest prick-tease in history, let me tell you it felt like it. All I can say is that I didn't press the point. She wasn't mine, you see. She was Penelope's. That was my consolation. Her love for Penelope was something we could both rely on as paramount, even if it was no longer requited. In fact the Mole relied on it even more than I did, now that Chance was subtracting himself from her life. For a long time Jenolan Pasha had surrounded himself with his women while retreating from the world, and now, it seemed, he was retreating even from them.

In the morning we did some more packing. Everything in the flat was going into boxes which would be strapped up to be stored in Battersea. 'I wonder why he isn't sending all this stuff to the Barbican?' mused the Mole as she stacked books.

'Have you asked him?'

'He's being vague. Pretty shitty, in fact.'

In the afternoon we were down at the beach to catch waves as the tide came in. The Mole rode Chance's boogie-board like a wicked child in a Bruegel snowscape sliding on a tray. Miss Pink Flippers did her forward roll. As I looked up from the prone position, the jailbait teriyaki glowed on the sea wall, like *Playboy*'s version of classical entablature. The old ladies were there again at the sea's edge to be tipped over. The young mother with the watered silk stretch marks wagged a fine-drawn finger at her little boy to stop him farting. My new young mother was there too, with her devastated offspring whom she could not leave alone for a minute. She had bought him a toy *chistera*. The basket hung from one uncertain arm as if aimlessness had been extended. He scooped sand and flung it inadvertently at a nearby pot-bellied male sunbather, who woke snorting, started to protest, saw, stopped, and fell back mollified by her smile of apology. That boy was always going to be a problem. He was heart-rending only when he was still. I could feel my heart hardening as I looked at him. Then I looked at her. She was better than I was. I was saved.

I must have been, otherwise I could not have borne the sense of loss when the Mole came dragging her long straight feet towards me through the shallow out-thrust selvage of the spent wave. A boy who had thrown a thin disc of plywood on to the film of water and taken a running jump on to it went sliding past behind her, creating a parallax effect which made me feel as if I had been sent instantly sideways but without inertia: a dream world. 'I was *mad* not to get a trim in Switzerland,' said the Mole, pulling at her hair as she sat on her heels. 'The minute I go home I'll have to get it all done again.'

'Don't you like doing that?'

'Yes, but it costs money. And I might not be a kept woman exactly but Chance does give me the odd few bob. Or did.' She rolled down the top of her costume. Exactly equal, her breasts

173

looked all set to outdo each other, like two shapely coupés lined up for a game of chicken. Remember *Rebel Without a Cause*? The Mole didn't even remember *American Graffiti*.

'I could afford a haircut for you.'

'Not this one,' she said with a firmness that I tried hard not to be miffed by. 'You like my hair, don't you?'

'I love it. So natural.'

'Well, it wouldn't look so natural if Nikky at John Frieda didn't cut it. Hair has to be cut really cleverly if it's going to look good whatever the wind does to it. See the way the fringe at the front looks like a layered cut until I sweep it back like that? Two and a half hours in the chair. It costs money. Not an *awful* lot. Just more than a student's got, believe me. Ooh look, she's bought him a basket. Isn't that *sweet*?'

A break in her self-absorption was the most I could expect, having so recently attained the same standard myself. She was a good girl and soon she would be a good woman, but not soon enough for me. My responsibilities lay elsewhere. I swear that I could already feel myself turning towards them. The readiness was in me. They say that a Boeing 757 jet airliner, should both pilots die, will fly itself back to the factory in Seattle.

That night, after the Mole had been stroked to sleep, I found the manuscript. Lack of time had intensified the search. Originating from Rome, a phone call from Chance before dinner had invited us back to London the day after next. Movement orders. Before we went, I wanted to know his secret. Here it was: an Italian notebook of unlined hand-laid paper between marbled covers, with nothing printed on the spine. Roughly the same size as the famous green and gold first edition of A. D. Hope's *The Wandering Islands*, it had been slipped in beside that book and a later, more complete collection of Hope's verse, up on the Australian shelf along with the poetry of Douglas Stewart, James McAuley and Judith Wright. I would have gone on overlooking it if the spine had not been blank. When I took it down, I found the first half of it crammed with Chance's handwriting, distributed in the usual manner, notes and additions on the left-hand page, text proper on the right. The front flyleaf was covered with provisional titles, of which LETTER TO A YOUNG STUDENT had been inscribed latest and largest, in block capitals cross-hatched and edged, as in the work-book of a schoolboy who makes up with doodling energy for what he lacks in concentration on the actual work. In this case, however, the actual work turned out to be the most concentrated thing Chance had ever done in the essay form. From the first sentence until it petered out it was a megalomaniacal cadenza addressed directly to the Mole. In giving you the edited highlights, I don't mean to suggest that there were *longueurs*. This was a piece he had written as if his life depended on it. You could tell by the elaborations arrowed from the left-hand page into every second sentence on the right; the sentences rewritten to unscramble their overloaded structure; the words crossed out, replaced, and then restored with a STET after the replacements had been replaced. Here were the death-throes of a living style, the *Totentanz* of a technique.

The time will come when you have to forgive me for calling Rilke a prick. At the moment, as your higher studies begin and you face the dazzling prospect of having literature's political dimension expounded to you by Georg Lukács – or, more likely, the political dimension of Georg Lukács expounded to you by Terry Eagleton – there is no reason for you to be concerned with a poet so precious that he could not write a line except on paper made for him, paid for with money that he had to beg for, with letters to great ladies written on that same paper, in rooms they assigned to him in their palaces, glad to be needed by so spiritual a man. The joke is that he actually *was* a spiritual man. Keats put on his Sunday best before sitting down to write. Rilke took the same principle far beyond clothes, into cakes of soap, nail scissors, matched hair brushes with silver backs, manners, protocol, the perfectly wrapped gift, every detail of life. After you have finished the formal studies you have just commenced, and have begun the informal reading which will light the life you lead without me, you will meet him, and find at last, after so much transcendental literary theory has made you weary of abstraction, that there really *is* such a thing as the mind that moves above objects – but that it can do so only through knowing them to their depths. You will recognise yourself. The way he arranges his paper and pens is the way you cut onions, line up your little bottles, slip that MOMA silver book mark I gave you so carefully into place at the top of the page, and ache to interfere with the disorder on my desk. By how you listen to Jacqueline du Pré playing the Elgar, I can already tell how you will react to the *Duino Elegies* and the *Sonnets to Orpheus*, although I think you had better approach them through the lower slopes, the smaller set pieces like the poem about the carousel. *Und dann und wann ein weisser Elefant*. The German you learned at school in Lausanne, and from your ski master when you got stuck on the Triftji at Zermatt, will come in handy then. But if you want to jump the gun, you could always try his prose masterpiece in translation. *Letters to a Young Poet* is the real reason I bring up his name, because something of what he said to the obscure Franz Xaver Kappus I want to say to you. It hardly needs pointing out that I am a less well equipped teacher. To compensate, however, you are a much quicker pupil. There is no evidence that the young poet took in a word his mentor said. There were ten letters, written in, and scrupulously posted from, Paris, Rome, Viareggio, Worpswede, and several addresses in Sweden. Thus bombarded with the distilled wisdom of a lifetime, the tyro ignored it all. He might have been right, and perhaps you will be wise to copy his indifference. The advice of the old, said Vauvenargues, illuminates without warming, like winter sunlight.

That was the gist of the introduction, which despite its ground-swell of self-regard I thought charming. But after a few more paragraphs of mock-modest disclaimer the tone grew less relaxed.

You can grow to admire a precious poet. A robust novelist you can love immediately. Stendhal you will adore as if he were a beautiful woman. He half was, though a notoriously ugly man. (Henry James was almost as keen to point that out as to find *Le Rouge et le noir* 'unreadable'.) One of Stendhal's principles has always sounded to me like holy writ. I don't know where he said it, I only know that the film director Robert Bresson quoted him to this effect in an interview, but here it is. 'It's the other arts which taught me the art of writing.' For me, when I heard that, it was not a case of copy, learn and use, because I already believed it. All I needed was the courage of my convictions. But in loving the other arts, loving learning from them, I got too involved in them – or perhaps, in my case, they weren't art. Acting, speaking, performing, directing: these things paid for time to write, and a life to write about, or so I thought. So I let fame draw me forward, and lost my simplicity.

Now *here* was a confession. At our lunch in the Garrick he had blamed the press. Yet in these pages, which must have predated that conversation by almost a year, he seemed to be taking the responsibility on himself. A little further on, the matter was settled.

Montaigne's mutability of the ego was my ideal, until I realised it. Beware of what you dream, said Wilde: it might come true. Possessing the world, I thought it was mine to command. I still believed – and believe still – that the writer must pursue the magic sentence. But I had come to confuse the magic sentence with my jealously developed trickery. I thought that instead of being given, it could be generated. And then one day, preparing for a television interview with Primo Levi at his house in Turin, I was re-reading his great book *Se questo è un uomo* (*If This is a Man*, a humanistic triumph which I won't spoil for you by telling you it will help you grow) when I came across a truly magic sentence that reduced the best of mine to the calisthenics of a card-sharp. '*E all' alba i fili spinati erano pieni di biancheria infantile stesa al vento ad asciugare.*' Which means, roughly, 'And in the morning the barbed wire was full of babies' washing spread to dry in the wind.' The previous day, the Italian Jewish internees, who had been rounded up by the SS, had been told that the next morning they would be put on a train. All the adult prisoners knew that this meant a quick death if they were

177

lucky, a long agony if they were not. But during the night the mothers washed the nappies ready for the journey, and hung them to dry on the wire.

When I read this, I knew that I was finished as a writer. It was not just because Levi had been there and I had not. Believe me, his participation in these awful events was not what I envied; and, as I later discovered, he himself was too honest a spirit to feel that he had been in any way privileged. What I envied him was his science. Where else did the purity of his art come from? His real life in chemistry had kept him simple: brilliantly simple, symmetrically concentrated, able to contain, like a pressure vessel, the incandescence of the magic sentence when it finally arrived. He had earned, kept and cherished the right to speak the unspeakable.

Do you know what my best idea on that same dreadful subject had been? I had an idea for a long short story about an old concentration camp commandant dying six million deaths from fear in a Jewish hotel in Miami. Come to think of it, it's still not a bad idea. But an idea is what it would remain, even if I wrote it down with all the power of evocation I still might summon. And an idea is not a thing. When the words exceed the thing said, it is blasphemy.

On the left-hand page beside these paragraphs there was a note. *French bus with spastic children: say can't say*. The note had been left undeveloped. I half-remembered that a chartered bus full of children from a spastic school – or else the bus actually belonged to the school, which made it even worse – had crashed and burned on a fog-bound *autoroute*, killing almost everyone aboard. Chance must have planned to cite this as an instance of what could not be said by him, but had then realised he could not say even that. He kept it general. The generalities were frightful enough.

It would be an easy claim to scruple if I said that the world's horrors had got beyond me. They have; they did early on; and especially when the victims were children. If a terrorist bomb blows an innocent adult's legs off, the rest of him can at least guess why he has been chosen as he lies there. Randomness was the reason. Arbitrariness was the rationale. But for the ruined child, there is no explanation that begins to cover the case, either for her – in my mind it has always been her, and now the her is you – or me. I can give myself no points, however, for these fine feelings. The truth is that these worst cases are only the beginning of what I can no longer treat. If I had kept my innocence, though I might never quite have caught the whiteness of the children's underclothes on the barbed wire – or the pinkness of the inside of the starving child's enormous open crying mouth in Ethiopia, or the redness of the baby pulped by a grenade in the Roman synagogue – I could at least have kept track of my own happiness, my own luck. I could have told the real story of my love for you. But like the hero of Hofmannstahl's story *Brief des Lord Chandos an Francis Bacon* – another perfect stylistic pleasure you might embrace early by reading in translation – I had got to the point of being unable to say anything through having learned too much. Do you remember, on that first day at Mürren in the fresh powder, how our ski tips floated through the snow like the prows of Viking long ships slicing silently through the estuarine mist? And how I crashed into the deep drift and couldn't find my ski and you made your joke about my being pissed-off off-*piste*? You can't imagine how I would like to write about that.

You just have, I subvocalised with some impatience. But it was a rare moment of obvious fakery. The whole tract rang dishearteningly true, and the last paragraph reverberated like a passing bell, albeit a cracked one, because surely there would have been much more to come if the manuscript had not fulfilled its own prophecy by choking in full flow.

When the time comes to show you this fragile testament it will probably be too late, so why finish it? I will no longer be able to make that sort of claim on your attention. The chances are that I will be gone altogether, having shaken loose the gravity of my wordy knack and disappeared into the weightless effulgence of the inconsequential. 'Literature without tradition,' said the great scholar Ernst Robert Curtius, 'is destiny without history.' To my shame, consternation and regret, I think I have grown to like that idea. Just after the Second World War ended, Curtius met André Gide at an open-air café within sight of the rubble of Cologne. A civilisation lay in ruins. Gide took one of the first commercially available examples of a new invention out of his pocket and showed Curtius how it worked. It was a ballpoint pen. I merely record this fact. Soon that will be all I am good for: to note the details of blind renewal, the impulse, which not even mass murder can quite quell, to remake the world. Do I insult you when I say that half my love for you is for how young you are, and the other half for how I must let you go, when by growing older you move on to be someone else's and share your life with . . .

Him or her? He left *that* word blank, the mad bastard. Did he insult her? Boy, did he ever: comparing my darling – who even as I finished reading sent a little dreamy moan through the open door of the bedroom – to a ballpoint pen! The effrontery of it! But when I simmered down, it was not the tone of the piece so much as its timing that interested me. He had been preparing to get rid of her even as he met her. He was so calculating, so cold. I had to work hard to remind myself that I owed him my life. Deciding that if he had meant her to see this shameful treatise he would have had the grace to finish it, I dropped it into one of the packing cases and consigned it to oblivion, or the University of Buffalo, or wherever it was that the Man of Destiny's foul papers would eventually end up.

Next morning, while the Mole was locked in the bathroom doing whatever it was she did to make herself even more fragrant, *Screen International* arrived. With a glossy crackle it unrolled to reveal, in a full-page advertisement on the inside cover, the next stage of Chance Jenolan's apotheosis. So Clive James had scrounged a few days' work after all! He would be pleased to see that he shared with Robert Browning the honour of having his name misspelled in what seemed to me the most suicidal act of self-abasement since Jimmy Carter took up jogging. Obviously the advertisement had been written in Tel Aviv or Hong Kong, perhaps both. One could only assume that Chance had not seen the page proof. The result might help him to see sense.

PRINCIPAL PHOTOGRAPHY BEGINS!
UNDER THE PERSONAL SUPERVISION OF GUS DISTING
SIR GO-GO CHOW
IN EXTRAORDINARY COLLABORATION WITH
GRAPESHOT FILMS
PRESENTS
A CHOWSHOT PRODUCTION OF
CHANCELLOR JENOLAN'S

THE RING, THE BOOK AND THE SWORD

'*From a poem no one has read comes a film no one will miss*'
STARRING
HEFLIN DUSTMANN   AL MASSIMO
ANGÉLIQUE VISAGE   JONAS Q. SALK
AND
CHANCELLOR JENOLAN
Also Starring
DEAN HARLOWE   HARLOW SHAPLEY
RINGO KERR   CAROLINE MONROE
With Guest Stars
CHRISTMAS DAY-LEWIS   SNAP SPENDER
PUTTNAM ISHERWOOD   GORDON AUDEN
And Introducing
IMOGEN WECHSEL as 'MARIA'
WITH THE SPECIAL PARTICIPATION OF
DOUG CURTBLASTER in the role of 'THE OLD MAN'

Designed by PRESLEY SCHAUFENSTER
Music by TOMLINSON KLEINBOTTLE
Story by CHANCELLOR JENOLAN and
LANCELOT WINDHOVER
Screenplay by NICHOLAS CRANE and DAVID BENTLEY and
COLIN THINWALL and CLIVE JONES
Additional dialogue by SHIR HOROWITZ and
NAT HACKLEY
Based on the poem by ROBERT BROWNLING
Photographed in CHOWSCOPE
Other technical credits to be announced

The film produced and directed by
CHANCELLOR JENOLAN
(Billing not contractual)

'It's absolutely doomed. It's a disaster,' I told the Mole over our traditional health-giving breakfast. 'This will cost him everything.'

'Do you think that's why he's selling this place?' she asked, adding live yoghurt to the stewed fruit and brown sugar to the live yoghurt.

'I shouldn't be surprised. Nothing about him surprises me any more. But I didn't mean it'd cost him just money.'

'What else?'

'Reputation. Respect. All that.'

'I don't think he cares much about that,' said the Mole, sounding as old as the hills and innocent as a lamb. 'He's always found those things a bit too easy. I bet he's sleeping with that Presley cow.' From her fastidiously held spoon the Mole dripped bloblets of yoghurt along Presley Schaufenster's name.

'I thought you said he couldn't,' I coaxed hopefully.

'If it got him out of paying her he might just manage it. This is why he kept us away, I expect.'

'So he could operate.'

'He's not a doctor, silly.'

'No, it's an American word. Operator. It means a wheeler-dealer.'

'What does *that* mean?'

'An operator. Someone who does clever deals.'

'Do all Australians speak American?'

'I don't really speak American. Just old English.'

Yet my distance from her no longer worried me. I could see her better. While Chance moved towards disintegration, I moved towards coherence, as if energy were being conserved. Having finished packing, and with no beach because of the tide, we spent the late morning under the parti-coloured awning in front of the Bar du Haou. The rearrangement of my diary was taking a definite shape. I drew more arrows, renumbered pages, put whole paragraphs into reverse. Always careful to dote on the Mole only when she wasn't looking, now I forgot her presence for minutes at a time. It made the impact more delicious when I looked up. Wearing white jeans and a pale blue sloppy joe marked OUTRAGE SKI EXTREME, she was absorbed in Peter C. Bartelski's *Fiction Beyond Fiction: the Unlimned*

Character in the Modern Novel from Thomas Parke d'Invilliers to L. S. Caton. Periodically transmitting some insight she deemed especially profound, at any sign of resistance from me she would get het up as if by the sun. She was particularly insistent on the metafictional principle that any background information about a character should be withheld until it was too late to be useful. Suppressing all mention of Chance's manuscript – if I had read it earlier, how much more I would have understood about these last confusing months! – I based my dissenting vote on the precept that to postpone the background might well make a novel about Australians more mysterious, but could only empty a novel about Britons of all content. 'But that's what's *supposed* to happen,' she protested, and went on to explain how reducing the content to technique, and *demonstrating* that the technique constituted the *actual discourse*, was the whole idea.

She was still explaining while we bought fruit in the market for the lunch we would have down on the esplanade. I watched her mouth pour forth its meaningless music while her hands, which knew their stuff, floated over the wine-dark plums, sending down sonar signals to test their ripeness. The men in white aprons behind the counters fell over one another to serve us. They invited her to prod their peaches, suck their nectarines, burst their grapes against her palate fine. Down on the sea wall, we spread the feast on flattened plastic carrier-bags. When the beach grew big enough we camped on our rattan mats for the afternoon. All the female members of the cast were present and correct, I was glad to note. Less gladly I noted that the computer software tycoon Jeffrey Chaucer had appeared at the head of the stairs, taken a fix on us, and started walking towards us even as he waved. Though he was fully kitted out for the beach, his skin suggested that he had not recently spent much time exposed to the sun: only the very freshest radish could have been more white. A straw hat, sun-glasses, long shorts and leather sandals did something to cover him up, but he would have stood out even if he had not been accompanied by a man I immediately realised must be Mr Nagoya. They looked like Mandrake the Magician and Lothar, an analogy which held true even for their relative proportions, because Mr Nagoya was enormous. His whole attire a minuscule black satinised posing pouch in which for some reason he had positioned himself vertically, he looked Japanese only to the extent of wearing spectacles and having too many teeth for his mouth. Otherwise he looked like Arnold Schwarzenegger. While Mr Nagoya stood there with his hands behind his back as if waiting for someone to climb him, Jeffrey set down all his gear – mat, sponge bag, hotel towel, small portable refrigerator, word processor – and did the introductions.

'Hideo and I would have liked nothing better than to have been down here with you two enjoying the briny, Joel. I hope this nut-case has been looking after you, Antonia, my own lovely. But at the end of the day, the job has to be done, even if it takes weeks. And let me tell you it hasn't been a doddle, dealing with these French city engineers, especially when Hideo's English is hardly the most fluent, which Hideo would be the first to admit, am I right, Hideo?'

'My Engrish is not fruent,' said Mr Nagoya, smiling as if James Coburn and Burt Lancaster had been forced to share the same mouth.

'And of course theirs isn't either, so we've had no let-up.'

'What exactly are you trying to accomplish?' I made the mistake of asking. Jeffrey started to tell me how the whole town would be integrated into one interactive informational interface, starting tonight. There was a lot involved, and Jeffrey had the facts to prove it. The Mole snuck her headphones on and drifted off on a personal tide of 'Where Hides Sleep'. I could tell by how she pouted at the sky. Mr Nagoya stood immobile for a further five minutes, but then, as if actuated by an electronic signal, took off his glasses, set them down on Jeffrey's towel, and ran towards the water, moving only slightly more slowly than Carl Lewis in the final of the 100 metres at the Los Angeles Olympics. It was amazing how his legs were not bowed. Equally amazing was how there was so little diminution in his pace when the depth of the water obliged him to stop running and start swimming. He just swam straight towards Canada, not even diving under the wave on which Miss Pink Flippers surfed towards him, but punching straight through it like a torpedo set to run at constant depth.

' . . . so we got them watching Hideo's video, and at the end of the day the penny dropped. They finally agreed that the only way to monitor a potential power surge was to shut off the whole area for twenty minutes and run a dummy programme. Except for the hospital, of course. So it's all happening tonight.'

'At the end of the day,' murmured the Mole – rather too loudly, as one tends to do when wearing headphones.

'Ah, Antonia, you always were the sarcastic one,' said Jeffrey with undisguised admiration. 'What we could do with you on our sales staff permanently. Make her think about it, Joel. It's the future.'

Yes, I thought, it *was* the future. The cold future. But the future has to be cold, or there would be nowhere for all this warmth to go to. The arrow must have somewhere to land, or it can't fly. While Jeffrey droned on, I contemplated, for what I thought must surely be the last time, the women of my cure. They were as warm to the eye as they would have been to the touch. Miss Pink Flippers was teaching Mr Nagoya to surf. He didn't learn straight away. It took him several minutes. His main problem was to slow down so that the wave could catch him up. When it did, his head was there beside hers: two freshly installed gargoyles shouldering their way off the marble cornice of a cathedral. The mother with the palsied son was on her slow way down the steps beside him. Left behind by the retreating sea, there was still a trapped pool of water around the base of the steps. She set up camp next to it so that he could dig canals with the *chistera* that was already broken. Sometimes she took her eyes off him for a few seconds to sweep the beach with her dark glasses, like a radar dish. When she brought her gaze back to him, he was still the same. One of the old ladies had started her epic trek from the steps to the sea's edge, like an elephant on its last legs. Soon the heat would go out of her, into the ground or adding its few calories to the fire. Her sons must be my age. She was on her way to let the salt sea into her dry womb. To be scuttled. Behind me and high above, letting nothing into their bodies except daylight, the jailbait teriyaki looked seaward unmoved, as if there were nothing to choose between the young men who sat out there astride their potato chip surfboards, pulling the nose of the board up into the rising swell, floating fertility symbols waiting for the breaker. The boys waited for the waves and the girls waited for the boys. Their children were in the future. But it was the near future, where nothing was decided. Only in the long, long term was everything cut and dried, and cold. Here and now and soon were warm enough.

Having cleaned up the kitchen preparatory to our departure, that night the Mole and I took our evening meal at Le Sable d'Or. Madame made such a tremendous fuss of the Mole that we almost didn't get fed at all. The Mole's finishing school French being so precise, I didn't need to imitate a sea bass, so the old lady had no chance to bring me a double bass instead. We had two bottles of a reasonably effective Saint Émilion for old time's sake and barely made it down the dogshit-dotted cliff *trottoir* in the dark for a long walk around the point to the children's beach, where there was a roundabout on which the Mole had promised herself a ride. While I watched from a folding metal and wood chair that might have come from the Luxembourg Gardens – but more probably came from a plastics factory in which strips of rusty mild steel and slats of wood covered with chipped dark-green paint had been successfully imitated in polystyrene – the Mole rode, her back as straight as you might imagine, on a pinto pony that really *was* made of wood, you could tell from the grain in its half-missing haunch. In a white two-seater swan out of a touring production of *Lohengrin* rode the palsied boy and his mother. The other animals and cars and the little red Fokker triplane were all empty. There was no one else to be seen except the owner-operator, a weathered Basque who in ancient times might have hunted whales out in the ocean. He gave the boy, the boy's mother and my recurrently radiant darling a long ride for two francs. When the mother swung towards me she was carefree. When she swung away I could see her protective arm stretched tautly along the swan's back, above the poised tail and between the vertically held swept-back pinions. I could see the little wrinkles of the skin already loosening at her elbow as by turning on the spot she journeyed forward into time. Such a complex of emotions, such a complicated motion. She was both a wave and a particle. She was like light.

When the music wheezed to a stop, the Mole came back to me. She was quite peeved that I had spent so long looking at someone else, I was glad to notice. We walked out over the little bridge to the big rock where the Virgin stood floodlit. More floodlights bathed the foam that bathed the broken, tilted pieces of superseded cliff. 'Happy?' I asked like a fool, knowing that she was not. 'Tipsy,' she said, meaning no. The floodlights and every other man-made light in the area went out. The Virgin became a silhouette. Above me, where I looked for the first time in many months of nights, you could see the sudden difference. Without interference from the town's illumination, the sky grew distinctly brighter, as if it had all jumped forward a few inches. It was a switch-on.

There they were, with their names in lights: all the lucky ones who had been written into their subject. Hubble's Law. The Kelvin-Helmholtz Contraction. The Mohorovičić Discontinuity. The Schwarzschild Radius. Some of them had done even better. They had elevated their names beyond theoretical principles and into actual phenomena: the Van Allen Belt, the Seyfert Galaxies, Halley's Comet, Lilywhite's Quincunx. The all-star spectacular. Well, that would never happen to me. But there was a consolation. Halley's Comet had no idea of its own name. Nothing up there needed us. That was the first thing to grasp and the last to lose sight of. It was the basis of awe, which induces humility, which chastens curiosity and gives us science. Now that I had lost my pride, I had at last joined them, the mighty ones, if only in their eternal childhood. Up into the lights I stared, chosen and afraid, like an American footballer in a Monday night game preparing to receive the punt, or like Halley himself on St Helena in 1677, as he looked up at the hot point of Eta Carinae in the southern sky. If only I had stayed down there, I might have had my name up *there*. I could have been an Aussie with his monniker in neon, like Colin Gum, who in 1952 found the Gum Nebula, a huge hydrogen cloud between Sirius and the Coal Sack, a cloud whose curling filaments are made shiny by a pulsar. Only 11,000 years ago the Gum Nebula was ten times brighter than Venus. Imagine having your name on *that*. Doesn't the Court Nebula sound better than the Gum Nebula? Forget I asked.

Because envy was impertinence. It was all too glorious. 'The moth-soft Milky Way,' says Hopkins in *The Wreck of the Deutschland*, 'The leaves of desire.' To pin down the night sky we need all the poetry ever written, even the overwrought. What else is the Veil in Cygnus except an *art nouveau* intricacy, a frayed violet Liberty silk scarf with pink highlights, the drowned Ophelia's hair as seen by Gustav Klimt? 'Rivers of beer,' said W. C. Fields, 'flowing over your grandmother's paisley shawl.' We give no sufficient answer by calling it a set of emission nebulae, remnants of a supernova outburst 160,000 years ago, sending radio signals from the edge of its loop but strangely without a hot central star. When you call it a reef without an island, already the metaphors creep back. Science must guard itself against the seductions of analogy, the purely poetic connection. But the organising principle within us loves a likeness, and charged language leaps towards the attractive fact as your glance is drawn to the girl across the room, even while her beauty drains towards the future, the cold future. She is beautiful *now*. Her eyes are like stars.

And stars are like jewels. On the border between Ursa Major and Canes Venatici shines the eighteenth-dynasty Egyptian brooch of M106, a lapis lazuli oval with two long chrysoprase spiral arms and the other arms attenuated to amethyst-dotted mountings for the hinge and hook of the pin behind it. In Virgo, M87 is a galaxy surrounded by a shell of 4,000 globular clusters, a pimpled baseball of diamonds given added sparkle by the blue jet and counterjet of synchrotron radiation at the system's core. You could take it down and wrap it up for Elizabeth Taylor, if it were not so hot to handle. That jumbo bauble from Rodeo Drive contains a black hole the size of 2.7 trillion suns. Let it stay where it is. It looks lovely there. And how wrong would Angélique be to drool over the planetary nebula in Lyra, which is like a frozen smoke-ring for her little finger; over the pink lagoon nebula near the Great Rift; or over the star nursery M83 in the southern sky, a Celliniesque extravaganza of diamonds and sapphires set in beaten gold? She might go mad. They wouldn't care, being different now, or perhaps dead. But there is no now. Not up there.

And stars are *not* like jewels. The old astrologers who saw a sky full of animals were telling the truth. Look into the stroboscopic pinwheel of M51's turquoise spiral, whose arms of bright young Population 1 blue sparklers cradle tired old yellow stars in the blanks between them. You can follow those arms for one-and-a-half turns, like a somersaulting diver. The thing's a whopper. Slap down your darling's urge to pin it on her lapel and look harder. Do you see the blue Portuguese man-o'-war peeling the rind off an orange? You don't? You must be blind. You must be tired of life.

And where there is life, there is disease. The dim red glow of Barnard's Loop is Orion's ringworm. Did the Rosette in Monoceros blow out, or was the gas used up by the cluster? Either way, the centre is empty. Yet that dense annulus is a bursting boil. It pumps out new stars like brilliant pus. Radio observation puts the mass of the Tarantula emission nebula (30 Doradus) at half a million suns. One hundred hot supergiant stars at the centre fester like a carbuncle. The sky has acne.

And human skin has the sky's violence. It is no comfort to the poor adolescent whose cheeks are purple pizza – and an insult to the stricken adult who was told for so long that it would all clear up – but our idea of beauty leaves too much out. Aesthetics are abstract. Like those dedicated zoologists on television who let cockroaches crawl over them or who pose with garter snakes group-groping in their beards like Medusa's mad older brother, we should try to take more in. *Einfühling*, Einstein called it. The love for the objects of experience. Alas, with the electricity switched off we have only the eye, which sees so little. Emerging from my curative journey *a riveder le stelle*, I could show the Mole, my little dog star, nothing of the radio universe and less than I would have liked to of the optical one. All we had was our unaided orbs, which I was somewhat put out to find were more powerful in her case than in mine. She could see seven of the Pleiades against my six. That left 239 that neither of us could spot, so I told her all about them. In detail, I'm afraid. Drawing on old examination memories, imprints of all-night muggings-up, I read her the news, at least some of which must have been out of date. I told her about the flare stars, the faint red dwarfs that brighten up and die down within months. She liked the idea of faint red dwarfs. I told her, correctly as it turned out, that it was still in question whether the reflective nebulae visible around the brighter stars were continuous gaseous expulsions or the tatters of the original nebula. I told her that this and every other properly framed question must have an answer, however deeply it might lie concealed. *Raffiniert ist der Herr Gott*, said Einstein, *aber boshaft ist er nicht.* God might be tricky but He isn't plain mean.

The Mole liked the idea of continuous gaseous expulsions. She said that they reminded her of Amanda's friend Susie, who did a foof during her Oxford entrance interview. This revelation almost wrecked the mood of cosmic rapture but I repaired it with an eloquent evocation of what she would be able to see in the Pleiades through even the most modest telescope: wisps and streaks of nebulosity, diamonds and sapphires, all the westering weeping she could wish. When she wanted to know what *that* meant, I recited the lines with no, repeat no, ulterior motive.

> *The weeping Pleiads wester*
> *And I lie down alone.*

She wasn't impressed, so I gave her Sappho's original. She was impressed with that: less by my Greek – which was Greek to her, and no more than a parroted recollection to me – than by my suggestion that Sappho was her poet. Hers and Penelope's. 'Was she pretty?' asked the Mole.

'Famously ugly. But beautiful within.'

I got a kiss for that, bringing my average up to one a week. At peace with myself, I was attracting luck. The lights went on and the stars went dim. She got very sleepy, so we went to bed. Together, for the first time. After so many walk-throughs the performance was surprisingly maladroit on my part, perhaps because I was drunk. I won't go into details because I honestly can't. I'm sure it was very nice. Since we had established long ago that I could never take possession of her, it was no conquest. A friendly match. She was patient with me and I was rewarded. As far as she was concerned, though she gave her standard squeal and even contrived to include my name, I could tell that it was nothing wonderful. I could tell from how she let me in, let me stay, let me continue. I was there on sufferance. There was no – how shall I put this? – seizure. Leaving aside the unthinkable possibility that I simply didn't excite her, I could only conclude that although she was made for men she had no great feeling for them. Call it a lack of grip. There would be no firmness, no friction, no fighting back. She was delicate down there, mesmerically so, so I closed my eyes and concentrated on pleasure that was all subtlety, nothing but nuance. It was about time. Before I knew her well, I would have said that she was giving me nothing. Now I could tell that she had given me myself. Compared with what I had been, I was a new man. I couldn't precisely count her eyelashes with my tongue, but with my left arm under her back and my right hand holding her left hand, I could kiss her folded fingers softly enough to tell her something about her own frailty. There was no other way to say thank you. Flesh is such an awful word in English, almost as harsh as it is in German. *Fleisch.* For the most fragile of all things. One summer's day in Prague, while Kafka was working on *Das Schloss*, he looked at the girls in their summer dresses, the form and pressure of their living bodies. *How short life must be*, he thought, *if something so flimsy can last a lifetime.* Afterwards I retired to my own bed, where I pretended that I could not hear her crying in hers. For a while, naked except for a towel around the waist, I stood on our balcony looking at the stars. Things had quietened down up there, but it was still all happening. The Old One just went on building his maximum break. Fat Man, you shoot a great game of pool.

The next morning was our last before we flew the coop. It was like leaving home. These rooms had seen, if not my greatest, then certainly my most conscious, happiness. Luckily the Mole had already dismantled nearly all the signs of her prodigious gift for nest-building. The empty bottles of oils and unguents that she had placed strategically to sweeten the air – she would even peel the sample strips of perfume-impregnated paper from glossy magazines and stick them to the edges of shelves – had all gone into the big grey plastic sack. From the railed altar above the bathroom sink, all my favourite votive offerings had been removed, including the centrepiece, her lime-green and gold badger-bristle Super

Duster blush brush. The sheets we had made love on and under were in the last laundry bag, to be picked up by Marie-Maria, whose open curiosity would at last be gratified. After doing most of the thinking and organising for both of us, the Mole turned to her personal packing, which naturally took ten times longer than mine. Out on the balcony I looked down at the beach, which was now supplementing its late afternoon appearances with a reasonable showing before noon. It was a cloudless day. On my face I could sense no breath of wind, but the waves were running high. The surfboards were out at the furthest line of breakers. The boards were triangles when the riders sat waiting, ellipses when they turned and paddled, curved slivers when they banked to either side. Back beyond them, windsurfers were slicing sideways along the unbroken swell or jumping from it into the air. The most adept of them pointed the board vertically before flattening out. One of them did a complete back somersault, board and all. I knew it must be Jean-Louis, though he was past the limit of my ability to pick out faces. So were the people on the beach, but one by one I could deduce the presence of almost everyone I had come to know. I could tell from their saintly attributes. The reeling little boy with a rectangle at the end of one arm; the older boy throwing a disc on to the water; the pink triangles beside the girl lying face down. All the coloured shapes had attached themselves to a narrative. The abstract painting had become a drama. Its absolute music undermined by the anecdotal, the *paysage* was *moralisé*. The bourgeoisie wants art to tell a story. I stood condemned. Yet I could not feel otherwise than elated. The story was too interesting. Eventually, by hard observation without instruments, I figured out why the prone Miss Pink Flippers had too many arms and legs. She was was lying on top of the supine Mr Nagoya, kissing him endlessly, as if trying to suck out the few too many teeth that made the man of her dreams less than perfect.

PART FIVE

The Pale Gates of Sunrise

Look at the stars! look, look up at the skies!
  O look at all the fire-folk sitting in the air!
  The bright boroughs, the circle-citadels there!
Down in dim woods the diamond delves! the elves'
      eyes!

The grey leaves cold where gold, where quickgold lies!
  Wind-beat whitebeam! airy abeles set on a flair!
  Flake-doves sent floating forth at a farmyard scare!
Ah well! it is all a purchase, all is a prize.

        Gerard Manley Hopkins, 'The Starlight Night'

WE CAME HOME TO A FLAT SO EMPTY THAT IT ECHOED like an air-raid shelter. Except for the Mole's cubby-hole, Chance's Barbican command post had been gutted. 'Why didn't he *tell* us?' The Mole was too shocked to weep. Lonely on the living-room floor, the olive drab Princess Line telephone extension gave its plaintive chirp.

'Why didn't you *tell* us?' asked the Mole into it. Chance was calling from Cinecittà. I left her talking and went to the nearest bathroom, in which precisely one towel had thoughtfully been left behind. When I came back, it was my turn to listen. Chance told me to look after her, as usual. Sometimes the difference between him and Jeffrey Chaucer was purely linguistic.

'I think I'm getting sick of this,' I ventured, feeling that some degree of protest was in order, if only to look good in front of the Mole. Or sound good: she was out on the balcony with her back to me.

'Only four more weeks of shooting left,' said Chance. 'Sorry, but I had to sell everything in a hurry. You can camp there for as long as you like. Use it as a base while you get back in touch with Cambridge. Transferring the tenancy will take an age.'

'Have *you* been in touch with Cambridge?'

'Take it easy and you can talk yourself back in.'

'What's happening in Rome?'

'Chaos. Heflin brought his own writer with him. Al felt his way into the role of an Italian nobleman by exercising the *droit de seigneur* on both daughters of the Italian finance minister. Doug wants a crucifixion scene so he can show his wrinkled old grey armpits again. Gus is on his yacht in Monaco trying to get Steph for a walk-on part so her old man will give us the palace for a free location for the pick-ups we're bound to need because half the cast are locked into their hotel rooms on the advice of their agents, waiting for cash in a paper bag. Go-Go's got no credit west of Singapore. The Grapeshot boys have got the US Securities and Exchange Commission steaming into them because they estimated their training films for the Israeli Army Catering Corps at an asset value higher than *Gone with the Wind*. Presley and Shir are such an item I can't get a set dressed or a word written.'

'What about Miss Wechsel?'

'Angelic so far. Too much of an amateur to realise how unprofessional she could be if she wanted to, thank God.'

'You sound as if you're having a wonderful time.'

'Am.'

'What am I supposed to do with the Mole?'

'She knows the score. I've got no time for her or anybody else. Help her see the bright side. She's off the hook.'

'I really think that's . . . '

'Got to go. Big party at Presley's when we get back. Be there. Could be my swan-song.'

The Mole helped me buy supplies and then, having packed up her stuff, disappeared in a taxi to her bolt-hole in College Hall. When she made her traditional visit to me twice a week, we slept together in her stripped room, now mine. There was no music to listen to, no television to watch. All we had was each other. The nicest, easiest love affair of my life – probably because we both knew it was going nowhere – it cost me nothing except the obligation, which I fulfilled gladly enough, to hear the chapters of her long essay. ('If I don't get an A for this,' she said after every second paragraph, 'I shall be very pissed off.') I paid her out with long avuncular lectures about her future with Ambrose. When she wasn't there, which was most of the time, I usually wasn't either. In a Ford Escort hired with a credit card which I was now wielding with renewed confidence, I made many a trip to Cambridge. Sometimes I dared to make the journey so late in the afternoon that I was asked to stay the night. It was autumn now. Night was starting to invade the day. When I left the M11, the Plough was already visible at the horizon, and the dishes of the interferometer were basket-work silhouettes against the pale stars. I would come off the motorway an exit too early, just to enjoy them. To my no longer jaded eye, they looked wonderfully romantic, like the radio telescopes in *Deserto Rosso* which the clueless Monica Vitti hadn't known the purpose of. 'They're for listening to the stars,' somebody told her. Lauren had never needed telling. We had seen that film together, in Naples, the year it came out.

Every morning we had read *La Stampa* over coffee. Translated by Lauren, professionally illuminated and framed, an extract from an article by Primo Levi hung on the wall of my study. The azure calligraphy was uncomfortably reminiscent of the RAF's book of the dead in St Clement Dane's, but the exhortation thrilled me still, even in my defeat.

THE POET-SCIENTIST

These messages from heaven are a challenge to our reason. It is a challenge we must accept. Our nobility as thinking creatures imposes it upon us. Perhaps the sky will no longer be part of our poetic heritage, but it will be, indeed already is, vital food for thought. It is possible that the human brain is a *unicum* in the universe; we don't know, and probably never will; but we know already that it is an object more complex and difficult to describe than any star or planet. Let us not deny it nourishment, or give in to the panic of the unknown. Perhaps it will fall to them, the students of the stars, to tell us what we have not been told, or have been told badly, by the philosophers and the prophets; who we are, where we come from, where we are going.

But this was an influence which neither Lauren nor I owed to the other. We both owed it to Chance's enthusiasm, which in those days had been unguarded. He worshipped Levi, not to mention Calvino and Montale. Long ago in Rome, on a winter's day when the fountains of the Piazza Navona were plump with ice, all three of us were shivering at an outside table when Pasolini walked past. Chance's efforts to stay casual made Lauren smile. She was on to him. I thought then that she loved him, and found out now that she always had.

'Yes, you can come back if you really must,' she said. 'We all miss you. God knows why. Don't hurry, though. Take your time. Get a picture of yourself. You're a jerk, a creep and a thorough shit.'

'Thanks.'

'But at least you're less like a bowl of jello than when you left.'

197

'I didn't leave. You threw me out.'

'You threw yourself out. But you have to understand this much. If that man ever calls by, I'm his for as long as he wants. I belong to him, body and soul. Have you got that straight?'

'Explain it to me again.'

'You were just so fucking casual about letting me know you preferred someone else to me. Because she was new. Because she was young. Because her prissy little English cunt could whistle 'Greensleeves'. Well, this is a taste of how it feels. I prefer Chance to you. He's a pain in the tail but I know who he is.'

'You're sure of that?'

'Yes. Even if he isn't.'

'Did you sleep with him?'

'One hundred thousand times.'

'Just now?'

'For as long as I've known you both. Without him I wouldn't have been able to stomach you for five minutes. How do you like *them* bananas?'

It was a measure of the distance I had travelled that I was merely crushed. Large sections of my forebrain continued to function. Helping Benjamin with the Amstrad instruction book, I heard every second question, and when we went to watch Donna dancing in the school ballet I figured out what the libretto was about long before the end. The *corps de ballet* represented the solar system, which had acquired a few anomalous recruits in order to give everybody something to be. Into the solar system danced my daughter, tentatively co-starring as Halley's Comet. The other co-star, more confident if less graceful, was meant to be a scientist. In a white lab coat and a horsehair fringed prosthetic bald head she was a ringer for Sir Bernard Lovell. Together they danced a *pas de deux* through the rings of Saturn, the moons of Jupiter, the Milky Way and the Magellanic Clouds. It transpired that Halley's Comet had come to warn mankind against the dangers of the atom, played by five little girls dancing around each other. Some of the costumes must have cost the children's mothers a week of work. The music, specially composed, owed much to Holst and more to *Chariots of Fire*. The whole thing was excruciating but my fixed smile never slipped. Afterwards one of the mothers asked when I would be back on television.

Not soon enough, was the answer. There was no series in prospect. Various offers of one-offs and guest appearances were there to be considered, but even if I accepted them all, it would not add up to a regular income; and a university post was out of the question, what with the academic world contracting faster than the universe was expanding. With Lauren's wealth looming over us I had never really been the breadwinner, but now there was no doubt of the fact, and the fact was rubbed in by her new career. She had gone back into the biology business in a big way: not as a research scientist – she had lost too many years for that – but as an entrepreneur. Half of her time was spent out at the Science Park, where she was a director in charge of marketing of a small but already flourishing bio-technology firm: the next thing after microchips. The other half of her time was spent across the Channel, where she used her languages to open doors. I was still too dazed to grasp what it was that they were making and selling. I had vague visions of an eyeball hopping along on one foot. When and if I took up the offer to come home permanently, I would obviously have to do my share of holding the fort, even though things seemed to be dauntingly well organised already. There was a live-in house-maid, for example. She was living in my study.

So back I went down the motorway to see producers, consider my options, and cuddle up to the Mole. If my behaviour strikes you as deplorably pluralist, I can only plead indecision. To bless my dumb luck would sound like arrogance. Anyway, I didn't see all that much of my protégée until the night of the film unit's homecoming. I saw more of Clive James, as it happened. Coming back from Safeway one evening, I ran into him jogging, or rather he ran into me. Stopping immediately, he complained of aching hamstrings, while seeming curiously reluctant to blame these injuries on the activity he was so fruitlessly pursuing. He invited me in for a drink. Curious to see his living conditions, I acquiesced. Approached by a staircase leading down from the podium level, his two-room bachelor pit, though devoid of luxury, was crammed with interest. Apart from a few pathetic items of furniture, it was nothing more or less than a combined, and surely uniquely comprehensive, portrait gallery and archive of Australian sporting stars. Down from the otherwise undecorated walls stared the cheaply framed faces of Frank Sedgman, Margaret Court, Keith Miller, Ray Lindwall, Neil Harvey, Dawn Fraser, Murray Rose, Lorraine Crapp, Jon and Ilsa Konrads, Lew Hoad, Ken Rosewall, John Newcombe, Rod Laver, Tony Roche, Jack Brabham, Kel Nagle, Greg Norman, John Landy, Hector Hogan and many more. Evidently torn from an old copy of *Pix*, the famous group-shot of Marjorie Jackson, Betty Cuthbert and Shirley Strickland with their arms around each other in Helsinki was crudely Sellotaped to the side of the television set. There was a bronze bust of Richie Benaud.

'Injuries decide everything, in the end,' said my host as he gingerly removed his past-it Pumas. 'Pat Cash's back could play the same role in modern Australian tennis history as Evonne Goolagong's ankle or Tony Roche's elbow.'

'Are you really that fascinated with all this stuff?' I was genuinely puzzled.

'Too right. Also it helps pay the alimony. A thousand words on the resurgence of Australian tennis goes down well anywhere.'

'But surely you made a fortune from the film?'

'Nar. I'll never see a dollar of that. A disaster, a disaster.' He smiled with undiluted pleasure. 'The bastard's really screwed himself this time. Afraid you'll have to drink this out of a mug. Did you see how they got my name wrong?'

'That's plenty,' I said hastily.

'Have you been invited to the function?'

I said yes, wondering if no might be a kinder answer.

'Me too,' he said, licking his lips and wiggling his bare toes. 'Suppose I'll have to go. Yeah, the bastard's really done it to himself this time.' For the next half hour he sang an uninterrupted aria on the subject of Chance's lost integrity. The awful thing was that I found it hard to disagree. Finally I escaped, using the good excuse that my Loseley individual acacia honey and stem ginger ice-cream was melting.

If these and other haruspications and rune-castings were right about Chance's film, there was no telling from the all-star wrap party, which took place, as advertised, at Presley Schaufenster's modest stash in Docklands. Her palace of images turned out to be even more vast than I had thought. There was a whole extra floor which I hadn't seen on my first visit. All done out in what looked like throwback high-tech, it could have been the final assembly shop for the Heinkel *Volksjäger*. Dressed to the nines among lengths of grey scaffolding made of some strangely inert substance like zerodur, the world and his wife looked out through an acre of clear glass at a square mile of smooth water whose far boundary had the outline, never completely seen from within, of the old city by night. The Piaggio seaplane in which Angélique and Jean-Louis had arrived floated prettily below. Ranged under sodium lights along the near side of the dock, the cars looked like a *concours d'élégance* waiting for the judges. I arrived sober and separately from our girl, but saw her shining among the crowd, the long hair – had Nikky been at it again? – hanging straight down the back of her black jersey classic with the bow bustle effect. She gazed adoringly at Chance as if nothing had happened. She waved airily to *me* as if nothing had happened. To stand out in a crowd like that, she had to be outstanding. In being so proud of her I was being proud of myself, of course: do you think I needed telling? And soon she would be gone.

If not precisely out of it, I felt a bit beyond it, that night. My mind was occupied with practical matters: money, work, lack of work, the possibility that my agent might be a madman, the challenge of my unanswered correspondence. But I had begun to deal with the backlog systematically. I even planned to send Gael a postcard. I was a model of conscientiousness. With one or two exceptions. Nobody here had much to do with me any more. On the other hand, they were grist to my mill. Returned to life, I was the universal observer. *Nihil humani alienum puto*. Limitless though finite, homogeneous and isotropic both in space and time, my field of study stretched before me until it came back to me: a labyrinth without impediment.

'Sartre desired me,' said Angélique. 'We women know these things. But I could not do that to Beauvoir.'

'She spent a lot of time telling me how the *literati* had lost their commitment to social justice,' shouted Nimrod Plooey.

'Next time I saw her was at St Moritz. She was taking a ride in the Aga Khan's helicopter.'

'And what were *you* doing at St Moritz?'

'Writing a poem about snow.'

'C. P. Snow?'

'Not the stuffed shirt. The stuff.'

'It's what I told Polanski,' said 'Zoom' Beispiel to Tim Stripling's left knee. 'Solve your image problem and you've solved your visa problem. You think he listened?'

'In Beijing they trust me,' said Sir Go-Go Chow, 'because I make their plopaganda movies at good plice.'

Eric was in charge of drinks. He had his hand and his hook full. Luckily Di and Fergie were there to help. They were absolutely marvellous. I helped too, for a while, and got to hear fragments of every conversation in all directions. As I toured, the fragments made up a sonic mosaic which nobody else would ever hear. It was a kind of semantic hyperspace, through which I could find my way only at the price of becoming lost.

'Don't you think Martin Amis looks like a character out of one of his own novels?' asked Samantha Copperglaze.

'He's *in* one of his own novels,' said Monty Forbes.

'How's that?'

'*Money*.'

'Is that why he did it? I should have thought he had pots by now.'

'No, it was *called* that. *Money*.'

'You mean *Success*.'

'No, there's another one called *Money*.'

'I missed that one. Must have been while I was away.'

'Where were you, darling?'

'Oh, I was here. But they put me away. In this place for sick people. Until I got better.'

'Victor and Elena I see last night in New York,' said Gus Disting. 'Mit dot rider Zubin Mehta. He don't look blind to me.'

'That's Ved Mehta.'

'Zubin he was called. You think I don't know Jewish names?'

I was briefly startled, until it seemed right, to see Veronica

Lilywhite sitting in a place of honour. Jean-Louis was kneeling in front of her, juggling three oranges. Suddenly it was four. I had learned enough about juggling to know that four was hard. Then he made it five. The applause was continuous.

'For you,' he shouted, as the oranges flew uncannily through one another's orbits. If Gloria had been there she would have gone to sleep. The spectacle of Veronica taking all this as her due was less nauseating than I would once have liked. Glory became her, the way mourning became Electra.

'Medawar was right,' somebody told someone else. 'Cambridge was bung full of clever people. But the scientists had something to be clever *about*.'

'I should have thought that was pure Snow.'

'Is that an American expression?'

'Not the stuff. The stuffed shirt.'

'Look, it all depends on which of the Yanks you openly ape, right? You're either a Bellow man or a Roth man. *He's* a Bellow man. *I'm* a Roth man.'

'With or without filter?'

'Stay out of this.'

'Do you think it's possible that Monty actually *screwed* Horowitz before Presley took her over?'

'Wouldn't put it past him. Capable of any perversion.'

'Then he's an Updike man.'

'That's not bad.'

'I'm working on a novel right now, and let me tell you it's got *none* of that stuff. It's got a straight story. It's got characters. The reader is definitely not invited to participate.'

'What's it called?'

'*Wuthering Heights*.'

'Didn't somebody write that?'

'I didn't say I was writing it. I said I was *working* on it. Writing an article about it.'

'I'd love to be there, but I have to be in Stockholm to see Ingmar.'

'Nolan pulled off the same double for years. The Aussies thought he'd come home but actually he lived in Putney. Same principle with Raquel Welch. The Yanks thought she was big in Italy. Italians thought she was big in America.'

'How is that the same principle?'

'Yeah, I suppose it isn't. Is this champagne, or does it just look, sound and taste like it?'

'I think it's Australian.'

'How can you tell?'

'It's giving me an accent.'

It was Bollinger, actually. Having sampled some of the merchandise myself by now, I was an increasingly contented traveller. No amount of inner peace, however, could compete with the outward radiance of Presley Schaufenster and Shir Horowitz. Presley's eyes were snowflakes tonight, her scintillating Corfu-blue get-up the result of some intense alliance between Claude Montana and a junk-yard. Shir had somehow acquired a charcoal-grey pin-stripe lounge suit which had once belonged to Pierre Laval. She had topped off her ensemble with a basin-crop haircut copied from the dominant member of the Three Stooges. As ungraceful as it was possible to be and only two-thirds the height of her companion, she yet outshone her. They were a double star, a new Antares.

'I'd love to be there, but I have to be in Hull to see Philip.'

'She owns her own publishing house, so she decides how much her authors get paid. She owns her own club, so she knows exactly how much they drink. When she owns her own clinic she'll know when they're drying out. She's starting her own country.'

'And every day she has lunch with Carmen.'

'They're starting their own world.'

'Soon you'll be a second-class citizen if you stand up to pee.'

'Get it cut off now.'

'The main reason Europe can't produce a new Caruso is the shortage of synagogues.'

'Caruso wasn't Jewish, was he?'

'No, but every time he came to a new city he'd go to the synagogue on Friday night and listen to the cantor. Especially in Poland. It was Polish Jewish cantors that taught him how to make it seem effortless.'

'Buy anything by Raphael.'

'Can't afford it.'

'Not him. Her. Sarah Raphael. Amazing.'

'Still can't afford it.'

'Nobody in New York lives like this.'

'Iris, Rupert, may I split you two up?'

'No.'

'Do I have to read Bergson to read Proust?'

'Good God, no. Um, to give you an, um, ah, a short answer, er, it's true that, um, Proust's, ah, theory of duration is *based* on Bergson's, but, um, Proust's theory of duration isn't what's interesting about Proust. In fact, ah, it's only when the general idea, um, *crops up*, ah, shows above the surface, er, that he's ever boring or a tiny bit super, ah, superficial. The, um, *specific observations*, ah, are what make him so, um, so interesting psychologically. And, um, of course, er, in every other, ah, way. I mean, Heavens, um, Bergson was dated even at the, ah, time. About time. I mean, ah, his theories about time were thought pretty unscientific even then. You should read Revel. What's his first name? Um, Jean-François. That's it. Jean-François Revel. Tells you all about that in his little book, what's it called? *Pourquoi des philosophes*? Um, not that you need to read him either, although he's um, ah, a marvellous Proustian, by the way. But *Proust*, um, is the man you need to read about Proust. It's ah, it's all er, it's all *in* there. That's the um, short answer.'

'Thanks, Terry. What's this we're eating?'

Food had appeared. Now Di and Fergie really came into their own. All Falklands factor and stiff upper smile, they were more marvellous than ever. Yet not even they could have coped unaided. The Mole had volunteered to assist, and assisting *her* was the legendary Amanda, an asteroid I now glimpsed at long last, as I was on the point of leaving the system of which she formed a part. New groups formed to eat, but nothing stopped the talk.

'I'd love to be there, but I have to be in Rome to see Federico.'

'Presley's doing the design and I'm doing the words.'

'What's the subject?'

'Mussolini. But what's really gonna make it fantastic is Tomlinson's music. It's got *nothing*. Not even repetition. Beside Tomlinson, Philip Glass is Verdi.'

'Who's singing Mussolini?'

'It's a problem, because he has to sing his last aria hanging upside-down. Pavarotti won't touch it.'

'It was a real disaster when those two bores were allowed to define the terms of the argument. Snow was a mediocrity in both cultures and Leavis's brainwave about there being only one culture should have been sufficiently discredited by having a vengeful maniac like him as its representative. There *is* only one culture, but science is part of it. Always has been. No, wait a second. *Listen*. What do you think Lucretius was up to? And you ought to read Queneau's long poem about cosmology. Calvino translated it. Brilliant.'

'The same Queneau as *Zazie dans le métro*? Come on.'

'He's a genius, I promise. But the point to grasp is that there *is no division*. Nothing so simple, nothing so comforting. Instead there's the eternal requirement to explain, to be clear, to create understanding, before it's too late.'

'Before the bombs go off?'

'Before the humanities lapse into barbarism. Pseudo-science is killing them, and it won't go away until everyone knows what real science is.'

'I was in Prague trying to write a novel. Rather intriguing structure with five interweaving plots. But I couldn't meet any native Czechs. Spent the whole time talking to Roth, Bellow, Updike and Stoppard.'

'I'd love to be there, but I have to be in Tokyo to see Akira.'

Accompanied by a surge of not-quite-random synthesised sounds which I correctly guessed to be music from the film, the general light went down and the zerodur scaffolding lit up in various colours. It must have been made of optical fibre. All those featherweight pipes were suddenly filled with homogenised light. Scattered and bunched through the multidimensional polychromatic grid, the stellar presences did not pause for a second in the sending of their signals. Everyone talked more loudly than ever except Heflin Dustmann and Al Massimo. Separately, in widely divided parts of the limitless expanse, the two singularities talked as quietly as was possible while still making a detectable noise. Each had his own tightly clustered audience leaning inwards, unable to escape, sucked into the near silence of the event's enormous gravity. Talking very quietly is a Los Angeles star-status shibboleth which ought not to be valid in London, but there is a magnitude of stardom which collapses all barriers, bending light, pulling space into a curve. Out beyond the event horizon of the black hole superstars, the hubbub became a *tohu bohu*, a *brouhaha*, a corroboree.

'It depends whether you put more emphasis on rhythm than on content. Rhythmically, the best book title of all time is *The Deerslayer*.'

'Hemingway always avoided the initial "the". He would have called it *Deerslayer*. Would have been better.'

'Why?'

'The "the" sounds like nothing. Name me one good title starting with "the".'

'*The Long Voyage Home. The Mills of the Kavanaghs. The Lady's Not for Burning. The Big Sleep.*'

'All right, name me *six* good titles.'

'*The Fountainhead.*'

'Worst book ever written.'

'Good title, though.'

'*Those Without Shadows.* Wonderful title.'

'Doesn't count if it's in French.'

'It's not *in* French.'

'Still *sounds* like French. No mistaking that translated sound.'

'*A Certain Smile.* Wonderful title. Sounds perfectly English.'

'*Mine Own Executioner.*'

'*Absalom, Absalom.*'

'No, that's terrible. Repetitions are invariably terrible.'

'*Multitudes, Multitudes.*'

'No such book.'

'Is. Book that one of the officers writes in *The Caine Mutiny*.'

'*Bhowani Junction.*'

'*Manhattan Transfer*. Ideal title. Still sounds wonderful even if you don't know what it means. Great rhythm.'

'What about *The Sun Also Rises*?'

'Terrible title. Nobody knows where the emphasis goes. Does the sun also *rise*, or is it also the *sun* that rises?'

'No, I meant that it starts with a "the".'

'It's the Australian expatriate extravaganza style. They *all* write like that. Jennings, Jenolan, Huggins, Bartelski. Walter Waiter. Even that poor bastard James. Romaine Rand *talks* like that. So does Dave Dalziel. So does Waldo Laidlaw. They all pile it on. Kangaroococo.'

'Oz Pizzazz. Razzmatozz.'

'Exactly.'

'Can't see it, myself. They might think the way Mel Gibson looks, but they talk the way John Newcombe thinks.'

'Exactly.'

'Who's that angry guy with the thick neck who looks like Bob Hoskins?'

'It's Bob Hoskins.'

'OK, your starter for ten. Who wrote: *Each man starts with his first breath/To devise shrewd means for outwitting death*.'

'James Cagney.'

'How the Hell did you know *that*?'

'I was in New York last night and I saw the same obituary you did.'

'I'd love to be there, but I have to be in Sydney to see Sidney.'

Chance was disentangling himself from some invitation offered by Eva Brownlow. He had Imogen Wechsel standing as close to him as she could without touching. The beauty of her face was beyond words. Intersecting it above the eyes was a headache band like the belt of dust across the galaxy NGC4594 in Virgo. She smiled nicely when I told her this.

'Good to see you back on form,' said Chance, cutting in.

'Is the film all done?'

'Christ no. Pick-ups'll take months. Heflin's being very nice about it. If we give him the whole picture outright he'll do the dub. How did your diary turn out?'

'It's practically a book.'

'Let me see it. Week after next. Ring me on this number.' He wrote it down on the back of my hand. While he did so, I noticed how fleshless he looked at the jaw-line. There was less of the Denis Healey effect. Stress must have slimmed him.

We drifted apart. I curved away in search of other wonders. Louis XV called Messier the Comet Ferret. The piped music of Tomlinson Kleinbottle gave way to something you could dance to without acquiring Evonne Goolagong's ankle or Pat Cash's back. I watched the Mole dancing with Ambrose. Although Angélique and Jean-Louis drew a bigger crowd, I preferred the two youngsters. The Mole was just drunk enough to overcome *pudeur* and strut her stuff. Her dancing was eloquent. One idea followed another without repetition. If she ever learned to write like that, the world would hear from her. As she bumped and ground in a tight circle with her wagging left hand held high, its thumb and forefinger formed the secret Masonic sign, intelligible only to me, which meant 'Yes, I am wearing no knickers.' Ambrose was the ideal foil. With his right hand held out trembling in front of him as if he were fly-fishing with an invisible rod, he just stood there looking thin, scruffy and handsome in his frayed trainers, pipe-cleaner jeans and damaged bomber jacket with the peeling painted Stars and Stripes on the back. Had that same jacket kept some previous young occupant warm as he waited, with the other survivors of his crew, in a goat-herd's hut in Valtellina for the guide who would take them above the tree-line in the dark and through the deep snow to Switzerland? No, it had not. It had been manufactured very recently in Taiwan. *Das Kunstwerk im Zeitalter seiner technischer Reproduzierbarkeit.* The work of art in the age of its technological reproducibility. Walter Benjamin really *had* waited for guidance across the border, despaired of its coming, and killed himself. The young men in their bomber jackets had arrived too late to save him, and now they, too, were retreating into death. Only their images flew on.

Breaking in with a proprietorial smile, I corralled the Mole alone against the window, looking out, my guardian arm around her shoulders. With her sharp eyes she could just see the angel of justice on top of the Old Bailey. I helped her to remember the Virgin shining on the rock. It was my time for the lecture about the comets. ' . . . it's an event, Mole. A mass extinction. The comet storm comes ripping in and kills just about every living thing. Happens every 26 million years. You can tell from the ocean that there have been eighteen of them already. Every time it happens there's an evolutionary jump. A saltation. Or anyway, that's what the saltationist evolutionists think. The gradualists think otherwise. They argue very well, very sanely.

But they can't argue the comets away. Because the comets have these black skins. You see, according to Hoyle and Wickrama-singhe, the parent molecule for cometary radicals is an organic polymer. Interstellar dust being biological. And Shirwan Al-Mufti, by lab spectrocsop, sorry, lab spectroscopy, predicted that cosmic infra-red sources at huge distances would show the signature of micro-organisms. The first spectra of the galactic centre confirmed this. And now we know that Halley's Comet is as black as Egypt's night. Can't get away from it, Mole. Black comets gave us your white skin. That's how we got from a blob on a rock to you. A gradualist evolun, a gradualist evolutionist would die rather than admit it, but it's . . . '

'God almighty.' There was a tear on her cheek. I was moved. I didn't realise I'd been *that* impressive.

'God all bloody mighty,' she went on. 'The way you bash my ear about your things. And when I tell you about *my* things you shift from one foot to the other.'

'Hold hard,' I said feebly. 'I'm usually lying down.'

'Nobody except Penelope ever really listens to me. And *she* doesn't listen to me.'

'She will. She will.'

'Have you *listened* to how boring that Imogen is? Has *he*? None of you can hear a thing. Eyes bigger than your stomach, the lot of you. Oh, shit. Shit shit *shit*.'

Give me credit for finding her distress so hard to bear. I resolved to do something. The supreme sacrifice. Her head on my shoulder told me that I wasn't really hated. Just not very much loved.

'You got that from me,' I said.

'What?'

'That word. Ear-bashing.'

'Oh, you're in my life, all right. If you want to be. But sometimes I miss her so much I think I'll die.'

And of course we couldn't have that. The Mole and Ambrose left not long after. People drifted away, yet somehow the party declined to thin out. Perhaps my apprehension of it was swelling to fill the gaps. But no, the general drift was towards elsewhere. As the stars in the Taurus stream move from all over the sky towards their point of convergence in the Hyades, everyone was making progress towards the door. But where *was* the door? I must have missed it. I was helping Di and Fergie to collect the plates and glasses. They were saving for their holiday in Val d'Isère. Last year they had gone as Supertravel chalet girls. This year they wanted to have some fun, OK? Finally they went home in their little car to Whistler's Walk in Battersea, and I was left there with Eric. He had a cigar in his hook and much to impart about his favourite subject.

' . . . it's his hands, every time. He always gets into the character through the hands. What about the way he checks the magazines of his grease-gun in *Hell is for Heroes*, remember that bit? Two magazines taped together with gaffer tape, remember that? The way he shakes the shotgun cartridge beside his ear in *The Magnificent Seven* to see if it's properly packed. Spins the chamber of his long-barrelled Colt, same picture. Checks the back-sight on his Lee-Enfield in *The Sand Pebbles*. Whacking that baseball into his catcher's mitt in *The Great Escape*. Best scene in *Bullitt* isn't the car chase – terrific though that is, mind. It's when him and Dalgetty are going through the mystery man's baggage. The way he riffles through the packed gear as if it was cards. Magic. And what about the *real* cards in *The Cincinnati Kid*? How he just touches them when they're lying face down. And how he holds that coin before he tosses it against the wall. That's why the one role he could never play was Thomas Crown. Nothing to do with his hands except fly that glider. His hands do the talking all the way up to *The Getaway*. Some people say Ali McGraw did him in, but you can tell from how he didn't use his hands any more that he was sick. I can't watch *Tom Horn*. Just can't watch it. Tragic. That was how I knew it was all over. When he started hiding his hands. But up till then he was beautiful. What about *Le Mans*, when he had nothing showing but his eyes? Told you about that before, didn't I? Right, wasn't I? No wonder the girls didn't go and see it. But I was watching his hands on that steering wheel. He was always like that, always. Right back to *The War Lover*. The way he pulled the throttle levers in the B-17 . . . '

As Eric droned on relentlessly towards sunrise, I gradually realised that I was in the presence of my superior. Here was a true theory of acting, based entirely on properly observed detail. *God*, someone had said, *is in the details*. The vaunted philosophical opposition between the particular and the general does not, or at any rate should not, exist in science. By that criterion, Eric was much more of a scientist than Roland Barthes had ever been. No structuralist, Eric reserved his concern for the living fact, the *punctum* impregnated with personality. Barthes would have seen two or three Steve McQueen movies and said something glibly arcane about capped teeth. Eric had seen everything his hero had ever done and had penetrated to the underlying truth that made the obvious significant. Barthes had been knocked down and killed by a car. Perhaps Eric had been driving it.

'Spend much time in Paris?' I asked casually.

'Can't stand the place. Only good time I ever had there was when I saw *The Blob*. You know he was called Ste*ven* McQueen in them days? With an "n"?'

'No, I didn't know that.'

Like Plato's symposium we had been overtaken by the dawn. As the Shostakovich Piano Quintet started again on the hidden sound system – the strings and the keyboard reconciled at last, now that I had come back across the water – I looked down at Jean-Louis's seaplane, which had rocked noticeably for several hours after he and Angélique had climbed aboard. What had he been doing to her down there, and what with? Now it was still. There was not a ripple on the water. Sunlight went past me westwards into the city. Tower Bridge was an empty frame as the sky undarkened. *The pale gates of sunrise*, wrote James Joyce, of all people. As I explained to Eric, this was a synopsis of what will happen when the universe ends. The sky will grow lighter as the stars are wiped out through a long morning. In a paradox that no living creature will be there to experience, when night falls on the stars it will look like dawn.

In Cambridge the following week I bumped into Penelope. Knowing that she had come up early to read under supervision or else get ploughed, I would have tracked her down soon enough, but by a nice coincidence out of Anthony Powell she came coasting down Castle Hill on her bicycle at the very moment when I exited the paper shop where I had been settling the bill so that we could go on having the *Sunday Times* ripped to pulp by being pushed through the front door in one piece. As the traffic lights changed and she came to a halt, I could give myself no points for recognising her. It was only surprising that Hunt, Millais and Rossetti didn't come running down the hill after her. I jay-walked through the traffic and introduced myself. 'Oh, hello,' she said, barely audibly. 'I already knew what you looked like. Saw you on that science thing.' Seemingly depleted by the effort of saying all this, she looked at the ground on the right side of her front wheel. Her hands fiddled with her bell, brake handles and the empty bracket for a headlamp. Compared to the Mole, she was big-boned, even a touch acromegalic at the extremities. The seraphic face was on a large scale. Probably it had to be. For a nose to register as dead straight, it has to go on for a while.

'Look,' I said, 'I have to talk to you about Antonia.'

'All right. Talk now.'

'All right. God knows there's not a lot to say. It's simple, really. She can't understand why she always has to write the first letter. Always has to arrange the meeting. She's done nothing to deserve that.'

'I know,' murmured Penelope. Having grown tired of looking at the ground on the right side of her front wheel, she looked at the ground on the left side: a revolutionary shift of viewpoint.

'No, you don't know. You'll look all your life and never find a friend as good. You're using up the world's resources of gold as if it was lead.'

'I know.' The lights changed but mercifully she did not start riding. While cars went past her, she stood there engaged on fundamental research into the trigger of her bicycle bell. The ball of her thumb checked it for texture. Yes, it was some kind of metal.

'She misses your friendship,' I said, scarcely daring to break the sacred hush.

'It's . . . difficult,' Penelope managed to articulate. 'We were so far apart and I had all these new friends. By the time I realised how shallow they were compared with her, I'd let things slide too far. I suppose I got . . . embarrassed.' I could tell this was the biggest speech of her life. Her chest was heaving.

'Just get in touch,' I said, trying not to sound brisk. 'She'll take care of the rest. She's a very capable girl.'

'I know.'

It was time to let her go, but the lights changed to red again. She occupied the time by checking a brake cable between thumb and forefinger. A slow glance earthward on each side of her front wheel confirmed that the roadway was still there. Yes, there was more of it under the back wheel too. Finally, having run out of vectors in which to avoid my gaze, she looked at me. Her eyes were stunning; helpless and powerful at the same time, like those of an enchanted rabbit which could make a car dip its headlights. 'All right?' I said cleverly.

'All right,' she replied. ˋ

'You know where she is?'

'I know.'

Then the lights went green again and she cycled off. I watched her over the hump of Magdalene bridge. Young men whistled at her only if they were in groups. On their own, they had that stricken look.

A week after that, I reported to Albany as ordered. I had never been there before, but found it easily enough by going to Hatchard's first and then crossing the road. Imogen Wechsel's set of rooms, which presumably her family was paying for, had been done out by one of those interior decorators who comb through about five centuries of luxury, picking out everything that will harmonise. Vertically striped cloth covered the walls and variously framed pictures covered the cloth. A Dibbs Buckley drawing of Chance, and his portrait painted by Jeffrey Smart, were among them, as if they had been there a long time. Perhaps they had: I hadn't noticed either of them at the Barbican, and in fact had last seen the portrait in Tuscany, the day it was completed. Chance indicated that Imogen was just about to leave. Dressed in some caped and hooded creation against the autumn chill, she looked literally divine, as if the Virgin Mary, bound for exile in Egypt, had been kitted out by Issey Miyake.

'You be OK?' asked Chance solicitously.

'Yes, I can make it,' she said, staring at him as if to commit his features to memory, in case she was kidnapped. Then, with

214

a brave uplifting of the chin, she turned and strode out, shutting the oak door behind her.

'Only going to Fortnum's,' said Chance. 'Somewhere between forty and fifty yards. But she likes to play a scene. Got the book?'

'It's not actually a *book*,' I said, proferring my revamped diary.

'Should bloody well hope not. Can't have you doing one of those straight off.' He leafed through my manuscript, pausing occasionally to read a paragraph. 'There'll never be a movie of *this*, thank Christ.' The bookshelves, I noticed, enshrined some of his best treasures. They couldn't have been Imogen's. 'Let me keep this,' he said. He didn't say much else. When I asked him how the film was going, he told routinely amazing stories about Gus Disting's use of digitalis at critical moments. For once in my life I didn't listen to him very hard. I couldn't believe that the film was important. Nothing he could now cause to happen was as interesting as what was happening to him. I had been the faint dwarf component, Sirius B to his Sirius A. But now, when I looked at him, *he* seemed to be growing faint. His jaw-line, I could now see for certain, had been neatened surgically. That explained the Swiss clinic. I was as embarrassed as if he had taken off his shirt to reveal a tightly laced corset, or expressed a wish that I should address him as Your Royal Highness. It was strange to see him stroke the angle of his jaw as he read. What did he feel?

'Is this your official residence now?' I asked.

'Moggy thinks so. But I might have to move on.'

The next big move, however, was made by me. I was in Cambridge when one of my sisters phoned from Sydney to say that my mother had died suddenly. No illness, just old age: out like a light. So I flew out of the gathering English autumn into the dazzle of the Australian spring. My sisters took care of the funeral. It was my job to sell the house. There was no prospect of keeping any money. It would take a good sale just to pay the debts. The house should have been sold long ago, but she wouldn't have understood.

When I told Chance I was going out there, he kindly gave me permission to use his flat in McMahon's Point. The view of the city at night was stupendous. There was, however, a price tag. Chance was selling the place to raise cash for post-production. So I ended up supervising two complete sets of real-estate transactions. At least I had somewhere to live. I could never have faced moving back into my old room. All my old stuff was still in it, starting with *The Modern Marvels Encyclopaedia* and ending with my University Medals, which in a fit of bravado I had left behind when I sailed away to conquer the world. Now their hardwood mountings looked to me like the very confirmation of mediocrity. Every day I caught the little ferry from McMahon's Point over to the Quay and then caught the bus out past Rushcutter's Bay and up the hill. I could have hired a car but the trip across the water was too refreshing to miss. It could have been that at that juncture I was subconsciously inclined to renew my acquaintance with the amniotic fluid. Freud would have known. Everything he ever published was up there on the shelves among my father's library.

'Dr Korth?' asked the punctilious young man from the antique book dealer's. He must have been given a key.

'Court. I changed the name.'

'Oh yes. Naturally.' He looked about him with an air of appreciation that I could tell was unfeigned. 'Are you *sure* you don't want to send the whole lot to Europe and break it up there? In Munich, say?'

'I'm sure.'

'Most of it will end up there anyway. No Australian public library would want to pay so much for reading copies and there aren't many new private collectors with these interests.'

'No. You do it all.'

'Your father must have been a close friend of Zweig, judging from the inscriptions.'

'An admirer. He was very young at the time.'

'You're aware that just those Peter Altenberg first editions would fetch high prices in Vienna?'

I was. It was very nice of him. Always shaded from the ruinous sunlight by my mother's peachy curtains, the books looked as if they had been printed yesterday. Most of them inscribed by the author in terms of affection, every book that mattered up to the Nazi seizure of power in Germany and the

Anschluss in Austria was present and perfect, the buckram lustrous, the embossed gold glittering. Paper wrappers weren't even chipped.

'He must have handled them like a jeweller,' said the dealer. 'That's what he was, really.'

He had been, in a way. My father was the crystallographer who pioneered the artificial opal. His version wasn't quite as convincing as the Gilson synthetic opals are now. With the Gilson, you can't spot the fakery until you get it under a proper microscope and see that tell-tale lizard-skin effect of the polygonal cellular structure. You could rumble Dad's opal with a magnifying glass. But few people carry magnifying glasses to parties, so his patent made him a fortune. The artificial opal was the second bright idea of his life. The first bright idea had been to get out of Europe in good time. Much older than my mother, he persuaded her to abandon first her orthodoxy and then her roots. They said goodbye to it all. Everything was left behind except the culture. The crushing culture. My sisters escaped most of that, but I, arriving last, copped the lot.

When I saw my music stand, still there in the middle of my room, my palms broke into a sweat. It reminded me of my first day at Cranbrook. I was sent there in our chauffeured Chrysler Imperial and I thought I would die of shame. For a long time I couldn't look at that car: a great pity, because it was easily the most elegant imported American car of the late 1950s. Ours was emerald green. The egg-shaped ruby tail-lights were attached to the top of the tail fins by chromium brackets. You had to have a chauffeur, or people would break them off while the car was parked. Even in Australia, there was envy. Stendhal called envy the third force, but I can't remember if he said what the other two were.

So you get to hear about my background at the moment of its dissolution. Honestly, I would have put it first if I'd thought it mattered. The last thing I want to perpetrate is any kind of technical trick. The same applies to Chance's origins, which were the polar opposite of mine. But you can have polar opposites only on the same planet. He came from a long way out in the Western Suburbs: somewhere like Panania or Revesby. His family name was Janilowitz or something like that. Not

Jewish: quite the contrary. His old man was a Latvian *Wehr-macht* draftee who managed to surrender westwards after a long walk. The first time Chance came to dinner in our house – it was my freshman year at university – he revealed these facts while drinking our wine as if it was water. My mother turned thoughtful, but I think she was just afraid he might pass out.

As far as I know, the McMahon's Point flat was the last piece of property in Chance's global village. By the time I had finished all the arrangements, mine and his, it was almost Christmas. Back in Cambridge, there were scenes verging on the festive. I gave my presents and even received some in return. I got a letter from the Mole, announcing her forthcoming engagement to Jeffrey Chaucer. Half-way through January, term started again and I was able to phone her in College Hall. 'But Jeffrey is a schmuck!' I protested. 'This is a marriage of convenience.'

'So it would have been with Ambrose,' she said, as if explaining something.

'So why are you getting married at all?'

'Well, I'm quite ordinary *really*. I think Ambrose quite likes Penelope, you know. He's such a dreamer, and she's perfect for that. It would all work out nicely, if that happened. I don't suppose it will.'

It didn't, quite. The Mole and Jeffrey did get married, but Penelope and Ambrose are just friends. Not long after the Mole graduated with First Class Honours, she and Jeffrey drove up from their new house in Dorking to be our guests for dinner in Cambridge. Lauren arranged it: her firm was calling Jeffrey in as a consultant on their computerised accounting, which is very complicated when it gets down to paying for individual cells. At dinner by candlelight, the highly *soignée* Mole impressively carried off the behavioural challenge of having known me well but not all *that* well. Her good influence on Jeffrey was already apparent. Several times he stopped talking about organic computers and put on a show of being interested in what someone else said. He made about a dozen references each to Olympia and Biarritz but Lauren had no cue to look long-suffering if the Mole seemed unflustered. Not that it mattered: for Lauren, this was no question of jealousy. I had ceased to deserve it. I was jealous about Jeffrey, but shortly afterwards I met the Mole in the Barbican conservatory for the first of our now traditional quarterly jungle strolls, followed by lunch *tête-à-tête* at Le Mistral in Smithfield. She put my mind at rest.

'Are you seeing Penelope?'

'All the time. It's marvellous. Dear sweet Jeffrey doesn't mind a bit.'

'Are you going to have a baby?'

'I expect so. After I get my PhD.'

'Are you really going to let Jeffrey be the father of your child?'

'Well, Penelope can't, can she? Don't be such a stick-in-the-mud. And stop leaving all the Roquefort to last. You're supposed to eat it *with* the walnuts.'

'Are you still bossing me about?'

'It's my way of saying thank you.'

'What for?'

'For bringing her back to me. She's a bit hopeless, you know. Fancy having to be *told*.'

'Is it as good as before?' Prurient question, but I had to know.

'Let me think.' She thought for a while, chewing. She swallowed. Then she closed her eyes for a few seconds before opening them wide straight at me and fluttering her eyelids with maximum histrionics, these signs of lewdness being counterpointed by a ladylike pursing of the lips. She can make me smile even when my heart hurts like a finger crushed in a car door.

And there, for the purposes of this narrative, I have to leave her: still in my life, but further from me than ever. She misses Chance terribly, I know, but if *he* was never the centre of her existence, imagine how much less I was, and am. I will never know what she and Penelope are really like together. I wouldn't know even if I was there beside them. Nobody can see feeling. In my mind's eye they flare up when they touch. They light the room. My picture of them doing so is the purest thought I have. How their passionate involvement with one another will turn out in the long term is anybody's guess. Perhaps it's already a back number, now that our permissive age is on the turn, and life, which had been a bad movie about men with half-shaves holding machine guns, becomes a worse movie, about the killer virus. I suppose a lot depends on how Jeffrey behaves when he's off evaluating edible calculators in Japan, and on what Penelope's male lovers, if she decides to take any, get up to when they aren't bombarding her with sonnets. There are such a lot of bugs about. They're multiplying as I write. Apart from that, I don't see how the two girls can catch anything from each other except tenderness. I feel fear when I think of them, but it is not fear *of* them. It is fear *for* them, and the world they live in, its terrible simultaneity. At the very moment when they kiss, some girl in Chile is being violated with a cattle prod. In my imagination, the two lovers embrace to the melodic pulse of the greatest thing I know, the *adagio* of the Schubert String Quintet in C. Perhaps my imagination is overdoing it. But when I conjure up my mental video of their innocent heads thrown back in pleasure, I can't shake the similarity of that image to the most oppressive emblem the real world offers, that of innocent heads thrown back in pain. I am not tempted by the resemblance into even a brief flirtation with the idea that the two things might be related. In my belief, there is no connection, no matter how deep you go. The one is the essence of benevolence, the other of evil. The difference between consent and duress is not one of degree. No militant feminist can tell me that for a man to rape a woman merely lays bare the politics of his love for her. Nor can any military sadist tell me that the same woman really wants to be outraged. Love and rape are not two points on a continuity: they are fundamentally opposed, the one the epitome of co-operation, the other of domination. The friendship between those two young ladies is an article of my religion. Nevertheless there is always a moment when a man seeks to make himself indispensable. It does him good to be dispensed with; to know for certain that somewhere else, by someone else, the mystery is being attended to without him. 'Not only queerer than we suppose,' said J. B. S. Haldane about the universe, 'but queerer than we *can* suppose.' He was more right than he knew.

The rough cut of the film was a surprise. Chance showed it to me in a small preview theatre in Wardour Street. He left me alone in there a few minutes after the start and came back a few minutes before the end, so for most of the running time I was free to lie back in the absurdly plush armchair and be stunned. Every frame looked fabulous. Imogen Wechsel was clearly going to be the biggest sensation since Nastassia Kinski. Chance's own performance was a testament not only to cosmetic surgery but to his love of language. The film looked like *Diva, Mephisto* and Carlos Saura's *Carmen* all rolled into one. But that was just it. All it did was look like something. It didn't sound like anything. Heflin Dustmann and Al Massimo could scarcely be heard. Engaged in a knock-down, drag-out competition to see who could speak more softly, they made sounds that were all amplitude, like Sylvester Stallone blowing bubbles. Except when Chance himself was talking, and not always then, the film had no voice. He had given himself away. 'It's tremendous,' I said when the lights went up. 'But you're wasting your time.'

'Wasn't much of that left anyway.' He said it abstractedly, leafing through my manuscript as he had done when I saw him last. 'I'd like to have one last crack at a novel but I'm short of a story. Can I use yours?'

'There's nothing *I* can do with it. I'd only get thrown out again.'

'What I hoped you'd say.'

The film got murdered when it came out a year later. Richard Toole, recently appointed editor of the tabloid he had written gossip for under a shorter version of his first name, wrote a full-page editorial blaming Chance's self-indulgence for the current collapse of the British film industry. Toole's grammar had been in better shape since he had risen to a position where his subordinates could be given the task of writing his signed pieces for him, but on this issue his feelings were so strong that he expressed himself personally.

The oh-so-famous Chance Jenolan (I had to ask several young things around the office befor I found his name rhyming with Marc Bolan) has finally flaunted one rule too many, it seems. Already cursed with chronic unemployment in the arts field, Mr Jenolan always was one more Aussie expatriot than Britain needed. Do we need *any* of

221

them? Its been a mute point up to now, but arguably it should be hauled out of the airing cupboard into the cold light of day. If the cobbers think their dingoes are so dinkum, we'll keep Dundee and they can have the crocodiles! No offence, sports, but that's how a lot of us feel here in the land you once were glad enough to call home.

The young, however, took to the film as if it were *The Rocky Horror Picture Show*, no doubt because the news of Chance's demise fuelled his legend. How the book will do is another question. Presumably the unabated interest in his disappearance won't hurt it. Joni Dankworth, who has kindly agreed to be my agent, assures me that the manuscript indeed exists. She says he wrote it in a tearing hurry but with no other aim than to have a hit. He told her that he wanted to provide for his first wife and their children. When she asked him why he was talking as if his life was over, however, he just laughed.

My own guess is that he's still laughing, but I have to admit that in the preview theatre he gave me a large hint about his plans. 'I might have to go and join Harold,' he said. I thought he meant Harold Pinter, and that he was going to write an enigmatic book. I was fairly sure that he didn't mean Harold Lloyd. Harold in Italy? It didn't occur to me that he meant Harold Holt, the Australian prime minister who left his clothes folded on the beach and disappeared, having given himself, presumably, to the sea and the sharks.

Chance left his clothes folded on a beach in Rio, or so the headlines said. It was my first reason for having doubts. Stories about the virus started immediately. Angélique had a blood test on French television but the rumours only accelerated. It was said – it is still said, and unless he comes back it will always be said – that he had gone where Liberace plays the piano. Some say that that was why he had his face fixed: he made himself perfect to meet his fate, like Gelsey Kirkland for Balanchine, or Mishima for the sword. Far from believing any of that, I could never bring myself to believe he had left us at all. His quick fade had all the signs of a *coup de théâtre*. Any clothes left folded on Copacabana beach would be worn five minutes later by the winner of a pitched battle between muggers. Chance hated Rio. He always called it a bad place to drown yourself, because there was no choice. The surf was such a killer that there was no prospect of swimming out in a dignified manner to meet your doom. Chance was a great one for dignity.

Recently I was riding a Ski-doo across an Antarctic snowfield in search of meteorites, which lie around down there like chocolate chips in lemon ice-cream. If my producer had had his way, I would have been shouting a piece to camera as I bounced along, but nowadays, with my duty clear, I am a bit better at saving my dignity while making sense of the script. Popular science isn't my second string any more. It's my calling, so I try to do it well. Having insisted on doing the words as a voice-over later on, I was free to think, lulled by the howl of the motor. Somehow I knew that Chance was still alive. He was hiding out in the only place anybody can. He hadn't done a T. E. Shaw or a B. Traven. He had gone home. He was back there in the Western Suburbs, getting ready to start again. Like a character in *Dallas* he would return in the body of another actor. He would never voluntarily give up the power to make things happen.

'For both our sakes I'll have to fiddle with this a bit,' he had said to me the last time I saw him, patting my manuscript as he led me from the preview theatre to the lift. 'Might have to make her a dyke or something.'

'And what will you make me?' As I stepped alone into the lift I was genuinely curious. I turned to face him. He was smiling, but right past me, into the mirror behind me on the lift's back wall.

'Already decided that,' he said, and chuckled. The door had started to close before he let me know my fate. 'I'll make you an astronomer.'

Suddenly I knew the kind of book it would be.

All Pan books are available at your local bookshop or newsagent, or can be ordered direct from the publisher. Indicate the number of copies required and fill in the form below.

Send to: **CS Department, Pan Books Ltd., P.O. Box 40, Basingstoke, Hants. RG21 2YT.**

or phone: 0256 469551 (Ansaphone), quoting title, author and Credit Card number.

Please enclose a remittance* to the value of the cover price plus: 60p for the first book plus 30p per copy for each additional book ordered to a maximum charge of £2.40 to cover postage and packing.

*Payment may be made in sterling by UK personal cheque, postal order, sterling draft or international money order, made payable to Pan Books Ltd.

Alternatively by Barclaycard/Access:

Card No.

Signature:

Applicable only in the UK and Republic of Ireland.

While every effort is made to keep prices low, it is sometimes necessary to increase prices at short notice. Pan Books reserve the right to show on covers and charge new retail prices which may differ from those advertised in the text or elsewhere.

NAME AND ADDRESS IN BLOCK LETTERS PLEASE:

Name

Address